THE UNITED FEDERATIO[N]
LYSANDER T[V]

BOOK 4
ESTHER'S STORY:
SPECIAL DUTY

Colonel Jonathan P. Brazee
USMC (Ret)

Copyright © 2017 Jonathan Brazee

Semper Fi Press

A Semper Fi Press Book

Copyright © 2017 Jonathan Brazee

Illustration © 2017 Jessica TC Lee

ISBN-10: 1-945743-11-5 (Semper Fi Press)
ISBN-13: 978-1-945743-11-5

Printed in the United States of America

Acknowledgements:
I want to thank all those who took the time to pre-read this book, catching my mistakes in both content and typing. Thanks to best_editor1 for her editing. And once again, a special shout out goes to my cover artist, the award-winning Jessica Tung Chi Lee. You can see more of her work at:
http://www.jessicatcl.com/news.html.

Original cover art by Jessica TC Lee

Cover graphics by Steven Novak

WINSTED

Chapter 1

Captain Esther Lysander, United Federation Marine Corps, plummeted towards the planet's surface, her heart pounding in her chest. The shell surrounding her started to glow as the heat built up. She was not a happy camper at all as the vibration grew, and the vessel that had carried her across the Black began to disintegrate.

"Come on, Lysander, just keep it together," she said out loud, her voice cracking after several days of disuse.

Esther had made several HALO drops from Space Guard ships, and they had been a fun kick-in-the-ass. None of those jumps had prepared her for this, however. She didn't consider herself claustrophobic, but getting locked into a tiny one-man Inert Atmospheric Insertion Capsule, or "duck egg," at the outer edge of the system and shot like a railgun round at the planet had wreaked havoc on her nerves. The blood thinners given to her to fight deep vein thrombosis had the side effect of keeping her more alert, exacerbating her stress. Her father had often told sea stories about his duck egg inserts, but his had always been with another Marine, and none of them had taken the 68 hours that Esther had been alone with nothing but her imagination.

And now, fully alert as she plunged thought the atmosphere, her imagination was working overtime. A thousand things could go wrong, and any of them would result in her component atoms being spread over half of the continent far below her.

Shouldn't this stupid thing be releasing me by now? she wondered as the vibrations increased.

If the duck egg's outer shell didn't completely disintegrate, she wouldn't be spread out over the continent, just sunk ten or twenty meters deep into the dirt at one location. Either way, she wouldn't be around to know.

In most ways, being inserted by duck egg wouldn't have seemed like an odd endeavor a few months ago while she was with Recon. There was nothing unusual about that. But when she'd accepted the APOC orders, this had been pretty far from her mind. She wasn't sure what she'd envisioned, but playing secret agent wasn't it. She hadn't even known what her orders had meant; when she had accepted the APOC orders, she hadn't known whether the "C" designated "At the pleasure of the commandant" or "At the pleasure of the chairman."

It turned out that the "C" meant "chairman." Esther was a Marine, but she was being controlled by the man himself. Not that she had met him. All her contacts so far had been made out of a non-descript office in a non-descript building in a non-descript Martian industrial park.

And now, she was hurtling towards a meeting in the jungle wilds of Winsted, hoping to connect with the Sword of the People, an insurgent group attempting to overthrow the government. The young woman back on Mars who'd briefed her hadn't minced words. The Sword of the People weren't nice folks. The Federation had been tied up in legal battles with the government of the independent world, however, and the chairman would be happy to see a new government, one that owed the Federation a favor, put into power.

The vibration of her egg increased, and Esther thought she'd be shaken apart. Something was wrong—until it wasn't, and the green LED lit up. She had only a few seconds to tuck into position before the egg split open, thrusting her into the atmosphere with a blow that knocked her dizzy. She held position, knowing that an errant limb could get broken with the force. Within a few moments, she had stabilized and was slowing down. Carefully, she extended into the age-old freefall position and started the next phase of the long insertion.

OK, we're good now, she thought with relief. *Just a little freefall, a little glide, and we're home free.*

At 10,000 meters high, Esther had a good view over hundreds of kilometers in all directions. Still in daylight, which better hid the light of the duck egg's entry, she could see the line of dusk approach below her. Somewhere in the growing darkness, at a spot she couldn't see but to where she was trusting her foil AI to get her, someone from the Sword of the People would be waiting. Esther hoped he or she would be waiting with good intentions.

Esther's entire descent was out of her hands, from the deployment of the foil to the glide path that would take her to the DZ. If something went wrong with the system, she had an emergency ripcord, but if that happened, the rendezvous was off, and she'd have to exfiltrate to her safe house for further instructions.

Right about now, she told herself, hand edging to the manual ripcord, but five seconds later, her foil automatically deployed, jerking her descent, her legs flailing high until she swung back down.

Her hands rose instinctively to take the controls, forgetting for a moment that for this jump, she was simply a passenger. With a rueful smile, she brought her hands back down and settled in for the ride. Even without control of her descent, this was a hundred times better than being in the duck egg. At least she could see where the foil's guidance was taking her.

Esther's AI was the only powered piece of gear with her, and it was heavily shielded. Both the positioning system and the steering of the foil were entirely mechanical, which was an amazing piece of tech. An active system was literally child's play, something children's toys had used for centuries. A passive system like this, with this degree of accuracy, was a far greater technical achievement.

The foil, with its 30 to 1 glide ratio, enabled Esther to cover a lot of territory, and between the rotation of the planet and her own progress, she passed over ground already shrouded into darkness. She was still in the light, however, and could be visible to prying eyes below her. At 1,500 meters, she, too, dropped out of the sunlight, which was a relief.

Seven minutes later, she took over from the little foil AI, flaring out for a standing landing. She was on the ground.

This was Esther's first APOC mission, and she wasn't feeling the comfort level. The three-week mini-course she'd completed on the remote Gryphon II did not a superspy make. To be honest, she still wasn't 100% sure just what her job was. Not for this specific mission, which seemed straightforward, but her overall job description. As a Marine, she'd have thought that she would be some sort of assistant or eyes and ears on military matters, not making clandestine rendezvous with insurgents in the middle of the jungle.

Esther turned on the foil's self-destruct. An extremely low current flowed from the battery, too weak to be picked up by all except for the most powerful surveillance devices. The molecules in the foil, however, picked it up and oriented in long strands, strands that almost immediately began to separate and break apart. Within two minutes, not much was left of it.

"Rey Alamosa?" a voice called out from the dense jungle surrounding the small DZ.

Esther wanted to reach for her Brockmaster, the sweet carbine that was still strapped to her thigh, but she resisted, saying, "Yes, that's me."

A few moments later, a man stepped out into the DZ, twenty meters away. Six more soldiers followed him, all pointing weapons at her as they approached.

"I'm Comrade Blue," the leader said as he reached her, neglecting to offer a hand.

"And I'm Rey Alamosa," Esther replied.

Which was all pretty stupid, she thought. She'd spoken to General Simone several times before leaving for Mars. Between the two of them, they'd decided that while she had an excellent combat record, she'd been offered these orders because of who she was, namely daughter of Ryck Lysander, former Commandant of the Marine Corps and Chairman of the Federation. More immediately pertinent to the Sword of the People, her father had been the leader of the Evolution. Her pedigree was considered an asset. It could also be a liability, however. She might be there as Rey Alamosa, Federation Citizen, but she wasn't the most inconspicuous person in human space. The Sword of the People didn't need to access the secure Federation databases to see that "Rey Alamosa" was the duly registered DBA for Esther Lysander.

And from the expression on Comrade Blue's face, he knew exactly who she was.

But from her "spy mini-course," she knew there was a legal reason for this. She might be on the planet as Rey Alamosa, and she might have been inserted without going through proper channels, but if she was compromised, the encrypted data dump from the chip in her wrist could be sent to the Fifth Ministry which would confirm who she was. Under the arcane rules of the Smythetown Agreement, this made her a registered agent, subject to certain protections, and not a spy outside of the accords. Her "Rey Alamosa" chip allowed her to move about freely, but it also made her a legal entity of the Federation, sort of a legal spy.

As opposed to an illegal spy, Esther had thought when she'd been told this.

Being a Marine was much more cut and dried, but while this and other aspects of her new job seemed crazy to her, they still were a little exciting to a girl who'd grown up watching every spy flick to come out. She might not be *Rebeth Tsung, Shadow Spy*, but still . . .

It was pretty obvious that this Comrade Blue knew who she was, but he didn't correct her. Even with insurgents, she guessed there were rules for this kind of things, formalities to observe.

"I've been asked to meet you, Mz. Alamosa. I need to tell you, though, that you're wasting your time. We have no interest in throwing off the yoke of the Dupris government only to accept the Federation's yoke."

Well, that's a fine hello, Esther thought.

She'd been briefed that some of the insurgents were essentially anarchists, and most were wary of the Federation, but that Comrade Brown (who had been identified as a Dr. Tor Allison, a former linear calculus professor on Watter's World) had initiated the first contact. Esther was supposed to meet with him and his staff as part of the glad-handing necessary to seal the deal.

"The F . . . the people I represent have no wish to yoke anyone. I'm here to learn about you and your cause and see where we can help you achieve your goals. We believe in self-determination of all peoples."

Esther didn't need to see the roll of the man's eyes to see how that statement was being received. She'd almost choked herself when she'd said it.

"Your, uh 'people's' past history would lead me to believe that you are blindly mistaken at best or a damned liar at worst. Either one doesn't make me inclined to cooperate with you in any way."

When Esther didn't respond, he added, "I might as well shoot you right here and bury you in the mulch. Jump accident, you know."

Esther had to keep back a smile. She wasn't particularly concerned with the threat, which she knew was a test. He might want to do that, but he couldn't afford to antagonize the Federation. But by saying "jump," she knew he had no idea how she'd been inserted. He probably thought there was a stealth aircraft hovering overhead somewhere.

When she didn't say anything, he said, "So let's say we allow you to assist us, how do we know you won't desert us like you did the Gravitors?" Comrade Blue asked.

Good question. We did leave them in the lurch, she had to admit.

The Gravitors was a small band of agnostics who chaffed at the Brotherhood's "benevolent" control. They'd received financial, public relations, and military equipment support from the Federation's Fourth Ministry—which had lasted until the Third Ministry reached an unpublicized agreement with the Brotherhood. Without Federation support, the Brotherhood Potestates quickly rounded them up and shipped them off to re-think camps where their "counter-thoughts" would be exorcised. Neither the Federation nor the Brotherhood had admitted that the Federation had been even peripherally involved, but not much escaped the myriad of tentacles prowling the undernet.

For a moment, Esther was tempted to hold to the party line, but looking at Comrade Blue's face, she knew that would slam shut a door that might never be reopened.

"Winsted is not the Brotherhood, Comrade Blue," she simply said instead.

It might not reflect well upon the Federation, but she hoped the pragmatic aspect of what she was saying would sink in. Winsted, an independent world on the edge of human space, was not the Brotherhood, and the Federation was not as concerned as to how the planet's central government would react to Federation interference. Sure, the Winsted president could complain to the United Assembly of Man. Despite a small resurgence of support for the UAM over the course of the Klethos War, however, it took that august body an inordinate amount of time in deciding just what salad dressing to serve at the UAM cafeteria, much less take action against the largest—and still most powerful—government in the galaxy.

Blue stared into Esther's eyes as if hoping to burrow into her very soul, and Esther blandly looked back, trying to exude confidence, something that she lacked.

After what seemed to be forever, Comrade Blue nodded and said, "Follow me, please. Comrade Brown will want to talk to you."

Esther nodded, only letting out a long breath after Comrade Blue had turned to lead her on, three of the six soldiers at the fore, three behind her. She felt relieved to get this far. Yes, the Federation had been invited, but still, she was an infantry Marine, combat-proven, but not some Four operator. Technically, with her APOC orders, she reported directly to the chairman himself, but she knew "Four," the Fourth Ministry, had their fingers all through this type of thing. She figured Four had thousands, if not tens of thousands, of operators who were better trained and more suited for this, but someone thought her the best person for this mission, her first since leaving Recon. It might be a softball thrown her way to get her feet wet, but it was still a mission, one for which she felt she was unqualified.

The eight of them walked up a narrow jungle path, almost overgrown in a hundred subtle shades of darkness. The smell in the still air was part freshness and life, part decaying death. Esther wasn't gagging, but the dichotomy confused her senses. She considered activating the face shield on her helmet, but she knew she was being observed, and if the insurgents could handle it, she could as well.

As they climbed a small rise in the trail, the path turned slippery, and Esther had to concentrate on keeping her footing. It wouldn't make a good impression for her to fall on her ass and knock down a few of the soldiers behind her like bowling pins. She managed to keep on her feet until the jungle opened up into a small clearing, the light of the planet's single moon providing enough illumination to give them some better visibility.

Esther relaxed ever so slightly just before the impossibly bright flare of an energy weapon lit up the clearing in stark relief. The point man was enveloped in a corona of blue light as Esther and the rest dove back into the minimal cover offered by the trees. A burst of automatic fire cut through the night air, the rounds splintering the trunk of the tree Esther was using for cover, sending splinters flying into her unprotected face.

She had left her Brockmaster in her thigh scabbard as a show of good intent, but it was long past time for that. She released the catch and brought it forward, her finger reaching for the safety as she hit the cheek pad, bringing down her face shield and activating the night vision mode.

Comrade Blue was yelling out orders to put fire on the ambushers. Two meters to Esther's right, one of the soldiers was attempting to comply while still hiding face-down behind a tree, holding his ancient Gescard out with one hand and blindly firing it. Rounds were hitting the tree immediately in front of him, and several looked to hit the body of the first soldier, still out in the clearing.

Both sides seemed content to merely fire at each other from 30 or 40 meters apart, all with minimal effect. If the soldier to her side was any indication as to the rest of both ambushers and ambushees, then Esther understood why. But even a blind squirrel can find a nut every once in a while, and with the number of rounds and the blasts from the energy weapon, given time, people were going to die. Esther was tied to the insurgents, so if she wanted to make sure it was the ambushers on the dying end, she had to act.

The Immediate Action drill when ambushed was to assault through the killing zone and take it to the ambushers. With the wild firing—from both sides—Esther thought a direct assault could result in her taking both enemy and friendly fire. Her bones inserts should be able to stop any of the kinetics she heard being firing, but the energy weapon, which she was pretty sure was a high-joule plasma rifle, would cook her just as it had cooked the un-armored point man.

Flank them it is, she told herself.

Her command mind started to shout out orders, forgetting for a moment that her companions were not trained Marines, and they did not seem to want to stop hugging the ground. She knew this was on her shoulders.

"I'm going to illuminate with my helmet torch, so don't fucking shoot me!" she shouted out as she stood and darted backwards.

"No! Stop her!" Comrade Blue shouted out.

Esther ignored him, and no one followed as she ran down the slope 20 meters, then made a hard-left turn, circling around the clearing. It was dark as Hades under the triple canopy, dark even with her night-vision app, but the sound and sights of firing were her guide. Every ten or fifteen seconds, the plasma gun went off, momentarily lighting up the jungle and giving her a target.

Like a wraith, Esther moved back up the slope, this time approaching the far side of the clearing. Branches and wait-a-minute vines reached for her, but she pushed through, her focus locked onto the enemy. With the night vision activated, she could see what was in front of her, but her depth perception was essentially gone, which made engaging a target more difficult.

And then she saw it, the tiny spark coming out of the muzzle of a rifle, her helmet's night vision blowing it up almost into a flare. Esther cut the night vision and hit the helmet torch at the same instance, catching a prone soldier in the beam. He turned to his side, one hand up to shield his eyes as Esther put three rounds into his chest.

A round hit her in her side—her left side, the side towards her contacts.

Friendly fucking fire! I told them I'm illuminating my torch!

The STF[1] armor, her "bones," stopped the round, but she didn't need to be taking fire from both sides. If they were aiming at her torch, then it was better off, and she cut it.

Someone ahead of her shouted out, and Esther bolted to her right, then forward, almost stumbling on a prone figure. She didn't cut on her helmet torch but put two rounds into his back before he could react.

A blast of light almost blinded her before her helmet killed the NV. The air around her crackled, and her left thigh blossomed in pain, almost dropping her to the ground. The plasma gunner had engaged her, but too early. The trees, some now with flames reaching out from the trunks, had absorbed most of the blast, shielding her. If he'd waited until he'd had a clean shot, she'd have been toast.

Ten seconds!

She should have timed the gunner's previous recycling rate, but it had to be at least ten seconds. The Confederation's P-Series Normans could recycle in seven seconds, but she didn't think whoever was out there would have one of those.

She flipped on her torch, and with her leg screaming in protest, bolted forward, knowing she had to find the gunner before he could fire again. She swept the beam from her torch back and forth, spotting another soldier who swung his weapon around to her. She snapped off a quick shot, but she couldn't spend any time on him. She had to get the plasma gunner.

Three, maybe four rounds slammed into her—whether from the ambushers or her own insurgents, she didn't know nor cared at the moment, trusting her bones to keep her safe. The plasma gun, on the other hand, would cut her down, and if hit in the head, beyond hope of resurrection.

Frantically, with the torch on spread, she swept the area as she ran forward. The tiniest whine reached her, barely a tickle in her right earphone. She dove to the ground, swinging to the right. A soldier was kneeling, five meters away, an immense plasma rifle to

---

[1] STF: Shear-Thickening Fluid

his shoulder. Her torch beam, even spread out, caught the soldier in the eyes just as his rifle charged, making him flinch.

That was all Esther needed. She snapped off two quick shots. The first .30 caliber "Concave" assisted round hit him just above his right eye before keyholing. It must have hit the back of the soldier's helmet and ricocheted forward because almost instantly, the front of his face exploded outward. Her second round probably hit as well, but she couldn't tell—nor did she care.

She swung around to the soldier who had fired at her a moment before, but to her surprise, her snap shot had taken him out.

She turned back and was immediately hit once more on her chest, which meant there was an ambusher deeper into the tree line. She switched back to night vision, turning off her torch, and taking a quick two steps to the dead plasma gunner. Just ahead, a soldier was standing behind a trunk, barely peering around it in the general direction of where Esther had been.

The tree was giving him cover, and Esther couldn't get in a kill shot. She did have a target, though.

The Brockmaster was not a sniper rifle: it was designed for quick employment and close-in work. Still, the soldier was only about 15 meters away. She could pull out her Ruger and hit him, but she wanted something with a bigger punch. Flipping up the digisight, she brought the barely-glowing crosshairs to bear and fired off a single round, hitting the soldier's protruding ass and dropping him. His screams filled the night like a banshee seeking revenge on humankind.

Ignoring him, Esther pushed forward, but the outgoing rounds began to peter off, and a moment later, the sound of retreating feet reached her. With her wild up, it took her a moment to realize that the ambushers had broken and were running for their lives. Esther didn't think the fleeing soldiers knew that she was in among their lines. More likely, the screaming of the ass-shot soldier, along with the silence from the plasma gun, had convinced them that their cause was lost.

Esther was fine with letting them get away. She wasn't on a kill mission.

Another round hit her, this time in the back. Her insurgents were still peppering the trees, most of the rounds going high, but at least one at her level.

Esther dropped down to a crouch and screamed out, "Cease fire you fucking morons!"

Oh, great diplomacy, Esther.

There was a short pause, then the firing started again.

"I said, cease firing! We are clear over here!"

There was another pause, then a voice called out, "Who's that?"

Mother Mary and the ass she rode on!

"It's Es . . . it's Rey Alamosa! I've cleared the ambush."

There was yet another pause, and she heard some mumbling. She turned up her helmet gain, but she still couldn't make out what they were saying.

"Come on out into the open with your hands up!"

Esther was tempted to clear them out as well, but she took a deep breath and shouted, "You've already hit me half-a-dozen times, so, no, I'll pass on that."

She knew she should just comply, but the adrenaline of the fight was still coursing through her, and she was not in a forgiving mood.

"We're sending over one of us," the voice called out after a 20-second break.

"Roger that."

Esther moved to the edge of the jungle and waited. A moment later, a soldier crept out, Gescard at the ready and looking very nervous. He slowly edged his way across the opening, stepping over his dead companion and continuing to the edge of the jungle.

"Are you there?" he asked, his voice almost a whisper.

"It's me," she said, stepping out while taking off her helmet and turning the torch on low and pointing it to her face.

She could see him startle, then as he recognized her, he turned and shouted out, "It's her!"

Four soldiers slowly appeared and walked across the opening until they had joined their companion.

One of them raised his rifle at her and demanded, "Where did you run off to?"

The oldest-looking soldier pushed down the muzzle of the first one's rifle and said, "Use your eyes, Gerry. She was clearing out the milties."

He turned to her and asked, "How many did you get?"

She did a quick head count, then said, "Four, I think. There's another one dead over there. I think one of you got him. Then there's our friend back there," she said, thumbing her hand over her shoulder.

The screams had faded to moans, but there was no mistaking who she'd meant.

"And where's Comrade Blue?" she asked.

"Dead," the older soldier told her. "And that's Elvin, dead behind us."

"So, what now?"

The man hesitated, then simply said, "Gerry," while pointing behind her with a tilt of his head.

Esther flinched, but then with a force of will, didn't object. As a Marine, whether on this mission or not, she was bound by the Accords. A wounded enemy had rights. But she'd been briefed on "interfering" with breaches in the Accords by others, even to the point that a lawyer assured her she'd have no legal liabilities if she had no authority over someone breaking the Accords. That didn't make her feel any better.

She stood there her heart pounding, refusing to even look in that direction, as the crying man's moans were suddenly cut off, to be replaced with the sound of a struggle, and then, silence. She'd just killed four men on her own, but to know that the man she'd wounded had just been executed hit her hard, and she had to swallow down the gorge that threatened to come spewing out.

A moment later, Gerry joined them again. He didn't say a word but simply nodded at the older insurgent.

Forcing herself to maintain her composure, she asked again, "What now?"

"Well, I don't rightly know, to be honest. We're just grunts here. But I'm thinking that if you're still willing, we take you to Comrade Brown."

"That's what I'm here for, so lead on."

It took the five soldiers a few moments to reorganize and step off. Esther fell in behind the second insurgent, but this time, she had her Brockmaster at the ready.

She tried not to think of the bodies they left behind. She'd been in battle before, and she'd felt the thrill of victory, she'd felt relief at being alive, she'd felt sorrow at fellow Marines lost. What she'd never felt was dirty.

Until now.

Chapter 2

Twenty six hours later, her mission completed, Esther stepped through the doughnut. She trusted the Federation's ability to defeat the scanner, but she half-expected to hear the alarm and for the "milty" police to swarm her.

Instead, the AI's generic school teacher-like voice said, "Gate 103, Mz. Alamosa. Have a pleasant journey."

Esther had been on Winsted for 31 hours, but "Rey Alamosa" was leaving Winsted, after a three-day business trip. There was a trail of her arrival, her hotel stays, her food and drink bills, and everything else that evidently passed the government's security system. None of the subterfuge really surprised her—she'd been weaned on Hollybolly flicks which made these types of capabilities the expected rather than the amazing. But she still didn't understand how her face passed surveillance. She'd had no modifications, yet the doughnut accepted her as Rey instead of Esther Lysander. The chip part was easy, but her face was her face. That boggled her mind, frankly, and scared her, too. If the Federation could do that, then she was sure other governments could as well.

Not for the first time, Esther wondered if she should have accepted her APOC orders. The Marine Corps was so straightforward. Missions were taken head on, and for the most part, the enemy's capabilities were understood. All of the shadows of her present job didn't leave her a chance to get comfortable—and as Mr. Vox had told her during her training, "comfort" would get her killed. She could never afford to let herself become complacent.

Esther shouldered her pack and followed the signs to her gate. She'd just missed the last shuttle, so she had 47 minutes before boarding the next one. In another three hours, she should be on the *AR Scally* and leaving the system first to the Confederation's *Falstaff Station*, then from there back to Mars. There was a bar next to her gate, and for a moment, she was tempted to take a seat and grab a drink, but she hadn't bothered to ask if Rey Alamosa had hit the bars during her stay. The chances were a million to one that even if the electronic trail didn't show a bar for the last three days, her ordering a drink would raise a red flag, but that was one chance too many. Instead, she sat down, slouched into her seat, and closed her eyes as if napping.

She'd given her initial report at the safe house three hours earlier. She'd assumed that her mission had been a success. Comrade Brown had agreed to open a line of communication—and material goods—with the shadow company set up by the Federation. There hadn't been much of an attempt to hide just who was behind the company, but forms had to be followed.

She'd also given a full account of the ambush, to include the execution of the wounded government soldier. Her report had been accepted without comment, and she was given her itinerary and told to proceed with her return to Mars. There would be a full, in-person debrief upon her return, and she was still not comfortable with the thought of that. How does a person, a Marine officer, tell someone she allowed a prisoner to be executed? In the Marine chain of command, that would be a career-ender, probably prison time.

The thought of getting into trouble, though, was minor compared to her self-image. Esther had always thought of herself as one of the good guys. She hewed to all the 12 leadership traits as taught to every Marine. Number one on the list was "honor," and the lack of legal ramifications did not alter what the word meant.

Something landed on her foot as a voice said, "Oh, sorry ma'am!"

She opened her eyes to see a young—very young—man in his Legion *Tenue* T22's, pulling up his seabag which had fallen onto her foot. His shoulder epaulet was bare, meaning he was a Legionnaire de 2e Classe, or someone right out of basic training.

Winsted was an independent world, so, young men and women who wanted a broader military experience enlisted in other larger forces. Some joined the Federation Navy or Marines, some the Confederation Army, but the Foreign Legion tended to be a popular choice.

Local governments often encouraged their young men and women to serve. After their sons and daughters returned home, they brought with them a wealth of military experience and knowledge that they couldn't have acquired at home.

Esther had fought the Legion on Nouvelle Bretagne, her first combat as a platoon commander. As with many Marines, though, she had respect for the Legion. Sometimes the Marines and Legions were opposed to each other, sometimes they were on the same side, and while each would swear they had the toughest warriors, they both were wedded to the concept of brothers in arms. They tended to feel a kinship with each other.

"You just get out of *La Ferme*," Esther asked, using the Legion nickname for their boot camp.

"Yes, ma'am. Two weeks home leave. Now I'm going back to Ahaggar."

"The hard part's over, son. Just stick with it," she told him.

"Were you in the Legion?" the young man asked, sitting back down.

What was Rey Alamosa? What would she know about the military? Esther wondered. *Screw it. If they're monitoring this and it sets up an alarm, let them come get me.*

"No, but I served with them. Good soldiers."

With . . . against . . . who's being particular?

The young man, who looked barely more than a boy, beamed with pride. As he should. He'd made it through the Farm, and not everyone accepted managed that. He was just starting out on his journey, his military career ahead of him. Esther hoped it would make him a better man.

"Just remember, *mon Legionnaire*, always serve with honor."

"I will, ma'am, I will."

You, too, Esther Lysander. Serve with honor, she told herself.

Jonathan P. Brazee

MARS

Chapter 3

"Come on, Major. One more? Get back at me?"

"Right, like I have a chance at that," Major Stephen Lent said, half collapsing against the wall of the court. "And I've still got to get the monthlies done. So, no, I'm done."

"Already finished mine," Esther said. "Signed, sealed, and delivered."

"Logging in all the field shitters in the Corps hardly takes much time there, Captain. But I have to say, the job fits you."

Esther was tempted to give the good major the finger, but despite their low-key relationship, that might be a bit too far, even in jest.

"No job's too small, sir, and it all comes out in the end," she said, going light with her response. "And if that gives me time here on the squash courts, so be it."

"It all comes out in the end? Come on, Captain, you can do better than that," he said with a dramatic groan. "But yeah, there's that. Our work load's not the worst. But I got behind last week, and I'm waiting for the division reports, so, back to the salt mines," he said, pushing himself off the wall, then turning to leave the court. "If you're up for it, give me a shout on Thursday."

"Roger that, sir."

The major was behind the curve because he'd been "BTG," as in "Broke the Glass," the term they used when referring to the missions that were their raison d'être. Like fire extinguishers, they waited behind glass windows until needed. Esther didn't know what the mission statement was for any of the other 18 Marines with a "special status." For all she knew, they could be APOC just like her, or she could be the only one. No one asked questions, and no one took notice when another one of them disappeared for any length of time.

All 19 of their select group were ostensibly assigned to the Marine Corps Logistics Command, which was a tenant command of the Navy's Station 1, although they were physically at the Leinart Annex on Mars' surface. The nineteen Marines, ranging from two staff sergeants up to a full colonel, were assigned actual billets. Esther's was as the Field Hygiene Deployment Officer, which meant she really did keep an inventory of the 4,332 field heads owned by the Corps, but also the water units, trash immolators, and about a hundred other SKUs. The work mostly consisted of gathering the various flag command reports and compiling them into a single Corps-wide report.

That very demanding job took her less than five hours each month, which gave her plenty of time for working on her off-campus Tac 1 course, PT, or anything else she wanted, such as playing squash. She'd never even heard of the game before; it was an ancient racquet sport played on an indoor and enclosed court. Before Mars was terraformed and the colony was still domed, squash had been rediscovered, and it was now a planetary tradition. Esther tried to play daily, and she was becoming quite good at the game, probably better than everyone other than Top Forrester.

But she could only PT so much while she waited for her glass to be broken for a real mission. A few of the others seemed to be constantly gone, but over the course of three months following her mission on Winsted, Esther had gone out on only two more assignments, each one as nothing more than window decorations on government missions. One of those was with the second minister and one was with the chairman himself. This was what she'd feared. The new chairman, probably anxious to cement his bona fides, understood that having a Lysander in his party would be to his benefit with the powerful Evolutionist faction, so Esther had dutifully stood by in her dress blues while the chairman had given a speech to the UAM and then spent two days bird-dogging him on the diplomatic social circuit. Esther hadn't liked her mission on Winsted, but at least she'd been doing something, not standing around like a wind-up doll on display.

Esther did not excel at quietly sitting on her ass. She needed to go out and do something, anything. She watched the days slide past, fully aware that while her peers were gaining the experience and schooling needed to keep climbing the career ladder, she was marking time, and Marines did not advance by merely marking time.

The stress was getting to her. She was able to sweat out some of the stress on the court, in the gym, and out on the track. She tried to bury herself in her course, resenting that she wasn't at the brick and mortar school on Tarawa, but knowing she at least had to finish the off-campus course. But other coping methods had her concerned. One was that she was shopping again. Esther had been a clothes horse before enlisting, a slave to the latest fashion. The Marine Corps boot camp had been cold turkey for her, breaking her of that particular addiction. Now, with so much time on her hands, she'd been finding herself at the Ruby Run, Harris Dome's universally famous shopping district. Originally a single street between G and H girders, when the physical dome had been removed after terraforming, "RR" had spread out to cover ten blocks of every high-end brand name known to man.

Shopping was bad enough, but she had a governor on her actions based on her salary. She simply could not pay for the latest Jin Hai bag, so there was a limit on what she could buy. The other habit she'd picked up was far more concerning. Esther had always enjoyed the occasional drink, almost always in social occasions. Over the last two weeks, however, she'd found herself walking alone into bars several times for a few drinks. She hadn't gotten plastered yet, but drinking alone worried her. Alcohol had ruined more than a few careers, and with her current clearance, she was positive that her purchases were being monitored. She knew she should lay off, but the fact that she hadn't stopped gave her pause.

Even now, as she stood in the squash court, covered in sweat, the thought of slipping into some quiet bar and sipping on a Blue Moon was very alluring.

Not today, Esther, she thought, shaking her shoulders as if to shrug off the thought.

She retreated to the locker room, put her racquet into her locker, and flicked the shoe selector from "court" to "run." Her footwear loosened around the ankles while the sole thickened. Pushing all other temptations out of her mind, she opened the back door and broke out into a slow run to the track.

If she could run herself into oblivion, she could go back to her apartment, get something to eat, and collapse in bed, another day down and one day closer to when she was back in a real infantry billet.

ARRIVAL

Chapter 4

"You ready to strut the catwalk, Captain?" Lieutenant Commander Spence Eitel asked, sticking his head around the corner.

"Yes, sir, primed and pampered," Esther replied, giving the bottom of her dress blues blouse on more tug. She turned around, held her hand out to her side, and asked, "Do I pass the inspection."

"You sure do. How about me?"

He stepped into full view. Esther gave him the once over, then reached forward and straightened the Federation Nova hanging at his neck.

"Probably not the first time you've done that," he said.

"No, sir. My dad hated wearing his. Said they stuck him in the throat."

"One is bad enough," the commander said with a laugh. "I can't imagine having two. But if we're all gussied up, we'd better get going. Mz. Allison's probably about to have a heart attack."

Mz. Juliette Allison was the first minister's protocol officer, and she'd been riding herd on the delegation. The night before, she found the two of them at the hotel bar, enjoying a drink, and Esther thought the woman was going into a conniption, reminding the two officers that they were representing the Federation and that they had to be on their best behavior.

Esther didn't understand her concern. It was true that a good portion of the Brotherhood population didn't consume alcohol, but some did, and this was an international hotel with a very well-stocked bar. And it wasn't as if either one of them were drunk. Feeling good, perhaps, but not drunk. Both of them were on per diem for the trip, and technically, they were supposed to return any of their daily allowance that they didn't use. At least, that was the excuse the commander had used when he invited her to meet him in the bar.

Not that Esther needed much of an excuse. Lieutenant Commander Eitel was one of three Navy officers on active duty who wore the Nova. Esther was not particularly in awe of the Nova as a medal. She'd been around them enough growing up, but the fact that the commander was awarded his for saving Marines bumped him up a notch or two in her estimation. The fact that, as with her father, Hollybolly chose to make a flick about him, might have edged him up another half-a-notch. Beyond that, though, the man was simply gorgeous, which was a major reason why he was probably the most recognizable face in the Federation military. He'd had some well-known affairs with more than a few celebs, and he'd been voted as the Federation's most eligible bachelor for two years running. For him to ask her out for a drink had been an ego boost she couldn't turn down, and he'd proven to be as charming as he was good looking. The evening had been enjoyable until Allison had cut it short.

Esther didn't read too much into the evening, though. The two of them were the only junior officers in the delegation, so it made sense that they'd socialized with each other instead of with the higher-ups.

Esther followed the commander out of the Federation suite, which was acting as a green room for the delegation.

Mz Allison was coming down the hallway, evidently to round them up, saying, "There you two are. Can you please join us? We're about ready to enter the ballroom."

Esther gave the commander a light punch in the back, hidden from their minder by his body. He'd been the one who said they had more time and suggested they sit and relax as the rest of the delegation started to filter out.

The suite was on the top floor of the Mövenpick, as might befit a Federation minister, but that meant a long elevator ride to the ground floor and the ballroom. The commander, looking nonchalantly to the ceiling, gave Esther a quick hip check. Esther got in a quick finger-poke to his side as the door opened.

Like high school kids, she thought as she struggled not to smile. *Real professional, Lysander!*

Allison turned and told them to hurry up, and a few moments later, the delegation gathered in front of a table of finger food. Esther looked at the spread with interest. If she'd known they had food, she'd have come down earlier.

"That's everyone, sir, and I think it's time to take our table. If you'll lead us in?" Allison asked the first minister.

The great man nodded, and accompanied by the Second Vice-Minister for Political Affairs, led the 15-person party into the grand ballroom and to their tables. The ten highest-ranking members took the main Federation table, one table to the left of the middle and in front of the head table. Esther, the commander, and the five hangers-on split off to the left, up against the far wall and three rows back.

"Welcome to the children's table," Sandra Oh said as they took their seats.

"Just as well, Sandra," the commander said. "The First Brother won't see me if I pick my nose during the speeches."

Sandra, who was 80 years old if she was a day, laughed out loud, a deep, robust laugh that belied her small frame. Esther hadn't had much time to talk with the career bureaucrat, but her initial impression of the woman was quite positive. She made a mental note to get to know her on the return back to the home system.

Two more people joined them, a Brotherhood husband and wife who didn't seem overjoyed to be sitting with Federation peons. Esther couldn't help but wonder if they were just the business couple they professed to be or if they were there to watch over the five of them.

Not everything is super-spy, Lysander. Don't be so paranoid!

Except that it was, at least as far as she was concerned. Yes, she was there as window dressing, one of two Marine in the delegation. She was there to flash her two Navy Crosses, reminding everyone who her father was. Yes, she was there, along with LCDR Eitel, Captain Peterson, Brigadier General Hoker, and Admiral des

Plaines, representing the military and lending substance to the First Minister, who'd never served. But she also had two "spy" missions.

The first was as a simple observer. Esther had thought that was a little ridiculous, to be honest. The Brotherhood knew who she was, and she couldn't very well go wandering off around Brotherhood bases. But as she'd been briefed, it was part of hiding in plain sight. The Brotherhood had an improved Saul, their main combat suit. The two governments were on friendly terms. Between them, they provided over 60% of the gladiators fighting the Klethos, and they'd crippled the Seventh Revelationists through a joint command. However, the universe was not static, and life had a habit of changing. The Federation wanted to know more of the new Saul's capabilities.

Earlier in the day, the general and Esther had been taken to one of the Brotherhood Host bases and given the expected dog-and-pony show. Esther had been briefed on what to look for, and while the host team went through their demonstration, she'd looked for the telltale signs. She saw nothing. Either her briefer had been wrong, or the deployment of the new suits was not yet widespread.

Or the Brotherhood knew she'd be watching, and so used the older combat suits.

Esther knew that not seeing anything was still intel, but it had been a bit deflating. It would have been far more rewarding to discover some deep secret—not that she'd actually expected to while standing there with a posse of Brotherhood hosts around her.

Her second mission was the one that had her a bit more nervous. Once again, it relied on hiding in plain sight. But for this one, she had to actively seek out the intel. She wasn't personally at risk—she was on Arrival under diplomatic immunity. If she was caught, she'd simply be deported, blacklisted, and the Federation would suffer a degree of embarrassment. Her service to the chairman would be over, and while that might sound like a relief, chances are that she'd stay on Mars with her inventory cover billet becoming her actual job.

She glanced at her PA. She had 52 more minutes, which should still be during the dinner. Water had already been served, so she picked up her glass, draining it. While the entire ball/banquet room would be under surveillance, she highly doubted that a real person would be watching her. More likely, everyone's actions were noted by an AI, and by drinking her water, that should give her surveillance cover for what she had to do.

She turned back to the other six, trying to look interested and engaged. LCDR Eitel was in the middle of telling a story to the Brotherhood couple and both looked enthralled—the woman especially. Esther understood it. The commander had "it," no question. Esther had been contemplating her response, should he have initiated anything last night—or his response had she done the initiating—before things were taken out of their hands by the ever-present Mz. Allison. She had no illusions that the two of them had some sort of long-term potential, but a night with the commander would have been memorable, if undernet rumors had any truth to them.

"Ladies and gentleman, the First Brother," was announced, and all the guests rose to their feet.

Esther had seen the First Brother on holos, of course, but this was the first time she'd seen him. He hadn't been at the UAM assembly Esther had attended with the chairman. With surprisingly few people in tow, he almost glided through the general tables to the head table. As he stepped up on the dais, he motioned everyone to sit down.

"I guess no one else wants to sit with us," the commander said, pointing to the three empty seats. "That's OK with me. More food for the rest of us."

Seizing her cue, Esther grabbed the water at one of the empty place settings and drained it.

"Thirsty there, Captain?"

For a moment, she wondered if he knew what she was up to, but then she dismissed the idea. That was just more of his flippant, if endearing, personality.

"Yes, sir. Space-lag, I guess."

He raised his eyebrows, but said nothing as the serving staff rushed in with a well-choreographed performance. Each table's server reached his or her table at the exact same moment, as far as Esther could tell, no matter that table's placement. With a flourish, their server set down what looked like shrimp on a small piece of toast topped with a yellow sauce and what looked like tiny eggs.

Is that caviar? Esther wondered, both curious and repelled at the same time.

Her brother was the foodie in the family, always going on about "real" food. Esther was fine with fabricator food and was a little queasy at the thought of actual animal flesh. She picked up her spoon and poked at the tiny eggs.

"You can leave the appetizer for our three friends," the commander told the server, pointing at the three empty seats.

The server nodded, deftly placing the tiny plates at each seat, then whirling away from the table, once again at the exact same time as the other waiters left their tables. The Brotherhood was big on classical dance: ballet, hip-hop, and neurosynch. Evidently, their love of dance spilled over to serving food.

As the server left, the commander said, "They made it for us, so no use letting it go to waste."

Esther looked up to the head table. She'd been given her etiquette lessons after she'd first reported in, and she knew she had to wait until the guest of honor took a bite, and he seemed to be deep in conversation with his table companion. Finally, he looked up and saw the waiting room full of people, and with a half-wave and a smile, picked up his appetizer and popped it into his mouth.

Esther turned back to her plate and hesitantly picked it up. She wanted to scrape off the caviar, if that was what it was. It could still be fab caviar, not real, but even that put her off. She took a deep breath and took a bite, cutting the small dish in half. She could taste the toast, the shrimp, and mustard in the sauce. There was also a salty something, tiny globes that popped in her mouth. She took a quick drink of water, washing it down.

"You want one of the extras?" the commander asked her.

"No, no. How about our guests?" she said, pointing at the Brotherhood couple.

"To be accurate, I think you are our guests," the woman said. "Please, help yourself."

Esther held up her remaining half bite and gestured to the rest.

"Well, I'm not shy," the commander said, taking one of the extras.

You're welcome to it, Esther thought, quickly finishing hers and washing it down with more water.

She drained the second glass when the servers came out again, this time leading trundlecarts full of juices and other non-alcoholic drinks. She could use a cider, but she had to acknowledge a clear head was better, so she asked the server for something only found in Brotherhood space, and he poured her a glass of some red-orange fizzy liquid that was surprisingly good.

Over the next half-hour, Esther tried to resist checking the time as two more courses were served and removed. She began to feel the consequences of drinking so much water, though. The pressure on her bladder was getting intense, and she wondered if she'd made a tactical mistake.

She checked the time—six more minutes.

Esther laughed at something Sandra said, not that she knew what was funny, only that everyone else was laughing. Between her nervousness and her bladder, she wasn't really listening.

Get a grip, girl! You've faced down Legionnaires. This is nothing.

And then, at last, it was time.

"Excuse me," she said to the table. "I've got to use the head. The ladies room," she added to the civilians.

She got up, moved to the wall, and made her way back and out the doors into the passage.

Left. Then to the second head, she told herself.

If she was being watched, bypassing the first one might seem odd, but she had her instructions. As she reached the first one, though, there was a temporary sign blocking the entrance, on which was written, "Cleaning in Progress. Pardon the Inconvenience." Once she saw the sign, she acted as if she'd been planning on using it, made a show of noticing the sign, and then turned and looked around as if wondering where to go next. She shrugged, then continued, eyes searching for the next set of restrooms.

A woman in an evening gown walked towards her, saying, "If you're looking for the loo, it just around the corner."

"Oh, thanks."

"A nice hotel like this and they can't keep the closest one to the banquet open?" the woman said as she passed Esther, obviously put out by having to walk another 30 or 40 meters.

And then there is was. Esther entered, ready to primp in the mirror if the fifth stall was occupied. Luckily, it was empty. The entire restroom was empty. She almost ran into the stall and started to undo her blues. She barely made it to the can before gloriously letting loose. If there was surveillance in there (and that was a creepy thought), she was sure doing her part for verisimilitude.

Nature taken care of, she bent forward and reached around and below her, running her hand under the curve of the bowl, feeling for any imperfection. Her heart jumped when almost immediately she felt something. She slipped a finger under the edge of the tiny bump, hoping it really was her drop and not some natural toilet detritus, and pried it loose. With it under her fingernail, she brought it up to eye level. There was something there, something manmade, about the size of a grain of rice.

Her heart jumped. This was real spy stuff here, and Esther was part of it.

The tiny object had information that the Federation wanted. Esther didn't know what that information was. And her excitement was tempered by the fact that she was merely a mule, not part of the gathering of the information. But still, this was an experience that was new to her, and there was a certain allure to it all.

Of course, this was the easy part. The Federation and the Brotherhood might be friendly rivals in the political, military, and economic spheres, but they were also allies in the fight against the Klethos, pirates, and splinter groups such as the SevRevs. Each was also the largest trading partner of the other. As such, the Brotherhood worlds were not closed societies, and millions of Federation citizens were in the Brotherhood at any given time. A simple pass would be child's play. But Brotherhood scanning was the gold standard, and anything, even something as small as the little speck under her fingernail, packed with data, could be picked up.

Esther had to get the intel back to the Federation. Tomorrow morning, before leaving for the spaceport, she was going to drink a specially-prepared concoction that would supposedly screen anything in her stomach. And just before leaving the hotel, she would swallow the databank.

Why does all of this have to screw with my digestive system, she wondered, looking at herself, still sitting on a toilet.

As part of an official party, Esther was not subject to the same screening as regular citizens. They'd be surreptitiously scanned, of course, but those scanners could never be as effective as the normal spaceport systems.

And if despite the stomach screen, despite the tiny device's shielding, despite not going through standard screening, if they picked up the databank, Esther had diplomatic immunity. She might have to give up the device, which would take as long as it needed to get through her gut, but she could not be charged with anything. And, as her briefer informed her, they might not do anything as doing so would be to admit they had screened the first minister's party. Which everyone knew they would. Which they still wouldn't want to admit. Which the Federation knew they wouldn't want to. Which they knew the Federation knew, so there would probably be intel going out with the party. And more "which they knews," on and on. It all made Esther's head spin.

Esther lifted her medals up and took a tiny shielded case out of her dress blue's left breast pocket and carefully slid the databank into it. Letting the medals back down, they would give a little bit of cover should anyone give her a direct scan, but she was assured that the chances of that were minimal.

And that was that. She put her blues back in order and stepped out and up to the mirror. It would be natural for her to check her uniform alignment in the mirror, but her focus was on the pocket and if it seemed natural.

There wasn't much else she could do, so she left to go back to the banquet. She'd try to put everything out of her mind until she drank the shielding in the morning. For now, though, a tiny smile creased her face.

She may be a mule, but playing spy was still pretty freaking copacetic.

MARS

Chapter 5

Mr. Byzantine slid the plastisheet printout over the desk towards Esther. She already knew what to expect, but still, she reached over, picked it up, and scanned it. There was her name, her identity number, the reporting period, the billet: all the normal heading data. What was missing were the entries in the descriptive part of her fitness report. Every single category, from Initiative to Discipline, from Courage to Flexibility, were marked as "Non-observed." The narrative, which was the meat of the report and usually described both her duties and how well she performed them, was blank.

The first six months of her tour might as well never have happened. Winsted never happened. Arrival never happened. Cornūcōiae never happened. Heck, even her time compiling shitter reports never happened. Her service had been a black hole.

She looked at the bottom of the form. It was signed by one Alexander J. Hastings, Colonel, UFMC. Esther didn't know a Colonel Hastings, and evidently, Colonel Hastings didn't know her.

Promotions in the Marine Corps were based on fitness reports. There was wiggle room for interpretation of those reports, but the bulk of what was given to the promotion boards were numbers crunching and statistical analysis. The promotion AIs took into account scores, trends, descriptive words choices, and even the past reporting history of the reporting senior. All of this went into the "whirlpool" and was spit out in a relative ranking of all those eligible for promotion. That wasn't set in stone; if it were, there would be no reason to have real Marines sit on a board. But while the board members could move candidates around, the initial basis was the whirlpool ranking.

And while her contemporaries were acquiring more personal data, Esther was at a standstill. One non-observed shouldn't matter, but Esther was staring six of them in a row, six where she should be developing as an infantry Marine. She couldn't be officially penalized for a non-observed report, but the board members were humans, and they tended to read into anomalies.

On the one hand, such a period of non-observed reports could mean just what it did in this case, that she was on a special assignment of some sort. On the other hand, it could mean she'd been spending that time in drug rehab or in psychiatric treatment. Either case would show up reading as the same.

And being Ryck Lysander's daughter wouldn't make any difference. Jersey Quillion, whose father was the Commanding General of the Outer Forces, had failed selection for major the year before.

"Not much to this, is there?" she asked.

Mr. Byzantine didn't respond to the question but said, "If you have no questions, can you validate it?"

Esther brought the bottom of the sheet to her face, stared at the optiscan until the tiny light turned from red to green. Immediately, the sheet was flashed into public record. She folded the physical copy and put it in her pocket.

She knew what she was getting into when she accepted the orders. That didn't mean, however, that it didn't suck.

COPIA 2

Chapter 6

Esther pulled the GE Bumblebee to the side of the dirt road and took her foot off the accelerator. Unlike hovers, it didn't sink down to its skirts when stopped. It didn't have skirts. The Bumblebee was a half-track, and as the first non-hover vehicle she'd driven in her life, it had taken her a good 30 minutes back at the assembly point to get used to having tracks and wheels in direct contact with the ground.

I don't know how you do it, Noah, she told herself, not liking the feel of the Bumblebee at all.

As a tanker, her twin would have had no problem with the little vehicle, but without experience, she'd frustrated her local handler while she insisted on getting a feel for the small vehicle. Esther could be rather anal in her preparations, and that had kept her alive so far.

She turned off the engine, and with a sputter or two, it died, leaving her in silence. The planet's sun was sinking towards the horizon, and the trees surrounding the open field were just beginning to throw shadows.

"We've got seven personnel, 200 meters at your 290," an unnamed voice said into the tiny earbud that had been implanted deep within her ear.

"Roger that," Esther subvocalized.

That was more people than had been agreed upon, but it was hardly surprising. These were not the most honorable people in human space, after all.

Esther lowered the window and simply listened for a few moments. At 200 meters, she was well within range of a sniper, but she doubted they'd take a shot now. They might not want her to survive the upcoming encounter, but to simply take her out before they started served them no purpose.

At three minutes before the hour, Esther opened the door of the Bumblebee and stood up, looking across the field for any sign of movement. There was none.

OK, Lysander, this is it.

Slowly and deliberately, Esther removed first her shirt, then her bra, throwing them on the seat. She bent down, pulling off her gym shorts and panties, tossing them on her shirt. She contemplated keeping her shoes on—the field was overgrown with vegetation, and she didn't relish going barefoot, but the terms had been clear. They wanted the courier to be fully naked, so she kicked off them off. Opening the rear door, she reached in and pulled out the transparent case containing 500,000 Maria Teresas.

And then she simply stood there beside the car, staring off into the trees on the other side of the field, waiting.

"Go," the voice inside her head passed at the top of the hour.

She started walking.

Esther didn't have any nudity taboos. She'd been naked with fellow Marines at the Kentville resort on Tarawa, and she'd started her recon final exercise on Prime Davis stark naked until she and Sven Luger had managed to score some clothes from a Goodwill donation bin. But as she walked across the field, she felt naked—not naked as in nude, but naked as in exposed. She had no armor, no protection, as she walked into a dangerous situation. She tried not to glance down at the little roll of fat around her waist.

She knew full well why she was naked. Ostensibly, it was to ensure that she was not armed. But the Kalebites wanted a show, and for the Federation to send a naked woman into a life and death situation played to their base who would feel that no righteous government would ever stoop to that. Not that the Kaleb leadership cared one way or the other. They were a for-profit organization, bandits, pure and simple. But many of their soldiers were recruited from the more conservative, reactionary, and religious sectors of society. They claimed to want to return to the "old ways," and as has been the case throughout recorded history, that claim struck a chord with many.

Jonathan P. Brazee

Ahead of her, in the trees, would no doubt be some of those soldiers, men who thought they were on the side of right against the corrupt governments of man. They would see nothing wrong with what they were doing.

Their own prejudices would be working against them, however. They did not believe women to be their equals, so they wouldn't be concerned that Esther, especially naked, could possibly pose a threat.

Esther vowed that she'd disabuse them of that notion.

She kept walking, trying not to wince when she stepped on something sharp. She had to look passive, just a courier sent to make the exchange.

Behind her, hovering over her half-trac, were three newsdrones, their network logos prominently displayed. This was also part of their demands. They wanted the entire galaxy to see how they could force the almighty Federation to do their bidding.

The Kalebites were small potatoes, very small, in the grand scheme of things. They preyed on the outskirts of humanity, taking tiny bites of what they could grab. This was their first foray into the big time, and they undoubtedly felt they could use this as a recruiting tool. There were more than enough disenfranchised people in the galaxy, all looking for a cause.

Fifty meters before the tree line, a large circle had been cleared. Esther stepped onto the short grass and stopped. Within a minute, five people came out. Two of them, a man and a woman, dressed in paper-like full-length parkas, were being pushed forward by two men in military-type fatigues. Another man in the same uniform had his attention focused on Esther, his Confederation Hasta 21 aimed in her direction.

The male prisoner was Kristian Dymond, the female was Keenah Tokiyashi-Jules. Dymond was the head of the FAID mission to Copia 2, and Tokiyashi-Jules was an intern from the University of Hiapo, working on her doctorate.

Copia 2 was a member of the Alliance of Free States. But with the Alliance's economy in shambles, the United Federation Agency for Intergalactic Development, FAID, had sent a mission, headed by Dymond, to assist in developing potable water systems

36

for the planet's mining communities. A Kalebite snatch cell had killed Dymond's security team and taken him and Tokiyashi-Jules as hostages, demanding 500,000 Maria Teresas or they would execute the two prisoners. They demanded a female courier, who would deliver the money naked at a time and place to be revealed.

Enter Captain Esther Lysander as the courier.

And now, she stood 20 meters away as they came to a halt, and the two prisoners were forced to their knees. Dymond, an older man with graying hair at his temples, looked resigned to his fate. He must have realized that his chances of survival were minimal. He'd probably lost comrades, killed by the very people they'd been trying to help. Tokiyashi-Jules, on the other hand, looked petrified, and when the two guards standing over them took out matching 20-centimeter knives and held them to their throats, she gave out a squeal of fear and started to slump down. Her guard grabbed her by the hair to hold her upright.

"Turn around so we can see you," the Kalebite on Tokiyashi-Jules ordered.

Esther raised her hands, then slowly rotated, letting the men check her out for weapons.

"So, is that the money?" the guard asked when she was finished, pointing with the tip of his knife at the bag before returning the blade to the girl's throat.

No, it's my frigging laundry, you idiot.

"Five-hundred-thousand Maria-T's," she answered instead, trying to sound nervous while not overdoing it.

Maria Teresas, named after an ancient international trade dollar, were the currency of St. Filipo, an independent station dug into a moon in the Juko system. It was one of the few physical currencies in human space, which made it the currency of choice for shady or outright illegal transactions. Esther had often wondered why the larger governments didn't just shut them down, but Noah had explained to her once that those same governments might be the biggest users of Maria-T's.

"Bring it forward," the Kalebite said.

Esther picked up the heavy bag, then walked forward until told to halt about five meters from them. She put down the bag, then retreated five meters as the head Kalebite demanded.

"Check it, Jonas," the man said, and the one holding the Hasta 21, rifle still trained on her, stepped up and ran a counter over the bag.

"Five-hundred-kay," the man said, reading the display before stepping back.

"Hmph," he snorted. "No funny business. I'm surprised the great and powerful Federation didn't try to short-change us." He looked beyond Esther in the direction of the newsdrones that were recording what was transpiring. "Not that it's going to do these agents any good."

The fighter with the Hasta took his eyes off Esther to glance to his left at the leader, his eyes lighting up with excitement, and that was all Esther needed. She stiffened her right fingers and drove them through the pseudoflesh that made up the roll of "fat" around her waist. The "skin" split open, and she grabbed the small handgun concealed there.

Bringing it up in a smooth swing, she fired two rounds that caught the head Kalebite just as he started to slice through Tokiyashi-Jules' throat. The hostage screamed in agony as Esther dove to the ground, through the sweep of the armed Kalebite's weapon as he tried to bring it to bear, double-tapping him twice in the chest.

Esther continued her roll, coming up on one knee, knowing she was probably too late to save Dymond, but the FAID director had dropped to the ground, and the remaining Kalebite, his eyes in a panic, was struggling to pull his rifle from where he'd slung it on his back. Esther fired twice more, and the man fell back.

She jumped up and ran to Tokiyashi-Jules, who was screaming, her hand to her neck, blood pouring between her fingers.

"Let me see!" Esther shouted, pulling back the young woman's hands.

She'd taken a pretty deep cut, but the knife hadn't reached the carotid. They could get her back alive if she didn't bleed out.

There were shouts from the tree line, and Esther looked up to see two men, pointing at them. One had a rifle, raised to his shoulder.

Esther's Spectrum was a sweet little piece of high-tech weaponry. Made from calcium hydroxylapatite, collagen, and keratin, it fired another calcium hydroxylapatite bullet, using a glycerol-based propellant. In other words, the handgun itself was made from what was essentially bone and fingernails, and the "bone" round was fired using fat as a propellant. When Esther was scanned, as she most assuredly would have been, the weapon would have registered as normal parts of the human body. Good for about 500 rounds, the drawback was that its effective range was limited to about 25 meters. The two men in the trees were well over twice that distance.

Still, Esther fired off the rest of the magazine at them before pulling Tokiyashi-Jules to her feet and telling Dymond, "Help me with her!"

The Bumblebee was 150 meters away, and they had to haul ass. If the two Kalebites were aggressive, they could run the three of them down before they could reach it.

There was nothing to do but run, and Esther's back itched in anticipation of the round she expected to slam into her. But it wasn't a round that hit. Before they'd made 30 or 40 meters, the cleared area erupted in a massive explosion, sending a piercing pain into Esther's shoulder and knocking all three Federation citizens to the ground.

Her shoulder screaming in agony, Esther struggled to her feet. Behind her, clouds of black smoke rose into the air.

"Now, now, now, now, now!" she shouted, pulling Dymond to his feet. "While they can't see us."

Dymond seemed dazed, but he helped pull Tokiyashi-Jules up, and between the two of them, mostly dragged her in the direction of the Bumblebee.

Esther didn't know how long the smoke would obscure them, but she knew it would be limited. As soon as the two remaining Kalebites realized that they hadn't been killed in the blast, they could pick them off from across the field.

39

"We have indications that two personnel are recording," the voice in her implant told her.

Just frigging great!

Somehow, they managed to make it to her vehicle. Esther bodily threw the woman into the back seat before bending down, reaching under the side, and freeing the case there. She stood up and took out the M114 that had been concealed in the case.

"Can you drive this?" she asked Dymond.

"Yes, yes, I think I can."

Esther reached into the driver's compartment and hit the GPS, punching in the rally point.

"Get in and take it back. We've got a medical team standing by."

"But . . . but, what about you?"

"My business isn't over," she said.

"You're still . . . you don't have any clothes on!" he sputtered.

"No time! Go!" she shouted, breaking out into a sprint, ignoring the damage she was doing to the bottoms of her feet.

And she was right. If they were recording what had happened, Esther had to stop them. The "network" newsdrones were in fact property of the newsies, but on loan to the Federation. What they recorded would never reach the public. But if the two Kalebites had recorded the engagement, it would get out. Those things always did. Whether this was a "win" or not, the Federation did not want any of this public. They did not want to be seen as negotiating, and beyond that, they didn't want any of their techniques revealed.

Even the simple Spectrum was not common knowledge, but with the bloody flap of pseudoskin hanging from Esther's hip (which had been connected to her real circulatory system to keep it at the same temperature as the rest of her body), observers might be able to put two and two together.

"Subjects are retreating at 310 from your pos, that is, three-one-zero. It is imperative that you stop them."

The voice in her head had been pretty good about keeping out of the way, and she hoped whoever was on the other side would keep it that way, but that was good intel. She needed it.

She angled slightly to her right and tried to push into a higher gear. She was grateful for all the gym time she'd been scoring on Mars. At .376 Earth Normal, Mars didn't provide the same workout as if under standard G, and even with artificial gravity under the tracks, it wasn't quite the same, but it was sure better than nothing.

"Subjects are entering vehicle. Their only way out is to the north east. We're calculating that you can intercept at perigee if you adjust to zero-zero-five, distance 386 meters. You need to haul ass," the voice said with the first hint of emotion in his voice since the two had been in contact.

Esther wished she had a simple face shield display with the spot she was supposed to reach highlighted. But she'd been shown a layout of the field, so she knew the general direction to take for the 005 azimuth.

She also wished she had taken the time to put on her shoes, at least. The ten or fifteen seconds that might have taken to get them on would have allowed her to run faster. She just tried to compartmentalize the pain as she ran.

But one emotion flooded over her: excitement. She was on the hunt, and that thrilled her. Her first three missions had not impressed her, and she'd been second-guessing her decision to accept the orders since she arrived. True, the mission to Arrival had been exciting in its own way, but even that wasn't why she enlisted into the Marines. Federation Marines served their fellow citizens. That is what it boiled down to. And for the first time since arriving on Mars, she felt she was doing that. Dymond and Tokiyashi-Jules were Federation citizens just doing their duty to make the galaxy a better place. They were taken by thugs for financial gain, and Esther had saved their lives.

That was what a Marine did.

Well, they tried to keep bad things from happening, too, not just reacting, and Esther was pushing herself to cut off the escaping Kalebites. They had been complicit in what was to be an execution conducted for what was essentially marketing. That was reason enough for them to die. The fact that their recording could do damage to the Federation cause was only icing on the cake.

Esther darted through the trees, trying to keep on course. She listened for the sound of a vehicle, certain that it would beat her to the spot.

"Guide right ten degrees," the voice said.

She oriented herself slightly to the right and kept going. She wanted to ask where the vehicle was, but she couldn't control her breathing enough to subvocalize. She figured he'd tell her if she missed them.

Esther's mental clock, which was far from accurate, ticked off a minute-and-a-half before she ran up a small slope onto a dirt path. She didn't need her minder to tell her the vehicle was almost upon her. She could hear the hum and barely had enough time to orient herself back down the trail before it appeared through the trees. It was a utility hover, the type work crews used to get around the worksite. Without a roof, the two Kalebites were open to the sky. They saw her at the same time, and the passenger with the rifle rose over the windshield to take her under fire.

Esther was sucking wind big time, and when she brought up her M114, which was the carbine version of the M99, she jerked the trigger high, sending the small fusillade of darts over the gunman's head. He managed to get off two shots in return. Esther didn't know where they went, so she took a deep breath, let it half out, aimed right at the man's chest, and squeezed the trigger. Four or five darts shredded his chest, and he rolled over backwards and out of the cart. Esther shifted her aim to the driver, who was crouching below the windshield. She fired off another volley, and the windshield blossomed with cracks, making the driver swerve, but the hypervelocity darts didn't penetrate. Now only 20 meters from her, she saw the driver smile and turn right at her, ready to run her down.

Esther waited until the last moment, then stepped aside and twirled like a matador delivering the estoque, sending a stream of darts into the surprised man as he drove past her. He was dead before his mind could process what had happened, and the cart veered off the trail, smashing into a large tree.

Esther waited for a moment, her M114 trained on the man's back, but he was not moving. Limping forward, her feet now screaming in protest, she approached the cart. Nudging the man with the barrel of her rifle, she confirmed he was dead. Then she searched the cart. In the back seat, she found the holocam. It took her a moment to figure out the controls, but on playback, she confirmed that they had used it to record what had happened.

She didn't bother to scan to the point of the recording where she took out the three Kalebites.

"I've got the recording," she passed.

"Thank God, Robin," the voice said, using her call sign. "Good job. Check to make sure it is the only one."

Esther went over the cart, then checked the dead man's pockets before limping back to the first dead Kalebite and searched him. Unless they had some stealth recording capability, Esther had found the only one.

She didn't know how long it would take the local authorities to arrive on the scene, and she wasn't sure she should be there when they did. She had arrived on-planet with another fake identity, but the less fuss, the better. With one last look around, she turned and limped back towards the field. Once there, she could hike back along the road.

She had to stop twice to pull things out of her feet, one of them being a rather large stick. She was bleeding pretty good from her feet, from the pseudoflap of skin, and most of all, from her shoulder. She could feel the warm blood flowing down her back to her ass and then on down her leg. She just put it all out of her mind.

She reached the field and crossed to the far side when the familiar whir of a helo caught her attention. She didn't think the Kalebites had any, but she kept her M114 at the ready as she watched the black bird circle the field, then flare in for a landing. The back ramp opened, and a short figure stepped out and motioned for her to get onboard.

Esther didn't recognize the make and model, so she asked her handler if it was friendly.

"Roger that. That's your ride home, unless you want to walk back."

"Nah, I think I'll ride."

Standing tall, and trying not to limp, Esther strode to the helo and climbed up the ramp. She took a seat as the crew chief followed her in. Within moments, the bird had lifted into the air.

"Here you go, ma'am," the crew chief, a young-looking woman said, holding out a pair of unmarked overalls.

Esther took a look at the short crewchief, wondering how the overalls could possibly fit on her much taller frame, but when she unrolled them, she saw they would be a perfect fit. Whoever these people were, they'd come prepared, she'd give them that.

She got dressed, zipped the holocorder in her cargo pocket, and sat back down.

Her mission had been far from ordinary, a mission she'd never have imagined doing in a million years. But still, she felt a warm feeling of both pride and *belonging*.

It may have played out in a weird fashion, but she felt like a Marine again.

MARS

Chapter 7

"She looks cute," Esther said, which was about the best she could come up with.

Her niece did look cute, so Esther hadn't been lying, but kids were not something with which she felt comfortable. It wasn't that she didn't like kids. She did, at least as much as anyone else. But as a professional Marine, she'd put childbearing off. The implants the Navy docs had put under the skin over her triceps ensured there wouldn't be any accidents.

And now Noah had two of them, Chance and Hannah Belle. It was hard to grasp that. Her brother, her twin, was a father, and from what Miriam had just told her, they had yet another on the way.

As she watched the cooing little girl in her mother's arms, the briefest wisp of uncertainty passed through her, just brushing her soul. Was she doing the right thing in delaying her own child? Sure, she could wait, and there'd be time after she had left the Corps for a family, but prolonged exposure to the implants and advancing age could affect fertility once the implants were removed. She wondered for the hundredth time if she should harvest some of her eggs and keep them on ice.

"So, how's everything else?" she asked her sister-in-law, more to cleanse her thoughts of her own motherhood.

Esther had never really trusted Miriam, and she had thought Noah was making a big mistake in marrying her. But over the years, despite seeing each other rarely, she'd come to appreciate her sister-in-law. And now there was obviously something on her mind. She hadn't made the call from Quintero Crag just to show Esther her niece.

"Good, things are good. Mostly."

The "mostly" was laden with meaning, and Esther remained quiet, waiting for Miriam to delve a little deeper. It didn't take long.

"Ess, do people . . . does being resurrected change them? I mean, that and regen?"

"You mean Noah?" she asked.

Shit, Lysander, of course, she means Noah.

"Yeah, ever since St. Gallen, he's been, well, like different."

"What do you mean?" she asked, worried at what she might hear.

Noah had rammed his tank into a wall on St. Gallen, evidently saving hundreds, maybe more civilians. He'd been KIA while doing it, put into stasis, and brought back to the Naval Hospital where he'd been resurrected. For most zombies, while regen increased the probability of the "Brick," or Boosted Regenerative Cancer, there were normally few side-effects once they'd regenerated whatever part of the body was missing or damaged. For an unfortunate few, though, the consequences were much worse. Some broke down and committed suicide. The slang for that was "completing the mission." Others, became aggressive and abused those close to them. Esther hoped against hope that Noah was not hurting Miriam or the kids. If he were, she'd have to report him immediately. It would destroy his career, but he'd be able to get the help he needed.

"It's just, I mean, he's so distant. He spends all his time on base, ignoring us. He's getting out in six months, so you'd think they could manage to get along without him, but no, he's got to work on his precious *Anvil*."

The *Anvil* was Noah's tank, and he'd finally been made tank commander. It didn't surprise Esther that he'd be taking his job seriously, but she had a feeling there was more to it than that. At least he wasn't getting violent with anyone.

"You know, he didn't even have to go to St. Gallen. Fierdor told me."

Esther didn't know who Fierdor was, but she didn't interrupt.

"He could have already been working up at battalion, but he wanted to go. And that was right after Belle was born. Is there such a thing as post-partum depression for men?"

Esther shook her head. She sure didn't know, but it was something she could look up. She thought if Noah was acting different, and it wasn't just Miriam's imagination, then it wasn't just having a daughter. She knew Noah was a good father, and she knew he loved his kids. No, it had to be something else.

And then it hit her.

Maybe he doesn't want to get out?

She rolled the thought around in her mind for a moment, and it just felt right. Noah had just been made a tank commander. He'd already been awarded a Silver Star, and from the mission on St. Gallen, he was being awarded another CPM, but this time a Civilian Protection Medal First Class, not the Second Class he'd already been awarded. His career was finally on track, and he was almost assuredly a shoo-in for staff sergeant. He might not want to leave. Miriam had told her that Noah had been offered a job with their Uncle Barret back on Prophesy, and while Miriam hadn't said it, Esther was sure the pay would be significant. But he wouldn't be a Marine.

She and her twin were not as close as they had been growing up, and Esther blamed herself for pushing him away. But at this moment, it was like old times, when they knew what the other one was thinking before anything was said. She felt she knew what Noah was going through as if she was channeling him. Non-twins could never understand how that worked. Hell, Esther didn't understand it. She only knew that it did. She hadn't felt that way for years, but she would bet on it now. Noah wanted to reenlist.

"Miriam, what would you say if Noah reenlisted?"

"Oh, no, he's not going to do that. We're going back to Prophesy. He's got the job with your uncle."

"But what if he doesn't want to get out?"

"Oh, no, that's not what's going on. He wants to get out. He told me he wants to be a better father."

Yet, he's spending all of his time on base.

"Well, maybe you're right," Esther said. "But I tell you what. Let me give him a call and see what's up. If there is anything wrong, I'll try to ferret it out."

Relief flooded Miriam's face, and she said, "Thanks, Ess. I'd be so grateful if you could. I'm just worried about him, you know."

She took a deep breath, and Esther could see her forcing herself to change the subject. She spent the next minute trying to get Hannah Belle to wave at Esther, who sat on her side of the call and dutifully waved at the little girl. Hannah Belle wasn't interested in reciprocating.

A few minutes later, the two adults said their goodbyes. Esther stared at the blank screen for a few moments, marshaling her thoughts. She'd give Noah a call, but knowing him, he hadn't even made the decision if he should reenlist or not. He'd probably feel that he should get out, that he should take the cushy job. With two kids and another on the way, he'd need to make more than a sergeant's pay to support them all.

Even if he couldn't admit it to himself or not yet, Esther was as sure as she'd ever been about anything. Just like her, her twin brother was a Marine for life.

Chapter 8

"Happy birthday, Marine," Major Lent said, tapping her on the shoulder.

Esther put down her drink and said, "Happy birthday to you, too, sir."

"Not such a big deal here, I know, but wherever there are Marines—"

". . . we'll gather and celebrate, yes, sir."

Actually, Esther had been surprised that they'd even gathered the 81 who'd attended the small ceremony. There had to be a thousand or more up in orbit in Station One, but on the surface, Marines were a rare commodity. And with the secretive nature of some of their real jobs, they didn't do much in the way of advertising their presence. Of the 80 other Marines, Esther knew about 20. Anywhere else, she'd know each and every one of them.

"It's good to see dress blues," the major said. "I've been going through withdrawals."

"I know what you mean, sir."

And she did know what he meant. She'd been in her blues for half-a-dozen formal receptions by now, accompanying the chairman or some minister, but this was different. She wasn't wearing the uniform as a pampered pet to be shown off, but as part of the larger Corps. She felt good, recharged, to put on her blues and mingle with other Marines. It reminded her who she was.

"Did you get a piece of cake? I didn't see you up there."

"Not yet, sir. I came over here to get a drink and beat the rush."

The ceremony had been small. They'd been served dinner in a mid-sized banquet room at Mama Lacona's, a local Italian restaurant. A colonel from Station One had come to read the Commandant's message, and a small cake had been cut, the first piece going to the colonel as the oldest Marine present, the next piece going to a staff sergeant as the youngest Marine. It was nothing like any of the other birthday's Esther had celebrated, but that didn't make it any less meaningful. They didn't need a grand ball to celebrate being a Marine.

"Well, you'd better get there quickly. It was almost gone last time I looked."

"OK, thanks, sir. Maybe I'd better grab mine now," she said, taking her glass with her and wandering back into the banquet room. Several small groups of Marines were chatting, but she bypassed them, walking up to the head table. The cake itself was gone, but there were four pieces left on plates. Esther grabbed one, looking for a fork. But whoever had left out the last four pieces had neglected utensils. No one was looking at her, so with a shrug, she picked it up with her fingers and took half of it in with one bite. It was actually pretty good, and she finished it off with another bite, then licked the frosting off her fingers.

"Join, us, Captain," a lieutenant colonel from one of the small groups said as she started for the cash bar.

She glanced at her almost empty glass, but she dutifully obeyed and joined the group. The lieutenant colonel had his wife with him, one of the few spouses at the ball, and she was out to kill with a long live-cloth gown that was cut perfectly for her figure. Esther stared as the colors shifted seeming in random patterns, but it didn't take long for her to realize that the shifts were coordinated with her make-up. This wasn't fashion—it was choreography.

Each of the Marines seemed to know her—not that she was surprised. Very few Marines sported two Navy Crosses. But for once, no one seemed to pay much attention to her lineage. She was just another Marine on the Marine Corps' birthday. It was rather refreshing, and Esther quickly felt part of the group. The six Marines worked in small arms procurement, and from their conversations, it seemed like their jobs were actual, full-time jobs, not like the Marines in Esther's office. And as a grunt, Esther was frankly interested in what they were doing for the next improvement for the venerable M99. She forgot about the drink in her hand, and when the group was kicked out of the banquet room, they took over a table at the restaurant's bar.

To her surprise, when offered a drink, she asked for a mint tea instead of another single malt. Surprised and pleased. She knew she'd been boozing too much, and refusing now gave her a tiny sense of empowerment.

It wasn't just the six Marines in the group. Holly, the lieutenant colonel's wife, was a research Ph.D., studying something she deftly avoided mentioning when asked. She was the personable one of the couple, and she and Esther hit it off, talking about everything under the sun.

The group broke off at midnight. Holly and her husband had to get home to their kids, but she gave Esther her number and made her promise to meet up sometime. With a few last happy birthdays, Esther found herself alone. Two Marines were in deep conversation at a table in the corner, and Esther got the vibe that three would be a crowd. She considered getting a nightcap, but for the first time since shortly after she'd arrived on Mars, she didn't really want one. She was in a good mood, and she didn't want the night to end, but there wasn't much else going on, so she turned to leave. She could go back and make a few birthday calls, starting with Noah and General Simone. It was the day after for the general, but Noah still had a couple of hours left.

"Happy birthday, Captain Lysander," an older man said from his seat by the door.

"Uh . . . thank you, sir," Esther said, wracking her brain to try and remember who the man might be.

Nicely turned out, he was probably in his seventies or so, and although he had the tiniest accent that Esther couldn't place, she could sense that he knew her.

"Can I buy you one last birthday drink?" he asked.

Is he coming on to me? Really?

"I don't think so, sir. I'm done for the night."

He pushed a glass forward, and Esther could tell it was mint tea.

"Please, Captain, humor an old friend."

"I'm sorry sir, but do I know you?"

"Forgive me, Captain. How rude of me. My name is Titus Pohlmeyer," he said, obviously looking at her for any hint of recognition.

She shook her head.

The man sighed, then said, "I was a friend of your father's. I was hoping he might have mentioned me to you."

"No, sir, he didn't."

"Too bad. That would have made things easier. But please, give me five minutes," he said, hand out to the other chair at the table.

Esther hesitated. People regularly came to her saying they knew her father. She was sure many of them were lying and had ulterior motives. Something about this man spoke the truth to her, however. She took the chair and sat down.

She ignored the tea and asked, "So what do you want?"

"Pretty direct, Captain. Not much like your father, at least when I met him."

"And when was that?"

"When he was a major. On New Mumbai."

In the Confederation?

Suddenly, his slight accent made sense. Esther moved back a few centimeters as if she could distance herself from the man.

"And how did you know him?" she asked, almost not wanting to know.

"We were friends, I'd like to say. We respected each other."

"And what do you want with me?"

"Like I said, you are so direct. But it's standing you in good stead. You've done well in your career, and I don't just mean your two Navy Crosses. Your current position, for example. And I have to say, Copia 2? Now that was just like your father would have done."

Esther stood up, hitting the table with her hip and knocking over her glass of tea.

"Look, I don't know who you are, and I don't know what you think happened on wherever this Copia 2 is, but I'm leaving, and I suggest you do, too."

"Please, please, Captain. I'm not here for anything nefarious. I'm just here to offer you the same thing I offered your father, something he accepted."

Esther stopped, her mind warring with itself. This man was Confederation, and while the two governments were allies, he was obvious an agent of some sort. She should notify the Fourth Ministry and have the man arrested. But what if her father had been working with them? She didn't want to know, but she *had* to know.

"And just what is that?" she asked, steel in her voice.

"Nothing more than an open line of communication. It might not ever be used, but better to have it and not use it than need it and not have it."

"And did my father ever make use of this, this line of communication?"

"It is possible that he did," the man said calmly. "But I can assure you that it was in the interests of the Federation."

Esther paused. There had been rumors that the Confederation had been involved much deeper in the Evolution than had been officially released. Even her father's escape from the first minister's clutches was rumored to have been either conducted, or at least assisted, by Confederation operatives.

She stared at the man, trying to see the truth in his eyes. She saw nothing but an older gentlemen, polite and perfectly normal. But if he was some sort of operative, that was how he would present himself.

"Why me? I'm just a captain."

"And your father was just a major. But like him, we saw something in you. He rose to a position of power, and you could very well do the same thing."

Esther didn't know how to take that. It was a compliment, of course, but this was a representative of a foreign government, and Esther was a Federation citizen, a Marine. Her loyalties were to completely to the Federation.

She was just about to turn away and stalk off when he said, "Captain, I'm asking nothing of you other than to take this number." He pushed an old-fashioned business card across the table towards her. "If there is ever a time in the future when you think it would benefit the Federation to talk to us, then this is your way."

"And if I never do that?"

"Then we can rejoice that there never was a need."

"Am I the only one you are, well, reaching out to?"

He smiled and said, "Hardly. That wouldn't make much sense. No, we identify certain people who have the capability not only to rise within the Federation, but who are astute enough to know when communications would be in order."

"And only with the Federation? What about the Brotherhood? What about the Alliance?"

"I'm afraid I'm not privy to any of that information."

So, he's only the Fagin for the Federation.

Esther wanted to leave, to get out of there, but despite her common sense screaming at her, she somehow trusted the man. She was suddenly sure he had a hand in her father escaping the first minister, and she was sure the rumors about the Confederation and the Evolution were true.

Slowly she reached out and picked up the card. On it was printed a simple number, like any other number that could be connected to throughout human space. She stared at it for a moment, then slid it into her blues' breast pocket.

"I'm not saying I won't trash this in the morning. And I promise you, I will never, ever, do anything against the Federation's interest. I am not a traitor."

"We wouldn't have it any other way, Captain. Please believe me."

"I doubt very much that we will ever speak again, sir."

"I hope not."

She nodded at him, stepped back from the table, then strode out the door. She knew she should report the contact. That was SOP. But what if he was on the up-and-up? Only a few moments in real time had passed, but she was sure he'd been telling the truth about her father, and her father had actually made use of the contact to help save the Federation.

It was up to her to initiate contact, if ever, and it was sure not going to be for anything that would be at odds with the Federation.

She was not a traitor and never would be. She'd get a good night's sleep before she decided what to do.

She felt as if the card was burning a hole in her pocket as she hailed an autocab to go home.

MARS

Chapter 9

Esther nodded at Helen-Lee and stepped into Mr. Byzantine's office. To her surprise, a Marine colonel was sitting on the couch.

"Captain Lysander," the colonel said, rising to his feet, hand out to shake, "I'm Colonel Soeryadjaya. It's good to meet you."

Esther waited, hearing the unspoken "and" in his voice. He didn't disappoint her.

"I served with your father twice. The last time was aboard the *Admiral Kravitch*," he told her, which caught her attention."

Senior officers and staff meeting her tended to lead with their relationship with her father, but to be with him on the *FS Admiral Kravitch* was unique. The small Marine staff, along with the battalion on the *Ballston Shore* and part of the Navy crew, had been the ones to defy Admiral Kurae and the first minister, starting what turned out to be the Evolution. Normally, Esther tended to smile and gloss over the comments, but she'd love to pick the colonel's brain sometime to get his view of what had really happened on that pivotal day in Federation history.

She took the colonel's hand, wondering what he was doing there. Up to now, she'd never seen anyone in uniform in the building.

"Captain, we have another mission for you. Colonel Soeryadjaya will be in charge, so I'll let him brief you."

She shot the colonel another look. A Marine in charge? She liked the idea, but she wondered why. And who was he? He certainly was not one of her peers working in Logistics Command. Then it hit her. Of course, there couldn't just be 19 Marines in this type of billet. There had to be more with various agencies.

"Thank you, Mr. Byzantine," he said, then turning to Esther, "Have you heard of Kepler 9813-B?"

Esther racked her brain, sorting through the chaff. There were probably hundreds of thousands of Keplers, all designated since 2009, Old Reckoning, when the original Kepler satellite started cataloging stars and planets. Most of the viable planets in human's interstellar neighborhood were subsequently renamed and colonized. The ones not yet terraformed or not high on the list of priorities were the ones that still kept the original Kepler designation to this day. If this planet still had a Kepler number, it couldn't have been very important to humanity, Esther wasn't surprised that she didn't recognize the name.

"Fair enough," the colonel said when she shrugged her shoulders. "Let me give you the skinny version. Kepler 9813 is an ultra-cool dwarf. Its previous claim to fame has been its life forms, which basically look like weird Earth fungus.

"Kepler 9813-B is tidally locked. As a dwarf, Kepler 9813's gravity is so powerful that the gravitational gradient creates a synchronous rotation in the planet. So, as you know, the same side of the planet always faces its sun."

Esther didn't automatically know that, but she had no problem with the concept.

"This is not that rare of an occurrence, but usually, planets like this are blasted with too much solar radiation to allow for life. However, because Kepler 9813 is an ultra-cool dwarf, the radiation that hits the planet is in the habitable zone, but only along the rim between the day side and the night side. The reason I'm telling you this is simply to highlight that the world cannot really be terraformed. And while there are traces of O2 on the planet, the atmosphere is deadly to human life."

"Let me guess, sir. You're telling me this because the Marines have a mission on this planet."

"Not the Marines. The Council. The Marines are merely the tools to be used."

Esther nodded, acknowledging the legal difference, then waited for the colonel to continue. She couldn't imagine why Marines would be needed on a planet like that, though.

"What is of interest to the Council is that Allied Biologicals have found a biological structure on the planet that has tremendous potential to humanity."

"A biology that compliments ours? That's . . ."

"Yes, it is," the colonel said.

For the most part, alien life forms discovered so far were incompatible with human life. Capys could eat and survive on Earth food products, but most life seemed to be not only incompatible, but actively inimical with Earth life forms. If this fungus-life or whatever could benefit mankind, then the planet could be a potential windfall.

"Is Kepler 9813-B Federation?"

"We think so, but the Brotherhood has filed with the UAM that it is actually in their territory."

"Interesting that they just filed that now," Mr. Byzantine said, speaking up for the first time since the colonel had started his spiel.

"But if this fungus-thing has that sort of potential to help human life, then doesn't the UAM have to step in?"

The colonel looked at Mr. Byzantine a moment as if checking to see if what he was going to say was allowed before saying, "Allied Biologicals has established a research center on the planet, and the UAM has not been so informed."

"No license was issued?"

"No."

"And if the Brotherhood just filed to take control over the planet, then they know something is up, right, sir?"

"Not just them. There is an unknown commercial entity in the system."

"OK, sir, then why not send in the Navy to chase out the bad guys and put the FCDC on the planet."

"Because doing so will require a response from the Brotherhood now that they've filed the claim. And we don't want things to escalate."

Esther thought it over a moment. It made sense. What didn't make sense was why she was sitting here getting briefed on it.

"So that leads me to you, Captain Lysander. At the command of the Council, through the Second and Fourth Ministries, and with the full support of the First Ministry, you are going to lead a mission of Marines, FCDC troopers, and scientist-types to the station, both to ensure its security, and if that becomes untenable, to keep whatever has been discovered from falling into non-Federation hands.

"Sir?"

"You've been selected, Captain. You've got infantry and recon experience, you now work for the chairman, and no one will question your absence."

Esther tried to take it all in. This was a crazy mission, she had to admit. Still, it had to beat another diplomatic meet and greet, although with a Brotherhood ship of the line there, maybe this would turn out to be karmic payback for her mission during Arrival's Founding Day. Still, she was going back into the field, and that beat what she was doing now by a long shot. Her excitement level was already rising.

"Aye, aye, sir. Just tell me when and where, and I'm there with bells on."

TARAWA

Chapter 10

"OK, Staff Sergeant, let's take a look at you," Esther muttered, swiping in Staff Sergeant Carlito Rapa's MC-100.

As a fellow Navy Cross holder, she'd have known who the staff sergeant was even had he not been anointed "The Grey Death" by the press. His 52 kills on Florin-3, accomplished in two days and despite being seriously wounded, had been widely and intensely reported. But the MC-100 had every bit of data compiled on him from both during his service and prior, so she dutifully started going through it. Nicknamed "Bomba" within the Corps, his record was sterling, even before Florin-3. Esther knew that the SOP for choosing Marines for Level 1 (Spec) missions was to check the entire MC-100, but after two minutes, she shortcut the process, hitting the accept. If the staff sergeant wasn't qualified, then she didn't know who was.

Esther had spent the last 11 hours and counting going through the records of 34 Marine scout-snipers so far in order to select 16 of them for the mission. She had a few recon Marines she'd liked to have selected, but her ops orders were pretty specific in that all Marines needed to be snipers. She'd immediately tried to recruit the newly-promoted Staff Sergeant Bob Burnham, with whom she served on Elysium, but he'd just started the SNCO Academy, and pulling him out would set him back a year.

She reclined in her chair, tipping it almost to the point of no return, and rubbed her eyes. Her back hurt more than if she'd put five hours in the gym.

Come on, Lysander, just buckle down and finish it.

She knew that her list of Marines had been pre-screened, so all of them she'd reviewed so far would probably be fine for the mission, but she wanted to assemble the absolute best team she could. She had no control over which FCDC troops would be assigned to the mission, nor the civilian scientists, but this was the one input she had, and she wasn't going to rush it.

She looked down at her list. Gunnery Sergeants Manuel Chun and Gracie Medicine Crow had been fairly easy choices to make. Each was considered among the Corps' very best. There'd been something about Sergeant Tennerife Delay that had caught her eye, and Sergeant Spig McConnaughy had a sterling record. She'd hesitated over Staff Sergeant Tibone Mubotono. There had been a few oblique comments relating to his attitude, but his accomplishments in the field were impressive, so with only minor hesitation, she'd selected him. Now with Rapa, she was up to six. She had 13 in her maybe list, so if she didn't find the rest on the first go-round, she'd have to go back and re-examined the maybes.

Ten more to go, she told herself as she leaned forward and brought up the next record.

****

Two days later, Esther was standing in the back of the briefing room as Colonel Soeryadjaya briefed her 16 Marines. She and the colonel had already briefed Sergeant First Class Enrico Juarez and his FCDC Internal Security team. And as soon as their civilians arrived, they'd embark aboard the *FS Portoluma Bay* for the Kepler 9813 system.

Things were happening quickly, which wasn't that unique in the Corps, but this was just one more mission that fit the pattern for her, a pattern of deploying with Marines she barely knew yet. And this time, she had FCDC and civilians in her command as well.

Not command, she reminded herself.

The colonel had been pretty clear about it. Esther was in command of the Marines, and she could infer command of the FCDC troops (but he told her not to put that to the test if she could avoid it), but this was a Council mission, and Dr. Tantou was in charge of it. Officially, he wasn't even in one of the ministries. He was from Allied Biologicals. The colonel, however, had hinted that the man might be affiliated with the Fourth Ministry somehow, and he advised her to keep that in mind. Esther could step in for reasons of security, even over-riding the doctor, but for all other purposes, she took her orders from him.

She chaffed at this restriction, but it was no different than anything else she'd been doing for the last year. At least this time, she had Marines with her. She was an addict, finally getting her Marine hit.

She looked over her Marines as the colonel briefed them. Medicine Crow and Rapa were the big names here, but all of them were the cream of the crop. Sergeant Marco Piccolo had even served with her with 3/14—not in her platoon, but in Second Platoon.

"And this is Kepler 9813-B," the colonel was saying. "The planet's claim to fame has been its life forms, which look somewhat similar to fungus on Earth."

Esther kept back a smile. He'd used almost the exact same wording to her two days previous. She wondered how many other times he'd briefed this mission.

He switched the view on the table display to an image of the planet's surface, a section of land covered with what looked like rotting mushrooms.

"No terraforming, sir?" Staff Sergeant Rapa asked.

"Not worth it, Staff Sergeant Rapa. As you can see," the colonel said, switching the display back to a system image, "9813-B is tidally locked. Kepler 9813's gravity is so powerful that the gravitational gradient creates a synchronous rotation in the planet. That means, the same side of the planet always faces its sun.

"This is not that rare of an occurrence, but usually, planets like this are blasted with too much solar radiation to allow for life. However, because Kepler 9813 is an ultra-cool dwarf, the radiation that hits the planet is in the habitable zone, but only along the rim between the day side and the night side."

"Oh, like *Ribbon World*," Sergeant Shaan said.

The colonel gave Esther a quick glance, a small smile tilting the corner of his mouth. One of the FCDC soldiers had said the very same thing earlier in the morning.

"*Ribbon World* is a figment of some Hollybolly writer's imagination," the colonel answered. "The idea might make for an interesting setting, but the practicality isn't there. Yes, the trope has been alive in scifi books and flicks for centuries, but there is a reason why no tidally locked planet has ever been terraformed.

"Oh, sorry, let me get off my soapbox. The bottom line is that the planet has not been terraformed, nor will it be. You can't survive on the planet. There are only traces of oxygen, but don't worry about that. Before you could suffocate, the hydrogen cyanide would kill you."

If the colonel had been waiting for laughter, he was waiting in vain. The FCDC troopers hadn't laughed at the same word-for-word comment, either.

Esther watched the Marines as the colonel went on. So far, they all seemed attentive, but not too concerned. She wasn't surprised, but still, an MC-100 was simply a file of records. It could never be a total picture of someone, and the slightest change of expression could be indicative of a problem. They would be boarding the *Portoluma Bay* in about seven hours unless there was a glitch, but that left plenty of time to drop someone. Two of her alternates were here on Tarawa, and they could be brought in if needed.

"So, why not send in the FCDC?" the colonel said, bringing Esther back to the brief. "The problem is that if we send in the troops, we're essentially opening up a Pandora's Box. We're announcing to the galaxy what we're doing, and we need more time to develop the potential before we do that. Sending the FCDC, or a Marine battalion, will require a response in kind from the Brotherhood, and we don't want war."

"So, you send us in unofficially to protect the research station from the unofficial Brotherhood personnel and the unofficial corporate personnel, and no one raises a fuss, right Colonel?" Gunny Medicine Crow asked. "There's nothing really happening, after all."

"You got it in one, Gunny. That's about the long and short of it.

"And with that, I'm going to turn it over to Captain Lysander, who will be the mission commander. She'll give you your initial brief now on what you have to do to get ready, then you'll receive more on the ship. You embark in seven hours, so I suggest you pay attention. Captain?"

He stood, waving everyone else down as they started to rise as well, then nodded and left the room. Esther waited until the hatch shut behind him before speaking.

"As the colonel said, I'm Captain Lysander, and I'll be commanding this mission.

"First, I'm sorry to say, all of you have failed your interview for the CEAC."

This time, the Marines all laughed. The CEAC, or the Commandant's Enlisted Advisory Council, had been the purported excuse to draw the sixteen Marines here to Tarawa.

"But as the colonel said, we embark in seven hours, and we've got a lot to cover, so let's get down to it.

"First, we will not be on this mission alone. We have an FCDC team attached—"

There was a collective groan and a couple of muttered "Fuckdicks?"

Esther held out her hand to quiet them, saying, "I don't want to hear 'fuckdicks' for the duration of the mission, even when you think you're alone, understand?"

There were nods and mutters of assent, and so she continued, "And we will be working under a civilian team of scientists."

There were more groans, and this time Esther didn't stop them.

"I've broken you up into two sections with Gunnies Chun and Medicine Crow as section leaders. We're expected in the division armory in 20. Each Marine will draw the primary of his or her choice, but section leaders, ensure that your section has the full spectrum of weapons for any contingency.

"Gunny Medicine Crow, you are senior, so you are the SNCOIC of the detachment. Get everyone to the armory, then to supply for equipment draw. You've got full authorization at supply, so take what you think you need. Then meet me back here with full kit by 1400 for your deployment brief. Understood?"

"Roger that, ma'am," she said, then turning to the rest of the Marines, "You heard the captain. Let's move out."

Within moments, the Marines had gotten out of their seats and exited the room, all with minimal fuss, all without horseplay and grab ass. Digesting what she'd observed over the last 20 minutes, she was pleased. These were professionals, all proven in combat.

This is going to go without a hitch.

FS PORTOLUMA BAY

Chapter 11

"Ears, got anything?" Lieutenant Commander Chacon, captain of the *Portoluma Bay* asked.

The *Porto* was a schooner, a new class of small, stealthy ships with more surveillance and stealth capabilities than arms. As a smaller ship, she rated a lieutenant commander as a skipper. Most of the ships Esther had been on had been commanders and captains, but she'd also been on the Space Guard ship *UFSGS Manta*, commanded by the then Senior Chief Arleigh Carpenter, so this wasn't that odd. What did feel odd to her was that along with a few of the navy officers, she had the second highest rank aboard the ship.

Now, falling out of bubble space 900,000,000 kilometers from Kepler 9813-B, the *Porto* was running silent in full stealth mode, silently drifting while it tried to pierce the shielding of any other ship that might be in the system.

The *Porto* had Kylefelter meson cannon and Clovis launchers, so she packed a decent punch when compared to commercial freighters and pirates, but she was outclassed as a ship-of-the-line. If there was a Brotherhood man-o-war in-system, the captain wanted to know about her before her counterpart on the other ship knew about the *Porto*.

"Negative, sir. All quiet," Lieutenant (jg) Haddad, the Surveillance Officer said.

"Guns, stand down the cannon, but keep the missile tubes ready," the skipper ordered before turning to Esther and saying, "We'll just sit quiet for an hour or so to see if our arrival was noticed.

If there's nothing, we'll start moving in until the POC; then it's your call."

Dr. Tantou was the actual mission commander, or Chief of Mission as his official title, but LCDR Chacon had ignored the man, treating Esther as the mission commander. Dr. Tantou hadn't objected, so Esther hadn't corrected the man. Whether Tantou or Esther commanded, however, it was the skipper who was in charge of the mission at the moment, and he would remain in command until the ship reached the Passage of Command, a control measure that signaled the shift of command from the Navy to the ground element. From that moment on, the *Porto* would be the subordinate element.

Esther nodded and settled in to wait. She and the gunny were the only two Marines in the crowded bridge, and there wasn't much they could do except observe.

Ten minutes later, the first class petty officer in charge of communications, spoke out, "Sir! We've got comms going out. Putting it on the speakers now."

". . .don't know how much longer we can hold out."

"Who is that, and why are we just now hearing it?" the skipper shouted.

"That's Alpha-Three, sir, the research station. I've only just now got through the protocol for booting in-system comms."

"Any identification on who is attacking?" another voice asked.

"That's Goby Station responding to Alpha-Three," the petty officer said without being asked.

"Fuck! I think they just broke through!" a panicked voice said. "You've got to help us!"

"Ears, what's going on?" the skipper asked the lieutenant (jg).

"I'm picking up the same broadcast, but not much else. I don't know who's attacking them."

Esther's mind was whirling. That was the Federation research team being attacked, and a Marine's purpose in life was to protect all citizens.

"Captain, how long to get my team down to their position?" she asked.

The skipper looked to her master chief for confirmation, then said, "As fast as we could? Maybe eight hours. That's using the shuttle, not the duck eggs. Add another ten hours if you want to use those."

"We need help now! You've got to get here! I can hear them outside the door!" the operator from Alpha-Three said.

"Wait one," Goby Station passed.

"I can't wait!"

Esther knew they couldn't get down to the surface in time to help, and she felt helpless. She'd listened before when Gunny Monty Montogomery and his recon team had been lost, and she'd swore then never to go through something like that again, yet here she was again. But what could she do if they couldn't get down to the surface in time?

And then it hit her. They could make it seem like they could get down. They could spoof whoever was attacking. At the minimum, a threat of retaliation could make the attacker pause, leaving the station crew alive. At the worst, it could reveal who they are, and then revenge could be extracted.

"We can't make it," Esther said. "They're lost. But maybe there's something we can do."

"I'm all ears," the skipper said.

"First, if we initiate comms with them, can anyone trace us?"

"Depends on what kind, ma'am," the communications chief said. "On a direct beam, not likely, but possibly."

"I don't mean that. On the hadron comms."

As a Navy ship, the Porto had hadron comms, which weren't broadcast as in normal communications. Hadron repeaters were linked together upon manufacture, and through the magic of quantum mechanics, what was input into one was input into all of the other 15 twined repeaters. This allowed for instantaneous communications that were also secure. Esther knew that they were secure, but her plan was forming as she talked it through.

A Navy ship and large entities would have hadron comms, but they were expensive and difficult to manufacture. Most worlds had large hadron nodes that communicated with other nodes, bouncing around the network until reaching the intended recipient.

On a world like Kepler 9813-B, there would be no large nodes, so the first explorer ship would have left a satellite which would be linked to a node somewhere. Messages intended to go off-system would be sent to that satellite, and that message could be intercepted. If the Porto tried to communicate with the station, that would almost certainly be picked up by any ship in the system.

"Well, we could use the hadrons back to PEM302, then have it re-routed here and sent out under standard comms."

"And whoever is out there won't be able to pick us up?"

"No, ma'am."

"Captain, send a message to them to hold on, and we'll be there in two days."

"But we can get you there sooner than that."

"Yes, sir. But we can't get there in time. Those unfortunate souls are lost," Esther said. "We can't save them, but maybe we can flush out who're the attackers."

"Ah, I get it. Pass that, and then sit here and see who bites."

"Yes, sir."

The skipper paused for a moment, head tilted up as he thought about it, and then he grabbed a stylus and started scribbling on his PA.

"Pass that over the hadrons via NF3, Greg, and make sure it comes back over the node in the open."

"Aye-aye, sir."

Esther stood silent, her nerves on fire as she waited for the petty officer to sent the message.

A few moments later, the speakers broke with "K9813B Alpha Three, this is the *FS Admiral Miguel Posov*. We are on our way, ETA 40.32 hours. Hold on the best you can."

"I can't hold on that long!"

"Understand your situation. Get into your panic room and wait. Do not attempt to resist or secure property. God be with you."

"The *Posov*, sir?" Esther asked.

"Might as well make it something with a little more punch than we have. And I know she's out cruising right now. We sent

Jonathan P. Brazee

that out through Third Fleet, and they'll tell the *Posov* to keep low for the next 40 hours."

With the message sent, it was time to wait to see if anyone took the bait and reacted. It didn't take long.

Less than two minutes had passed when the comms chief said, "I've got an anomaly, sir. Probably a shielded ship moving closer to the planet."

"Brotherhood?" the skipper asked.

"I'm running the probabilities on that, but I don't think so. Looks commercial, probably Yantos-made, possibly GE."

Esther had been listening with every fiber of her body, and she was relieved to find out that the ship was commercial. They just didn't have the strength to take on most Brotherhood men-of-war.

Esther hoped that the message would save the lives of the station personnel. The message, however, gave the attackers a timeline, and whatever research was on the station would be taken and whisked away. Even if they launched now, Esther doubted they could get there in time to prevent that.

But we don't have to stop them on the surface, now, do we?

"Sir," Esther asked, "Are your lifeboats shielded?"

"No," the master chief, "Boats," they called him, answered for the skipper. "That sort of defeats the purpose of a life boat in being seen. Our rekis are shielded, though."

"You have rekis? I didn't see them on the manifest."

The *Porto* was not a full-sized ship of the line. There was no Stork or Navy fighter sitting in a hangar bay. As far as Esther had known, the ship only had her shuttles and lifeboats.

"I don't think they were originally part of the TE, but we've had them as long as I've been aboard. They're in C24. I can have them assembled in an hour."

"So, they're the R version?" Esther asked.

"That's affirm."

"Captain, I take it that you want to take your Marines and seize that ship out there?" the skipper asked her.

"Yes, sir. I'm assuming you don't want to break your own shielding by firing at the vessel, and I know the Federation doesn't want any of the research to get out of the system. We don't know what's being uploaded, but all the samples will need to be lifted off the surface.

"And there's another thing. If we're going to have to clear out the bad guys, I'd rather they didn't have any support the ship there can provide. I want them cut off."

The skipper seemed to contemplate it, but he didn't answer with a yes or no, and this was his call.

"Any more information, Ears?" he asked the JG.

"Their shielding is pretty good, but I'm getting enough gravitational disturbances to know they're out there, and it looks like they're heading to take up a position along a standard ascent profile for the station."

"How long to reach a launch point for the rekis, given full stealth?" the captain asked the navigator.

"About six hours, sir. Anything faster, and we'll start to lose stealth. If we launch the rekis, though, sir, and if there's a Brotherhood ship out there, she'll see the sleds," she said.

"She'll know something is out there, like I know we've got something out there, but she won't know exactly what," Ears said. "She won't know they're Federation rekis."

The captain chewed his lower lip as he processed all this for a few moments before making his decision, saying, "Nav, bring her in.

"And Captain Lysander, what's your plan?"

Chapter 12

The target ship, a Yantos Executive III, looked huge in the near distance, and Esther felt extremely vulnerable. Through the pinholes poked into the reki's tarnkappe, she could see the individual EVA crewmen offloading a shuttle into the ship. She felt as if one errant look by one of them, and they'd be spotted.

The R-version reki, was heavily shielded from normal surveillance, and the sled had a large version of the infantry trankappe, which essentially "bent" light around the sled, making it invisible to the naked eye when viewed straight on. Still, anyone from the side could see them. Esther trusted the Navy coxswain to keep the right attitude, but mistakes happened.

This was Esther's second space-borne operation. Traditionally, this was the Corps' bread-and-butter, but over the centuries, the Corps had become more of a land force. However, as the very first Marines, the Roman I and II Adiutrix, were a sea-borne infantry—something her history-loving father had pounded into her young head as a child—Esther felt the pull of tradition.

She still felt awfully naked and exposed, though, and even the knowledge that the *Porto* was only 20 short klicks away was not that much of a comfort.

Esther was leading the boarding section. Ahead of her, Gunny Medicine Crow was leading the clearing section. Her section would take out as many of the enemy as they could and secure the hangar, clearing the way for Esther's team to board and secure the rest of the ship. Their priority was to keep the hangar bay doors open. If they were closed before the Marine could board, then they would have to resort to the breaching chamber. That would probably result in either the ship's crew arranging for a hot reception or the ship merely taking off. The *Porto* wouldn't let that happen, but Esther didn't want her Marines in the crossfire between two ships.

Up ahead, less than 500 meters away, Esther could see the gunny's sled as it approached. They were on a comms blackout, so she had only a basic idea of what was going on. When the gunny opened fire, that would be Esther's signal to go.

Firing projectile weapons in null-G was not easy with weapons designed for planetary usage. However, Esther had noted that the gunny had logged hours upon hours on the null-G simulators, so aside from being the senior enlisted Marine, she was probably the most qualified.

"She's orienting her aspect," the coxswain passed on the hardwire comms on the sled.

Esther could see the reki rotating. The gunny had explained that while the orientation didn't matter in space—there was no up or down, after all—but from a shooter's perspective, they tended to be more accurate when the orientation was the same. With the artificial gravity, the ship had an up and down, and she wanted to be on the same axis. What that meant to Esther was that the assault was getting close to kicking off.

"Get ready," she passed on the wire to the rest of the section.

Suddenly, there was a flurry of activity around the ship. A crewman, dressed in his green cargo overalls, dropped just as he reached for the red emergency door button. It was eerily silent, with no air to carry the sound and the comms still off.

"Move it," she ordered the coxswain.

And then the comms silence was broken as the gunny passed, "Find the gunners!"

Esther kept off the net herself. She didn't want to alert the ship's crew.

They glided forward, and Esther wanted to tear down the tarnkappe to see what was going on. The pinhole was just too small to get the big picture. She could see the Marines enter the hangar, but she couldn't tell if they were winning or not.

The coxswain swung around to pierce the atmospheric curtain when the gunny finally passed, "Falcon One, we are secure."

"Roger that. We're 30 seconds out," Esther said.

Esther tore away the tarnkappe as they came in. The coxswain had the reki at a slight angle as she breached the curtain, and there was that slight moment of disorientation as gravity took control of their inner ears.

Ignoring the Marines and prisoners, her section rushed to the main hatch into the rest of the ship. Sergeant Piccolo set a small breaching device against the hatch, and ten seconds later, it erupted in a glorious display of purple, yellow, and blue sparks that reached out to fall slowly to the deck. Piccolo kicked the hatch, and it swung open. Within moments, Esther's team was dashing through.

Esther hadn't fought with any of the Marines before, and they'd had only half an hour to rehearse aboard the *Porto*, but this was when training kicked in. Everyone knew what he or she had to do.

Ahead of her, a crewman in engineer purples came out of a hatch, saw, them, and ducked back inside. Piccolo looked back as Esther for instructions, but she waved him forward. She didn't care about a lone sailor. She wanted to secure the bridge before the ship started to move out.

They'd pulled up the schematics of a Yantos Executive III before leaving, and so far, the schematics had been true to form. This ship had not undergone major modifications. Two minutes after breaching the hatch in the hangar, they were at the bridge—which was closed off.

Esther gave Staff Sergeant Cezar Constaninescu the signal, and he placed the charge he'd been carrying along the edge of the hatch.

"Fire in the hole!" he shouted, as the rest of them crowded back into the passage.

"Stop! Don't blow it!" a voice came over the 1MC. "We surrender!"

The staff sergeant looked back at Esther with a questioning look, but it was too late. She wasn't going to send him forward to try and stop the charge, risking it going off in his face.

"I'd get back as far as I could if I were you!" she shouted into the air.

A moment later, there was a muffled boom, and the Marines darted forward. Piccolo kicked in the hatch, which had been askance, and the rest poured into the room, weapons ready.

Five sailors were inside the bridge, all just getting to their feet, hands in the air. There was no fight in them

"I'm Captain Esther Lysander, United Federation Marine Corps. This ship is now mine."

KEPLER 9813-B

Chapter 13

"Roger that," Esther said, trying to keep her cool.

She closed the connection, resisting the temptation to punch the display. The comms "station," which was a grandiose term for what was merely a table pushed up against the wall with her gear on it, was in the research station's main room, and she was aware that eyes were on her. She couldn't let any one of her Marines see that she was frustrated with Dr. Tantou, to put it mildly.

Esther and her Marines, along with the FCDC Installation Security team, had arrived at the station two days earlier to find 16 citizens killed during the takeover. Three people had been discovered alive, but in a state of shock.

Esther had initially decided to leave the civilians in the team aboard the *Porto* until she could ensure that the ground situation was safe. Dr. Tantou had vetoed that idea, insisting that his team come down to "inventory" the station, which Esther knew meant see what might have been taken that hadn't been recovered.

Esther tried to get the COM to listen to reason, figuring he'd be concerned with his own skin, but to no avail. He simply told her that security was her bailiwick, so "secure it."

And that was what Esther was trying to do. The research station was designed for 30 people. With 17 Marines, 16 civilians, and eight FCDC station guards, the station's life-support systems would be taxed to the limit. The slightest breach in the station, whether caused by an accident or outside action, could push the station past the breaking point. The Marines could survive outside the station for a week or more inside their HED 2's or Hazardous Environment Deployment System 2's. They might not be as robust as the Marines' System 3's, but they would do. The FCDC troopers had their own suits that would allow them to perform outside the station for up to 48 hours. The civilians simply had vacuum suits that got them from the shuttle to the station's airlock. They were rated for 30 minutes in the planet's atmosphere.

If it came to a breach, the civilians needed to don the emergency enviro-suits that should keep them alive for 16-20 hours. The issue with Esther was that none of the civilians had ever put on the suits before.

It seemed logical to Esther that all personnel go through drills to make sure they knew what to do should a breach occur. With that in mind, she scheduled a drill for that afternoon (with no planetary rotation, there was no night or day, so they were using Earth GMT time). She'd summoned Tantou to the intercom—Marines and FCDC, who were openly—and dismissively—referred to as "muscle," were restricted from the main lab—and told him to get his people ready, and he'd flat out refused. They were "too busy," and she'd simply have to make sure there was no breach that could overcome the station's self-repairing capabilities.

In Esther's opinion, his reaction contravened the MOU between the three organizations. She had the final say in issues of security, and this was a security matter. So she'd marched over to the comms and, using the *Porto* as a relay, connected with her minder back wherever he was. The minder had blown her off, for all intents and purposes, so she'd contacted the colonel.

She didn't get the answer she'd hoped.

"Stand down, Captain," he'd said. "Feel free to drill your Marines and the FCDC troopers, but it's hands off the civilians. That's coming from on high. I trust I'm making myself clear?"

Esther was a Marine and would follow orders, even if she didn't like them. She had full responsibility for security, but she had no control over the group least trained to deal with a contingency. That contingency could very well become a reality.

The *Porto* had moved farther out from the planet, but not before running a full planetary scan. That scan revealed that there was a heavily shielded (not shielded enough, evidently) group of humans located about 2,000 klicks north of the research station. The *Porto's* Intel officer aboard the ship gave it an 86% probability that they were a mid-level corporate pirate group, hoping to grab a few discoveries and run back to the parent company where whatever they'd found could be exploited. Esther would most likely be tasked with rounding them up, but as they posed no real physical threat at the moment, that would only occur once the Federation station was secure.

"At the moment," however, was hardly a guarantee. The first station had not been protected as there had been no credible threat, and Esther could see how that played out.

Security was the Marine's highest priority at the moment, so Esther had to focus on that. With Tantou nixing the EA drills, she had to push forward with what she could control. She'd already had the FCDC team set up their hi-sec entrance to the station, and she'd given orders to the two gunnies to plan orientation patrols. They had to see the lay of the land if they were going to be able to defend it, much less go on the offense.

The first patrol might be for orientation, but some of the corporate mercs who'd killed Federation citizens were still out there. Just because they'd run didn't mean they wouldn't strike again if given the opportunity.

She looked back at the secured hatch leading into the lab, thinking dark thoughts about the COM, wishing she could throw them like mental daggers. That wasn't going to do any good, but the image of him reeling under her superpowers made her smile for the briefest moment.

This might be a long, long, deployment, she told herself as she turned back to her Marines.

Chapter 14

Esther listened with half an ear as Gunny Medicine Crow's team watched the entertainment screen. She could sometimes get lost in the programs, but each time she tried to watch, her mind came up with something new she thought she had to address. She'd only been in an independent command once, with her MARSOC team on Elysium. While the threat had been far greater there, she knew what she faced, and the action kept her occupied. Here, her mind jumped from one possibility to another, and no matter how unlikely each one was, she felt she had to plan for it.

She turned her head to see the large display where Verry Onkle of the Alliance Explorer Corps was managing another improbable crisis while relying on her rather extensive cleavage and sexuality. Esther couldn't refrain from rolling her eyes, and she wondered how Gunny Medicine Crow and Sergeant Delay could watch that crap, but they seemed addicted to it.

The alarm jolted her, and she was on her feet before it registered on her, slapping on her helmet. She'd ordered that the Marines and troopers keep on their suits at all times unless they were in the autojets showering, and their helmets had to be within reach. She'd run several drills, demanding three seconds for compliance. With her own helmet sealed, she was pleased to see that the gunny's entire section was suited up as well.

Ether checked the station readings: integrity was solid 100's across the board. So, it wasn't a breach. She stepped back to check the security screens, and on number 6, she could see that one of the FCDC guards was down, holding his leg. On the bottom of the screen, the guard's bio readouts showed him to be alive, but in shock and pain.

"Did he fall over his own feet?" Sergeant Ganesh asked.

Gunny Medicine Crow beat Esther to the screen, swiping a 60-second repeat. The guard's image appeared, with him slowly walking his post. He walked about 15 meters or so, then turned around. He paused for a second, and just as he started to move again, he fell to the ground, clutching his knee.

"First Team, out with me. Take cover and keep your eyes peeled. Second, cover the entrance," gunny told her section.

"Wha—" Esther started to ask, but then bit it off. The gunny wasn't hesitating, and if she thought she needed to move so aggressively, she didn't need her commander on her butt demanding an explanation. For a moment she wanted to follow First Team out, but she knew her place was right there at their mini-command center.

"Captain, what's going on?" Dr. Tantou passed through the station's sound system.

"Stay in the lab, Doctor," Esther told him. "We've got a situation out here."

"What kind of situation?"

"I don't have time now. Stay off the net," she said.

If I knew myself, maybe I'd tell you.

She looked back on the visuals. The gunny was leading her team, advancing in full tactical mode. Two of the IS guards, carrying the downed guard, met them at the corner of the station. The gunny had two of her team provide cover while the rest of them hustled the first guard to the airlock.

The gunny obviously thought this was an assault of some sort, but Esther didn't know why. It looked like the guard had twisted his knee somehow. She checked the surveillance drones, both the Marine dragonflies and the Navy drones, but there was nothing showing up that triggered any kind of alarm.

The front airlock was cycling, so Esther left the screens and waited at the door. When it opened, the three IS guards and three Marines stepped inside, and it was immediately evident what had happened. Spec Alfayed had taken a round in his knee. The joint was destroyed.

"Lay him down right there," Esther said, pointing to the deck right by the door.

Everyone coming through the airlock was hit with both a chemical wash and IR to remove the residuals of the outside atmosphere. But Alfayed had been shot in the knee, and that would have brought the poison into his body. He was contaminated, and the station's life support systems didn't need the extra load.

"Dr. Williams, please come out here now. Specialist Alfayed has been shot," Esther passed to the Allied Biologicals scientist who was doubling as their medical officer.

"Sergeant De Vries, get the decon kit off the bulkhead. Sergeant Ganesh, get the *Porto*. Tell them we've got one WIA. We're going to need a CASEVAC, but right now, I want them to run a trace and find out who did this."

Within moments, Dr. Williams entered, Dr. Tantou in tow. He assessed the wound, then started injecting the decon foam right into the wound. Spec Alfayed grimaced, squeezing Spec 5 Holsom's hands.

The airlock cycled again, and the other two Marines, along with SFC Juarez came in.

The FCDC team leader rushed forward, asking, "Is Farouk going to be OK?"

"He's got some regen time ahead of him," the doctor said. "But he'll be fine."

"Hear that, F-man? You're going to be fine," Spec 5 Holsom told him.

"He's lucky," Esther said, more to herself than to the gunny, who was standing beside her.

"No luck to it, Skipper," the gunny said.

"What do you mean?"

"That was a controlled shot. The sniper wanted to take out the knee. It was a message to us, and that trooper was the messenger."

Esther didn't have a clue as to how the gunny could say that with such conviction, but she didn't question her. The gunny was one of the best snipers in the Corps, if not in humanity. If she said Alfayed's knee was the intended target, Esther would have to accept that.

And then that left the message, which was pretty clear. Someone wanted them off the planet.

Chapter 15

"So what do we do, Captain?" Gunny Chun asked.

Esther ran through her options. She knew what she should do, but she had to consider all of the ramifications first. She wished the dragonflies were sending back clear intel, but even without that extra source of data, there was really only one course of action.

"I'm taking this as a potential threat to the station's safety. As such, it's my call, and my call is that we're going to get visuals on them, and if I still deem them a threat, we're going to take them out."

There was a chorus of "ooh-rahs" from the rest as the Marines expressed their joy at finally being able to do something.

"Specialist Khan, please get Sergeant First Class Juarez," Esther told the trooper on watch.

"And since Calcutta was in the port section's AO, Gunny Medicine Crow, your team's got it. Sorry about that, Gunny Chun."

She could see the gunny's face fall, while Staff Sergeant Rapa punched Gunny Medicine Crow's arm in excitement.

"But I'm going with you, Gunny," she told Medicine Crow. "To give weapons free in case our comms are being jammed."

That was reasonable, Esther knew, but she couldn't help but feel excited to be getting out of the station. She'd already gone out with both sections on patrols, but since Alfayed had been shot, there was an added degree of intensity.

The *Porto* had been able to run a trace on the round that had destroyed Alfayed's knee. It had been fired from 1,616 meters out. The bullet fragments the Porto's surgeon had extracted from the trooper's knee had yet to be analyzed, but they looked to be from a .3005—which was the caliber of the round typically used by Brotherhood snipers. It was bad enough that Intel was sure there was a Brotherhood ship-of-the-line in the system, but if they had put combat troops on the ground, the stakes had been considerably raised.

And now the seisos they'd put out had registered a hit at Calcutta, a ridge and one of the many registration points surrounding the station. At 4,600 meters, Calcutta was almost out of sniper range, but there were crew served weapons, such as a simple mortar, which could easily reach that far. And even if whoever out there simply wanted to observe them, Esther was not OK with that. She wanted to find out who was out there and to disrupt whatever they were trying to do.

Juarez cycled through the lock and reported to Esther. The sergeant first class had been somewhat of a pain in her ass. He seemed to walk around with a permanent chip on his shoulder, and after Alfayed had been shot, he'd bordered on insubordination while demanding that action be taken. Esther understood his protective posture of his troopers. It was commonly known that Installation Security was at the bottom of the FCDC hierarchy, and that could explain the way he seemed to be looking for something at which he could take offense.

Esther, though, wasn't going to take any shit from him. Taking the colonel's instructions, however, not to push the command issue, she was trying not to get too much into his hair and not to give him any orders that would go against their SOP.

"We've got contact, probably three people, on Calcutta," she started, seeing the immediate surge of interest cross his face. "Gunnery Sergeant Medicine Crow is going to investigate, and I'm going with her. As soon as we leave the station, make sure you've got our telltales registering on your displays. I want you to continue your security sweeps as normal and in full view of the ridge, but if anything goes down, take cover on the west side of the station. Do not engage unless ordered to. Understand?"

"Yes, ma'am. I've got it," he said, and Esther could almost detect something different in his voice.

A wistfulness?

Then it hit her. The guy was jealous. He wanted to go out and engage. That kind of attitude could be good or bad. He wasn't going to shirk his duties, but would he go overboard somehow, anxious to prove himself? She filed that away in her brain housing group for contemplation later.

Eight minutes later, the patrol was cycling through the auxiliary lock on the west side of the station. That kept them out of sight of anyone watching from Calcutta. The gunny had selected somewhat of a round-about route around the station and off at an oblique through a shallow depression that gave them concealment. The depression angled away to the south, but after 150 meters, it was bisected by a fissure, one that petered out just a few hundred meters from Calcutta. Not that they would approach that closely. All they needed to do was get eyes on the target to see what was there. A wrinkle above the fissure should give them that ability.

The patrol moved quickly up the depression, then turning into the fissure, had to slow down due to the uneven ground. Still, it was only 21 minutes after leaving the station that they reached the wrinkle. That was an amazing accomplishment, one that filled Esther with pride. But it was still more than enough time for the tactical situation to change, and Esther kept expecting the sound of an assault on the station.

The gunny nodded at Esther, then with Staff Sergeants Rapa and Mubotono, crept up and out of the fissure to take Calcutta under observation.

Esther chafed at remaining behind. She wanted to see the ridge herself. But she knew that the more Marines that could see the ridge, the more targets whoever was on the ridge would have a chance to spot.

The fewer the better, her tactical mind said.

Screw that, her emotional mind added in counterpoint.

Above her, the flat plates of the fungus (Esther knew they were not fungus, but it was easier to think of them as such) the Marines called the "shingles" reached over the edge of the fissure, like beach umbrellas giving shade. Nasty ugly beach umbrellas, umbrellas that made her shudder, perhaps, but that is how they struck her. Their redeeming feature was that they should give the gunny and the two others good concealment.

Ten minutes later, Staff Sergeant Rapa slithered over the side and back into the fissure.

"We've got an energy weapon of some sort and three pax," he told her.

"What kind of energy weapon?" she asked. "That's a long shot for beamers."

In space, plasma and meson guns had almost unlimited range, but on a planet with an atmosphere—and Kepler 9813-B's atmosphere was thicker than Earth-normal, even if it was poisonous to humans—the beams rapidly ablated.

"Can't tell. They've got some sort of shielding going on, kinda like a tarnkappe. But it's a big one. Crew-served. Aimed right at the station, too. Gunny thinks we need to engage it and wants your go-ahead."

Esther didn't hesitate. She'd pretty much decided already what she would do if there was someone there that posed a threat, and the gunny's assessment merely solidified her decision.

"Take it out. Take them out."

The staff sergeant nodded, then asked for Sergeant De Vries. His full surname was De Vries-De Jun, but despite Esther's predilection for by-the-book, she cut his name to De Vries (everyone else simply called him "Dutch.")

Esther felt a tiny pang of jealousy as the sergeant disappeared with the staff sergeant up and over the fissure.

I know what you feel like now, Juarez, she told herself, the Marine in her wanting to be at the forefront of any action.

Esther was tempted to try and tie into the gunny's display. But even if their comms were not being blocked, they were on complete emission-silence, so she had to wait blind. This was the gunny's show, and she had to trust her.

Trusting her subordinates had been one of the most difficult things for Esther to do once she got commissioned. It was still a struggle, even when serving with the cream of the crop.

The five Marines still in the fissure waited—and waited. Esther kept checking the time as five minutes, then ten passed.

What the hell's taking them so long?

And then a fusillade of shots rang out. Esther immediately climbed the wall of the fissure and started pushing her way through the fungus, oblivious to the white fungus-milk that oozed out and coated her HED as she crushed their lobes.

The four Marines had finished firing by the time she threw herself down beside the gunny and raised her binos.

"Three dead and the weapon probably put out of action. No sign of anyone else," Gunny told her.

Esther could see two bodies and what was probably a large crew-served weapon covered by a cloak of some kind. There was no sign of any movement.

She brought down the glasses and said, "Good job, Gunny. I'm sending Delay back now."

The Hollybolly war flicks never showed it, but in the modern battlefield, the use of messengers was not that rare of an occurrence. With all the interference blocking comms, Sergeant Delay had been designated as the runner to tell Gunny Chun to clear Calcutta.

Esther kept glassing, and 13 minutes later, Gunny Chun's Starboard Section was heading out in a tactical formation. Her plan had been to stay with the Port Section, but she changed her mind as the Starboard Section advanced. She got up and jogged almost 700 meters, joining up with Gunny Chun. She needed to get personal and up close with Calcutta to assess the threat.

Almost 25 minutes later, they reached Calcutta. Two bodies were on one side of the crew-served, one on the other. Esther knew immediately that they were dead, but as per SOP, Sergeant Piccolo checked them while the rest covered him. Esther's eyes kept straying to the crew-served.

As soon as the ridge was secure, Staff Sergeant Kneffer walked up to the crew-served and pulled off the cloak. She didn't recognize the make or model of the cannon, but it was a pretty impressive piece. The display had been hit and destroyed, so she couldn't read the power parameters, but there was no doubt in her mind that it would range the station with significant effect.

It was also too big to bring back to the station.

"Slag it," she told the gunny.

He pulled out a toad, activated it, and set it on top of the casing. Five seconds later, it erupted in a glare so bright that they all had to turn away, the HED's face shields unable to compensate. After another 20 seconds, half of the cannon was slag.

"I guess that's it, Gunny. Let's head on back," Esther said.

Esther had been confident as to the righteousness of her decision to fire. Nothing changed after seeing the cannon.

You come to play with us, you pay the price, she told the three dead men as she turned to walk away.

Chapter 16

Esther took another bite of her lunch, something generously labeled "Caspian Pilaf." She'd never heard of the dish before but had decided to give it a shot as one of the limited menu options on their field fabricator. She shouldn't have. The Mac and Cheese was a known quantity, and the fabricator could handle that. Still, it was calories, and that was what she needed.

Dr. Tantou was at the fabricator, along with Dr. Verone, arguing over something like children, and Esther tried to tune them out. The station was too small and too crowded, and Esther was surprised that nothing had boiled over yet.

The Marines and the IS troopers got along well. Even some of the civilians, like Dr. Williams, could be pleasant and personable. Within the civilians, however, tension was rising. Esther didn't know the details as most of the arguments took place in the lab, but it seemed as if many of the researchers were taking issue with Tantou's leadership and the direction of what they were doing.

None of that was in Esther's area of responsibility, but the constant bickering added to the stress levels of the pressure cooker that the station had become. She just wished they could act like adults and control themselves.

She'd reported the tension, but she didn't expect anything to be done. She only felt a tiny bit of guilt for covering her ass with the report. If the researchers escalated their little conflicts to where it affected the mission, Esther wanted it to be known that this had nothing to do with the uniformed members of the mission.

Not that the Marines and troopers were super-gung ho at the moment. After the takedown on Calcutta five days ago, things had gone quiet. Even the jamming had largely ceased, and comms were working again. The general consensus was that whoever had been trying to interfere with the station had taken their licks and withdrawn. Esther didn't buy into that—she couldn't afford to. But with Tantou continually pushing her to initiate offensive action against the known pockets of people, she was falling back on the "things are quiet" argument to keep him at bay. He might be the mission commander, but she had the final say on security matters. Whatever pockets of personnel were out there, they were not attacking. Esther didn't like leaving any potential adversaries out and about, but she was not there to conquer an enemy.

"And I tell you again," Verone was saying, her voice strident, "the data just doesn't support that. There was no reaction, and without that . . ." she said, trailing off as if that won the argument.

Esther didn't know enough to form an opinion. But the "Three Amigos," which the Marines and troopers were referring to Verone, Williams, and Mueng, seemed to think that there wasn't anything on the planet that would benefit mankind.

Esther rather liked the three, but the Federation and Allied Biologicals were going to a lot of effort for something that had no value. She was not an expert, but if she were a wagering woman, she'd be putting money on Tantou.

"This isn't difficult science, *Dr. Verone*," Tantou said, putting enough scorn into her name to use it as a pejorative. "If you simply had the ability to comprehend what's there, you'd realize that."

"The ability, Dr. Tantou? I'm not the one with a mail order Ph.D. I earned my doctorates the hard way, not by sucking some piss-crap dean's cock."

Esther almost laughed but studiously avoided turning to watch. There was a sound of flesh hitting flesh, which got her attention, and she turned just as Verone slammed into her, bouncing off and hitting the small table. Tantou stood over the woman, hands still extended from shoving her, his face a bright red.

Esther lost it. She jumped up, grabbed Tantou by the front of his shirt, and bulldozed him up against the bulkhead.

"You will never, I repeat never, put your hands on anyone in this station again," she said, her voice deadly serious.

"But . . . but . . ."

"No freaking buts. If you touch anyone else, I will personally beat the living shit out of you before pressing charges."

She could tell he was about ready to crap his pants, the fear was so palpable on his face. She was going to add something else, but she'd made her point. She let go of his shirt, then turned back to Verone.

"You OK?"

"Uh . . . yes. Thank you. Yes."

Half of her Caspian Pilaf was spread out across the deck where it had been knocked off the table. She shrugged, then knelt and started shoveling it back on her tray with her bare hands. She felt more than heard Tantou skirt around her to go back into the lab, giving her plenty of space.

Slowly but surely, the Port Section, who were in the station, turned away from the scene, resuming whatever they'd been doing before. Esther ignored them. She'd lost it, but she wasn't going to apologize or make excuses.

She dumped the tray in the trash, then took a long look at the hatch leading into the lab. Tantou had been thoroughly cowed, but he wasn't the type of man who would meekly accept what had happened. He was still COM, and he could make life miserable for her.

Fuck him, she thought as she walked over to the comms station to report what she'd done.

Chapter 17

It didn't take long for Tantou to reassert himself as the COM. Shortly after Esther had gone off on him, one of the dragonflies picked up something hidden about two klicks from the station. Gunny Medicine Crow and Staff Sergeant Rapa had been out on a patrol—on which Esther had sent them just to get them out of the pressure cooker that the station had become—so Esther had diverted them to check it out. To Esther's surprise, the two of them had returned riding a WCD Palomino, of all things. Esther had chewed out the gunny something fierce. Marines did not loot, period. But between the time the gunny had returned and when Esther was done with her, the Marines were already taking turns trying out the exquisite bike.

Esther knew that she should secure the bike, but the Marines, troopers, and even Dr. Williams were so excited, so pumped, that she relented, declaring it "abandoned property under Federation jurisdiction" with the warning that if anyone came to claim it, it would be returned.

This was contrary to every regulation she knew, but she put the morale boost higher on her priorities than following some convention signed by politicians who'd never marched to the sound of guns.

She laid down some serous restrictions as to its use. Break those, and the bike was going to be put up in storage.

And the temptation had proven to be too much for her as well. On the second day, after gunny offered, she'd relented and taken the bike for a short ride. It had been a blast, and she could see the allure. WCD made one sweet machine.

But it had given Tantou the ammunition he needed. If someone had used the cross-country bike to get into a position to spy on them, then there was still a threat. For him, that meant the known installation 2000 klicks away, and by going up his own chain, got a mission approved to take over that station. Esther had tried to object, but she'd been told to comply. Tantou's contacts evidently outranked hers.

Esther didn't think that the Palomino came from their target—that was too far of a trip on a bike. So there had to be others out there, people a lot closer. But her hands were tied, and now, aboard one of the Porto's shuttles, she was heading out with Tantou and his sidekick Dr. Polonov, the Port Section, and SFC Juarez and four troopers.

Esther was still angry at the mission creep. The Marines were there to provide security, not go arrest interlopers. Technically, while they could take prisoners of war in a battle, the restrictions concerning *posse comitatus* made it illegal for the Marines to arrest anyone, hence the IS team. They had police powers as part of their charter, so they were the point of main effort for the mission. Juarez had been so excited and full of himself that he was running around like the proverbial chicken with his head cut off, going as far as trying to give Esther orders—orders she ignored.

"Two minutes," the shuttle crew chief passed.

Esther checked her M99. She had no idea what they'd be facing. And while her Marines were among the very best in the Corps, they had not worked together in standard infantry ops, nor had any of them been regular infantry for quite some time. Individually, they were superb, but as a unit, they were largely untested, and that could prove fatal if they encountered a determined and well-trained opponent.

Esther watched the repeater as the shuttle pilot swept around the small, shielded dome. It looked barely more than a storage unit, the same kind used on hundreds of worlds. The entry airlock looked to be a low-grade commercial lock, and it was pointed to the dark side of the planet.

"Bring us in here, if you can," she passed to the pilot, touching the repeater at a spot corresponding to a cleared area about 20 meters beyond the airlock's entry.

The repeater display was in front of her, and SFC Juarez was leaning in to see, but the troopers were not the ones who were going to breach the domes, so Esther used her hands to indicate the lock's position to Gunny and her section at the back of the shuttle.

The pilot made one more circle as his scanners relayed data to the *Porto*. Both the shuttle's and the *Porto's* weapons systems would be searching for any threat, she knew.

Esther's hand strayed to her harness quick-release as the shuttle flared in, the G's pushing her deeper into her sling seat. The back ramp started to lower before they landed, and while still five or ten meters up, the Marines released their harnesses and stood. The shuttle hit with a light thud, and Port Section ran out the back, followed by Esther, the troopers, then the two civilians.

The five troopers fanned out in reasonably good form, oriented outwards, away from the dome. They hadn't picked up any bad guys in the surrounding area, but a complacent soldier became a dead soldier all too often.

Esther followed Port Section as Sergeant Ganesh, who was ready to blow the lock, tried to cycle it. To Esther's surprise, the outer door opened.

"Do we have your OK?" Gunny asked her.

There were two considerations. The first was tactical. Cramming Marines in an airlock made them easy targets. Someone with a crew served could mow them down as the inner door opened. Marines, in general, did not like to enter a building through a door or hatch. They had brought enough ordnance that could blow a hole in the outer wall, but depending on the configuration inside, that could destroy the dome's integrity, and it could injure or kill anyone just on the other side of the wall.

The second reason was more on a political level. At the moment, Esther could cancel the mission and leave. No harm, no foul. There would be little, if any, legal ramifications. The moment they entered the outer door into the lock, they would have crossed the line. Their actions could be considered something as mild as trespassing or as major as an act of war.

Esther was half-tempted to cancel the mission. She couldn't see any advantage to continuing, and as the ground commander of the operation, she supposedly had the authority to do so. But higher-ups had deemed the mission necessary, and she'd have to explain just why she'd failed to comply. She'd been hoping to find a valid reason once on the site, but nothing was jumping up and grabbing her attention.

"Proceed," she told the gunny.

The plan had been for the Port Section to enter the dome en masse, using tried and true clearing techniques. Once clear, the rest of the people, short two troopers who would remain outside, would enter. SFC Juarez would arrest anyone inside, and the civilians would poke around to get an idea of what the prisoners were doing. At the last moment, though, Esther joined the other Marines in the airlock just before the outer door closed. With nine Marines in HED's, it was an extremely tight fit, which made them a very tempting target.

There was no decontamination spray or irradiation. As soon as the lock pressure reached equilibration with the inner dome, the inner door opened, and the Marines darted in, moving in their assigned directions, ready to engage.

Which was overkill. Fifteen civilians were lined up in the middle of the front compartment, hands in the air. They were not in environmental suits, and they were offering no resistance.

"I'm Doctor Angela Boran-Smith, chief of mission. We are Confederation citizens," an older woman said after taking one step forward. "This lab is the property of Jindal-Fergusson, and you are breaking intergalactic law with your entry."

"Get Juarez," Esther told Sergeant McConnaughy.

"Please stay where you are for the moment," she told the civilians, not that she thought they would move a muscle with seven Marines holding down on them.

Most of the civilians looked positively terrified, and Esther couldn't really blame them. None of them had the "military" look, and to have nine weapons-bearing Marines barge in had to be disconcerting.

"I said, we are Confederation citizens," Doctor Boran-Smith said, her voice on the edge of cracking.

"And you are trespassing on Federation territory," Esther told her.

She shouldn't be saying anything, she knew, leaving that for SFC Juarez, but it was rather awkward just standing there. The Confeds were standing quietly, but she didn't want them to try anything in a panic.

"But we've got authorization!" the leader protested.

At that moment, the inner door opened, and Juarez and his troopers, rushed in, weapons drawn.

Esther pointed at the leader, and Juarez almost ran to her, making her flinch, and said, "I'm Sergeant First Class Enrique Sanderson Juarez, Federation Civil Defense Corps. I am placing you under arrest for Criminal Code 2002.1, trespassing on restricted Federation property."

"But we've got authorization! I just told her that," she said.

That seemed to confuse Juarez for a moment, so Esther stepped back into the mix and said, "I can assure you that you do not. But if by some stretch of reality you do have authorization, and that has not filtered down to us, then you have nothing to worry about. Until then, I suggest you comply with whatever Sergeant First Class Juarez tells you to do."

"Where are your labs?" Dr. Tantou, who'd come in with the troopers, asked.

Esther had to keep from rolling her eyes. The building was a pre-fab dome, and this front section was living spaces, to include racks that folded up into the bulkheads. The hatch leading to the rest of the dome, with the convenient handwritten sign on the door that said, "No food in the lab!" was a pretty good indication as to its location

"That's private property," one of the prisoners said. "You have no right to enter it."

Tantou started to argue back, but Esther pointed at the hatch, so he and Polonov disappeared inside. Two of the prisoner tried to follow but were restrained by troopers.

"Do you think they really work for JF?" the gunny asked her as they watched.

"Probably, or at least as much as all our civilians work for Allied Bio," she answered. "Not that it matters. Jindal-Fergusson's got offices and factories within the Federation, so the Federation can reach out to them if fines are part of what happens here."

"Uh, Skipper? I think you might want to see this," Sergeant Ganesh said from the far side of the compartment.

With one last glance at the troopers processing the prisoners, Esther, followed by the gunny, walked over and into a surprisingly roomy locker that was serving as an armory. The weapons racks were two-thirds full with an array of rifles, but right in the middle was a crew-served hadron beam cannon of the type that Gunny Chun had destroyed on Calcutta.

"Gunny, put four Marines outside and send Rheumer and Ford back in," Esther ordered.

Rheumer and Ford were FCDC, and she'd assigned them to take the outside. They made their living guarding installations, so it seemed like a natural choice. But if a third of the weapon's racks were empty, and as she was positive that none of the civilians were military types, that meant that there were probably others out there, armed Confed soldiers or mercs. If someone was out there and planning a counterattack, Esther wanted Marines out there, not guards.

But if there was anyone out there, they held off. Four hours later, the prisoners, the weapons, and quite a bit of scientific gear and samples had been loaded up on the shuttle. Juarez put an official-looking lock on the airlock and posted a form that placed the building under Federation investigation. The lock wouldn't stop anyone who was determined to enter, but forms had to be followed, Esther guessed.

As the shuttle took off, Esther's mind tried to make sense of what was slowly coming to light. The sniper who had hit Alfayed had probably been Brotherhood or was Brotherhood-trained. The crew-served that Gunny Chun had slagged now looked to be from the Confederation.

For three supposedly friendly governments, there seemed to be a lot of confrontation going on.

Chapter 18

Esther followed in trace of Staff Sergeant Kneffer. She knew Gunny
Chun was probably chaffing at having her with him again, but she
couldn't stay cooped up in the station. If she did, she'd probably kill
Tantou before the day was out. The man, with his petty demands,
was driving her crazy. There was a very evident divide within the
geeks, as the Marines and troopers called them, and Esther was
getting sick of it. Ever since she'd thrown Tantou up against the
wall, Williams, Verone, and Veer seemed to think that they could go
to Esther to complain, and while she liked them, particularly
Williams, she not only couldn't do anything about their issues, she
adamantly did not want to get involved. Going out with the
Starboard Section was just her way of hiding.

This was the second time in two days that she'd gone out
with Starboard, but the last time was on another raid, one that
ended up far differently than the one on the J-F installation. This
installation was 500 klicks to the south and just at the twilight line
at the edge of eternal night. The Marines had to breach the wall of
the small building, and inside, they found the bodies of three men,
all dead. They had suicided, complete with brain wipes. There
would be no resurrection, no recovery for them. Some of the
equipment in the installation was Brotherhood, but not enough to
make a declarative statement as to their origin one way or the other.
Even in death, their bodies screamed military to Esther. Without
uniforms, while they probably were not officially in a military
service, they had the look about them that they'd served. Their DNA
was scanned and forwarded, but if they were from the Brotherhood
PHM or another high-level security organization, there would be no
record in any public data base that they ever existed.

The patrol was trudging to a small spot that both gunnies
thought would make a decent sniper firing point. They were going
to check it first for any sign it had been used, then emplace some

ground sensors. They'd identified 112 such potential FP's so far and investigated 47 of them.

Esther brushed against another of the tall, brown, fanlike funguses. She tried to avoid touching any of the vegetation, but sometimes, it couldn't be avoided. Many of the fungus-types exuded either a white or a dark liquid where they were touched, a liquid that could burn naked skin. The snipers loved it, as they could tell if someone had passed by recently. But that went both ways. It could also tell anyone else where the Marines had moved. On a more personal level, though, was that any fungus-sap had to be removed in the airlock before entering the station, and the stuff was uber-sticky. It was a royal pain-in-the-ass to get off, even with the biojets blasting away at full strength.

"Cougar-Six, this is Cougar-One," Sergeant De Vries' voice came over—broken, but readable—over the net.

"Go ahead," Esther responded.

"The station has been hit with a rocket. There's been extensive damage, but no one's been hurt."

"Is the station secure?" Esther asked, her heart pounding.

"Roger. There was a breach, and there's contamination, but the breach self-sealed. The gunny's in the lab now assessing the damage,"

"Understood. We are on our way back now," she said, with Gunny Chun, who was listening to the comms watching, twirling one finger in the air and then pointing back in the general direction of the station. "I'm setting Alert Condition Alpha. Stay inside the station until our return unless the situation forces a reaction."

Gunny Chun had already started turning the patrol around. Esther checked her AI. They had almost 2000 meters to cover before they arrived.

Esther had been wondering if there was going to be a reaction to the two raids. She now had her answer.

Chapter 19

Esther was seething as she waited for the airlock to cycle, Juarez standing beside her.

It should never have gotten this far.

Since the first rocket attack that destroyed the lab four days ago, the station had been hit five more times. There was more activity in the surrounding area as well. Esther had sent out the Marines in a cordon to try and keep the bad guys at bay, but with the rockets being fired at up to ten klicks, that hadn't done much good. One of the enemy crews got too close, though. Two days earlier, Gunny Medicine Crow and Sergeant De Vries had engaged a team setting up a launcher with the gunny getting kills at 4,565 meters, which was going to be a new record, if the data analysis held up. But one kill did not stop the incoming.

With the lab destroyed, all personnel were now living in the commons, suited up 100% of the time. Esther had tried to send the civilians to the *Porto*, but she'd been overruled. They weren't getting anything accomplished from a scientific perspective anymore, so the decision had to be symbolic.

And that symbolism had just cost them a life.

The door opened, and Spec 4 Deledriay and Private First Class Lum entered, each holding an arm of the limp body of Corporal Vicky Espinoza as they dragged her in through the front hatch. The corporal was face up, her head, or what was left of it, hanging down, leaving a trail of blood and brain matter dripping onto the white deck. Esther felt her anger mount. The corporal was KIA for good with no chance at a resurrection. Whoever was out there was now playing for keeps.

Juarez cried out and rushed to help, lifting her up and laying her on the table.

"No POO,[2] but I've got an azimuth of 290," Sergeant De Vries said, from where he was looking at the sensor array.

If the *Porto* were still in orbit, her sensors could have pinpointed the POO, but now that it had been confirmed that there was a man-of-war in the system, she couldn't risk the vulnerability being in orbit created. She'd pulled out of orbit and could not provide much in the way of support. With only three Eagle Eyes the *Porto* had left and their own dragonflies, Esther was glad they had at least determined the azimuth the round had taken, letting her know from what direction the round had come.

She stood over De Vries, looking at the map taped up on the bulkhead. Reaching up, she ran her finger along a rough 290 degrees azimuth away from the station.

"Right there, that's where I would be," she said, pointing at a slight rise about 1700 meters away.

"Captain!" Sergeant First Class Juarez shouted out from where he was standing over Espinoza's body, tears rolling down his face. "What are you going to do about this?"

This has gone on long enough. We can't just sit here as a punching bag.

Esther slowly turned to look at the IS team leader and said, "We're going to kill the bastard."

---

[2] POO: Point of Origin

Chapter 20

Esther monitored the display as her Marines started out on their stalk. She hated sitting inside the station while the teams were in combat, but they had all gone through sniper training, and she knew if she just injected herself into the mission, she could be a liability.

Memories of Saint Teresa where she'd watched her Marines die while she stayed safe and sound back at the CP kept trying to force themselves to the front, and she had to fight to keep them at bay. She had to focus on the task at hand.

SFC Juarez stood beside her. He would not have any input into the counter-sniper mission, but she thought he, and through him, the rest of the troopers deserved to observe.

Dr. Tantou, however, was a different case. He was hovering, just behind Esther, seemingly eager to watch. If the lab were still intact, she would have sent all of them back into it, but with that not happening, she tried to ignore the man, choosing that over a confrontation.

"Re-calculate the optimal coverage for Dragonfly Two," she instructed the AI. "Emphasis on Goa."

The AIs used extremely complicated algorithms to determine where the Dragonflies should surveil, but sometimes, maybe often, human intuition was needed. "Goa" was a ridge far to the right of where the AI had calculated was the most probable POO, but before she left, Gunny Medicine Crow had told her that she didn't think the sniper's FP was where the AI gave the highest probability.

The array picked up a shot, and a moment later, Staff Sergeant Mahmout Brooke's avatar shifted to light blue.

"Shit!" Esther said, watching while hoping the avatar would not gray out.

Unlike the more robust 3's, or even the bulkier enviro suits the troopers wore, the HED 2's did not have the same degree of ability to close off breaches. They were designed for hazardous environments, however, so they had to take potential breaches into account. The school solution for the suits was that if the damage done was great enough, the suits attempt to save the life of the wearer by closing the wearer down—by killing him or her. Exposure in a toxic environment could be more damaging and decrease the likelihood of a successful resurrection and regeneration, so stopping all bodily functions kept the poisons from contaminating the body further.

Thankfully, though, the staff sergeant's avatar remained the steady blue of a WIA.

"Francisco, get Mahmout back to the station. The rest of you, keep your friggin' heads down!" she passed on the command circuit.

After a moment, the avatars started moving forward.

"Sergeant Juarez, if you could get two of your troopers to the outside door, please have them help Sergeant Rez get Staff Sergeant Brooke back inside."

The shot alarm went off again, and Esther snapped her head back, but all the avatars were their normal bright blue. Esther's heart had just started calming down when the shot alarm sounded once more. This time, Sergeant McConnaughy's avatar grayed out.

"Spig's dead!" Staff Sergeant Mubotono passed over the net. "Head shot! I don't think he can be brought back! We're still under cover, and there's no way we were spotted!"

"All teams halt!" Esther ordered. "Freeze in place."

How the hell are they being spotted?

The area in which the teams were advancing was covered by fungus. All of the Marines were among the best snipers in the Corps, and they should be able to move under the broad caps without being spotted. For a moment, she thought the enemy might have implanted their own sensors, but they needed more than that to be able to engage a target. A Marine activating a sensor would not be enough to aim in and hit him or her.

As an officer, Esther had been trained how to employ snipers, but that didn't make her one. She simply didn't know enough to think like a sniper and try to figure out what was happening.

Occam's Razor, however, would seem to support that the Marines were making mistakes. It seemed improbable, but what other explanation was there?

The shot alarm sounded again, but no one was hit. She had to act. Doing nothing would get another of her Marines killed. But she simply didn't have enough knowledge to make a good decision.

Maybe Chun or Medicine Crow will have something.

The alarm sounded once more, snapping Esther to the here and now. Sergeant De Vries' avatar grayed out immediately.

"All teams, immediate retrograde to the station. Do not continue!" she ordered.

"Bullshit, Captain! I'm going to get that asshole," an angry Mubotono passed.

"That's a negative, Staff Sergeant Mubotono. You will return to the station."

"We can't back down!"

"That's an order. Return to the station!" she ordered, putting more steel in her voice.

The avatars slowly started to return to the station. Five more rounds were fired, felling Staff Sergeant Kneffer and Sergeant Piccolo. Esther wanted to rush out to help, but she knew she had to stay at the console.

She called up to the *Porto*, requesting support, knowing the request would be turned down. She was right. The comms chief wouldn't even patch her through to the captain.

Sergeant Rez arrived first, Spec Potter helping him bring in Staff Sergeant Brooke. Potter went back out while Brooke half-hopped to the chair where Dr. Williams started on him.

"Sorry, ma'am," he told Esther, his face grimacing in pain. "I didn't think he could see me."

"Don't worry about that," she told him. "Let Doctor Williams work on you.

And then the rest started arriving. Within 20 minutes, everyone was inside the station. Three Marines were KIA with McConnaughy almost certainly beyond resurrection. Doctor Williams initiated stasis on each of them, and they joined the body of Corporal Espinoza. Two Marines were WIA and out of action. In less than an hour, Esther had lost more than 20% of her uniformed strength, and there was still an active enemy out there.

Esther was in slow burn mode. Something had happened, and she needed to figure out how they'd screwed up. Five Marines had been taken out, and not one had managed to get off a shot, much less spot the enemy.

"Gunny Chun, Gunny Medicine Crow, to me," she said once the dead and wounded were tended.

"What the hell happened out there?" she asked them, her eyes blazing.

"Whoever it is, he knew where we were," Gunny Medicine Crow said. "We were out of sight, and I just checked Dutch for a temperature gradient right before he engaged us."

"Then how the hell could he spot you? You must have made a mistake!"

"CO_2, ma'am. I think it was CO_2," Staff Sergeant Rapa said, breaking into the conversation.

"What?"

"Gunny Medicine Crow said she was on her back, but Dutch was on his stomach, so why did he get targeted and not her? I think it's because our CO_2 waste vents are here," he said, reaching his arm around to point at the vortex valve at the small of his back. "We're pumping out CO_2 with every breath. We're recovering some of that O_2 with the splitter unit on our back, of course, but not all of it, and that excess gets vented."

"And here on this planet, with its screwed-up atmosphere, that would stand out like a neon plume, if you have the right kind of scanner. I think he might be right, Captain," Gunny Chun said.

Could that be true? she wondered before coming to the conclusion that it probably was.

"If that's true, then how do we deal with it? It's not like we can go out without our HEDs, and even if we could, we're still breathing out CO_2."

"The IS Team's suits don't vent," Gunny Chun said.

"You want to do a stalk in those?" his fellow gunny asked him.

Esther understood her point. The FCDC suits were bulky and hardly something a sniper would want while conducting a mission.

"Well, no, but what other options do we have?"

"The emergency hoods don't vent, either, but those would be almost as bad to fight in. And they've got limited comms," Esther said, more thinking out loud than anything else.

"Maybe I've got an answer, ma'am," Rapa said. "But I'd need a bit of time to work it out. Can you give me 30 minutes?"

Esther looked to the two gunnies, but they said nothing, so she said, "You've got them."

Rapa grabbed Staff Sergeant Cezar and went into the supply closet.

"I hope he's got something," Esther said.

"We could always cut and run, you know, call in the shuttle," Gunny Chun hesitantly offered.

"Marines don't run," Esther said automatically before adding, "but if we can't figure this out, we might have to consider it. I'm not going to get everyone killed for some bio-patent."

"Cutting and running" was what she'd been trying to do as their position had become more dangerous. The civilians were currently doing nothing, and they were the reason the Marines and troopers were there. But now, five Marines and another trooper were down, and Esther didn't have it in her to meekly accept that and withdraw. It wasn't in her DNA.

But she couldn't let pride rule her. If there wasn't a way to prosecute the mission, then her pride was not worth another Marine getting needlessly killed. She had to accept that as much as she hated it, she might have to call it quits and run home with her tail between her legs.

Without really dismissing the two gunnies, Esther turned back to the wounded and dead Marines. The two wounded would make full recoveries, Dr. Williams said. She was optimistic that De Vries could be resurrected. With a shattered spine, he was facing a long regen, but he'd make it. He also thought that Sergeant Piccolo had a decent shot. He'd put Espinoza and McConnaughy in stasis, but when Esther asked about resurrection for them, he'd merely shook his head.

This was not the first time Esther had lost Marines, and if she ever managed to get another command, it might not be the last time. But it always hit her hard. On the one hand was the simple empathy a Marine had for each other and the knowledge that there were loved ones back home who would grieve. On the other hand, Esther couldn't help but second guess herself. What could she have done differently that would have kept her Marines alive?

Esther's father had ordered his own brother-in-law, Noah's and her Uncle Joshua, and three other Marines to their death. As a child, Esther had even played with the fatherless kids of Corporal Felicity, one of the other Marines who'd been killed. Somehow, her father came to terms with giving those orders. Esther hadn't actually ordered anyone to a certain death, but still, there was always a sense of guilt that somehow, it was a flaw in her tactical planning that had resulted in avoidable deaths.

She didn't wallow in self-doubt, however. She was confident that she was a good Marine, a good officer, and better than most. But even the best could be better, and she owed it to her Marines to be the best that she could be.

Dr. Veer walked up to her, offering a cup of coffee.

"Thanks," she said, taking the cup.

"This is . . . I just can't imagine what's on your shoulders now. But I want to say we have confidence in you."

"You do?" Esther said, a smile managing to make an appearance. She held up the cup and pointed at Tantou, who was studying the command array as if he was Sun Tzu. "Even him?"

"'Even him' is an idiot," Veer said. "All of us who count have confidence in you."

Esther was about to make some light remark when Rapa and Cezar came out of the supply closet. Esther broke out into a laugh, along with everyone else, looking at Cezar. The staff sergeant waddled, not walked, and as one of the Marines remarked, looked like he'd just taken a huge dump in his HED.

The laugh was needed, and if it sounded forced, that was to be expected.

"Staff Sergeant Rapa," Esther said. "Just what in the hell is that?"

"Just a simple gyvering, ma'am. The problem, we think is CO_2. So, I started thinking, what do we do with CO_2 here in the station? We scrub it. And we've got plenty of scrubbers here. I just took two and hooked them into JC's ass, then used duct tape to make sure they were secure. We've still got a tiny bit of leakage, but I think most of it is getting caught up in the scrubbers."

"Will it scrub his farts?" Spec Potter shouted out to renewed laughter. "If it will, give one to Lim! His are nasty!"

Rapa smiled, but he ignored the comment said, "This is the scanner for CO and CO_2. We can go outside and see if it works."

That made sense, so Esther said, "Let's do it."

Along with the two gunnies, Staff Sergeant Rapa, of course, Mobutono, and Sergeant Rez, Esther went back outside. She knew they might be presenting a target with all of them, but they'd been taken under fire from the other side of the station, so she felt they were relatively safe.

Esther took the scanner, pointed it at Rapa, and keyed it. The CO_2 levels jumped up, so the scanner was working, at least. She turned to Cezar, and the reading dropped to almost nothing.

"Jump up and down," she passed to him.

He did a few jumps, then dropped to his belly and jumped back up.

"Not bad," she said on the open circuit. A little leakage, but minimal. I think this might work. OK, everyone back inside."

"Staff Sergeant Rapa's contraption—"

"The fart-catcher, Skipper, that's what we're calling it," Sergeant Ganesh said to more laughter.

"OK, 'fart-catcher,' seems to work. So, I want everyone outfitted with one, and I'm the first in line."

She caught the two gunnies exchanging looks, so she added, "I'm going out with you."

That resulted in some raised eyebrows.

"Look, we're missing too many of us. I can work out ranges and environmentals. I can be a spotter."

"So can I, Captain," Biming Lum said. "Let me go, too. I don't have an HED, but I don't need one of those fart-catchers, either."

Esther was about to say no, but if she was going out, then the same logic was there for the trooper to go out as well.

"If he's going, so am I," Sergeant First Class Juarez said.

"No, you're not. I need you here in command. If anything happens to us out there, I need you to call in the shuttle and get off the planet."

She thought Juarez was about to argue, but as soon as she said "command," he quieted down immediately.

Rapa got to work, and with Dr. Veer assisting, the Marines had their fart-catchers installed within an hour. Esther had gotten together with the two gunnies to come up with their plan of attack, leaving the bulk of the details to them. They were the experts in this kind of thing, not her.

The plan was fairly straightforward. It relied on putting Marines into position so that skill would go against skill. Esther had heard the word "memitim" being bandied about. The Brotherhood memitim were renowned snipers in their own right, and that would explain the skill that had been revealed. But Marine snipers were supposedly the best—at least that was what they advertised. If they were right, then skill versus skill, even if that was one or more memetims out there, was a pretty good proposition.

With the five missing Marines, there had to be adjustments. She was going to take the place of De Vries and be Medicine Crow's spotter and Tash and Francisco were teaming up. Lum was going to be Rez' spotter, and the both of them were going to hang back and provide overwatch. Without a spotter, T-Bone would take the Barrett and stay back as well, ready to engage if he saw anything.

"Get a last drink and a bite to eat if you want," Esther said. "Don't forget to take a shit, too. With the duct tape on our asses, better to do it now since we don't have any FIBs.[3]"

It took almost 45 minutes to get everyone fed, through the station's two heads, and through their weapons checks, but finally, everyone was ready. Gunny Chun took a head count as everyone moved to the exit.

"Who am I missing?" he asked. "I'm down one."

It took a moment until Sergeant Ganesh said, "It's T-Bone."

---

[3] Fecal Inhibitor Protocol

"Check the other rooms," Gunny Medicine Crow said as Esther powered up her suit, bringing up her display.

And there he was. His avatar was already some 400 meters away.

"Shit!" she said. "He's out there already."

"Staff Sergeant Mubotono, what are you doing?" Esther passed on the command circuit.

There was no answer.

She tried again with the same results.

"You'd better answer me, Staff Sergeant," she passed, her anger mounting.

"He's not going to respond," Gunny Medicine Crow told her. "He's on a mission to prove he's the best."

Esther blew up when she heard that, swearing up a storm. She took some deep breaths to calm herself, then said, "He'd better hope that sniper nails him because I'll have his ass if he survives."

Then, on her external speakers, said, "Mubotono's already on his way. And so are we. Mount up."

Chapter 21

Esther was concentrating on not touching any of the toilet bowls, the name the Marines had bestowed on one of the squat types of pseudo-fungus, making them move and revealing their position, so she was not paying as much attention to the overall situation as she should have been. When the shot rang out, it took her by surprise. Immediately thinking it was the enemy sniper, she instinctively froze before realizing that the shot came from behind her, and it was the Barrett. Staff Sergeant Mobutono had fired off the big gun.

She waited, hoping for the confirmation that the staff sergeant had bagged the enemy sniper. When nothing was passed, the gunny's leg just started to move her forward again when Mobutono fired again.

A second or two later, a single, sharp report rang out from in front of them, and Mobutono's avatar went gray.

"Fuck!" Esther muttered just before three more shots rang out, almost in unison. She could tell that two were from the slug-throwing Windmoellers and one was from the quieter Kyocera.

"I didn't see anything," Esther said. "Did you?"

"That's a negative, but somebody did."

"Report," she passed on the net.

"Saw the shot and took my own. Probable hit," Staff Sergeant Francisco said.

"Not so sure I was on target," Sergeant Tash passed. "Took a snap shot when I thought I saw something."

"Same here. I'm sure we both spotted him, but I don't know if I hit him," Staff Sergeant Rapa added.

Three of you had him, and you don't know if you killed him?

"What now?" Esther asked the gunny. "I've never thought about what you guys do if you can't confirm the kill."

"Depends, ma'am. Usually, we don't do anything unless we're ordered to do the BDA."

"We've got one dragonfly still operable. I'm going to get the coordinates from Staff Sergeant Francisco and have it fly in for a look-see."

She made the connection to Dragonfly One and gave the AI the coordinates. A moment later, the little drone changed course, heading for the spot. She hoped that the Dragonfly would spot a dead sniper.

A minute later, a shot rang out, and the Dragonfly feed blacked out.

He hit the freaking drone? Holy shit!

"I guess I missed," Francisco passed, stating the obvious.

"Did anyone pick up anything?" Gunny Medicine Crow asked.

The net remained quiet.

Esther pulled in the Eagle Eye data stream, then asked the AI for a trace, hoping there was something for her.

It immediately popped up, and she passed, "The Eagle Eye trace shows one-seven-five degrees."

One thing was clear. The trace went nowhere near the spot Staff Sergeant Francisco had identified. Either the staff sergeant had been completely fooled, the sniper had been able to quickly move, or there was more than one sniper out there.

Esther wracked her brain for a course of action. With a normal infantry unit, she'd have options upon options. Supporting arms, air, naval gunfire—any of these could clear the area ahead of them. That sniper might be skilled, but he or she couldn't stand up against some of the Navy big guns. The problem was that she had none of those normal resources. All she had were the Marines with her.

"I think our target is using this to maneuver. Manny, I want you to shift left, then using Delhi as cover, get up and haul ass to an FFP in the vicinity of 22455-67395," Gunny Medicine Crow passed on the net while forwarding an overlay that showed a series of almost concentric ripples on some high ground to their fore.

The gunny turned to look at Esther as if for approval. Esther had been contemplating a more typical base of fire and envelopment, but with a sniper on sniper action, she gave sway to

Jonathan P. Brazee

the gunny and nodded. A good officer made the best use of his or her resources, after all, and Gunny Medicine Crow was a hellaciously capable resource.

"Everyone else, get into a good FFP, then stay put until Manny's in position. Manny, you and Riko keep your eyes peeled. If I'm right, you're going to have clear enfilade if the target tries to move between positions," she passed.

"Roger that. We're on our way."

"Now we wait," the gunny told the captain.

Chapter 22

When the gunny had said they were going to wait, she hadn't been kidding. For thirteen hours, the two of them laid still while the others maneuvered into position. Gunny Chun had covered 1900 meters, which didn't seem like much, but when he and Sergeant Rikoman were covering that on their bellies while trying not to be spotted, that took a little extra time.

Esther and the Gunny had traded off using her Miller scope to try and spot the sniper. While holding the Windmoeller, she had a daydream of taking action. She imagined seeing the enemy sniper, taking aim, and firing, feeling the rifle recoil back into her shoulder and watching the enemy fall. She'd earn the coveted HOG[4] designation and be able to hang the hog's tooth around her neck. She'd fam-fired the Windmoeller before while in recon, and she was confident of her ability to hit a range target, but she knew she wasn't a real sniper. If she spotted the opposing sniper, she'd hand the rifle back to the gunny.

Medicine Crow's plan was a simple one. With Gunny Chun in position, Esther and the gunny, along with the other five teams, would become bait. Their sole purpose in life would be to draw a shot from the sniper and making him reveal himself so Gunny Chun could take him out.

Esther was scared, her throat tight, her stomach threatening to heave. Gut-wrenching fear like this was pretty much a foreign emotion for her. It took her awhile to realize what was wrong with her, and that confused her. She'd been in some pretty tough spots before, and she'd been sure she wasn't going to survive the final assault on Mount Zeus on Elysium, so she'd faced death before. But she'd faced it while fighting, where she was absorbed in her mission.

---

[4] HOG: Hunter of Gunmen, the term earned after a sniper's first combat kill.

This time, she'd just be crawling along, waiting for Thor's hammer to strike her. Her mission was to get shot.

Part of her wanted to object to her presence as bait, and there was a by-the-book reason to justify that. Without false humility, Esther knew she had the experience and knowledge to be best qualified to bring everyone, civilians, troopers, and Marines, out of the mess they were in. But at this stage, the die was cast, and then maybe just ahead of Spec Lum, she was the least-qualified for this mission. If she fell, SFC Juarez had the capability to call in the shuttles and get the civilians off planet.

And with more than a little guilt, she knew that Gunny, with her Windmoeller, would be the prime target between them if they were the ones spotted. The enemy sniper would give Esther, with her little M99, barely a second thought when there was a Marine sniper on his trail.

Of course, all of the other Marines had been through sniper school. They'd passed their stalks. Esther had never done that. So, if anyone was going to make a stupid mistake and be spotted, it would probably be her.

Sucks to be you, Gunny. He might spot me and then latch onto you.

Finally, Gunny Chun was in position, and with a quick order to the rest, Gunny Medicine Crow turned to Esther and said, "It's time."

The gunny, with Esther on her ass, slid out of their hide and into a depression to their right. Slowly, the two Marines advanced, and Esther could almost feel the crosshairs centered on her back. She started to wonder how long the fart-catchers would work, and she imagined a plume of CO_2 rising out of their asses like a signal fire to pinpoint their position.

It was almost three hours later, while she and the gunny were only 400 meters from the rise, that the expected shot was taken. Immediately, Sergeant Ganesh's avatar grayed out, and another shot was fired. Staff Sergeant Cezar's avatar, right next to Shaan's, went light blue.

"Get ready, Manny!" Gunny Medicine Crow passed.

Esther froze, waiting for the gunny to fire. Nothing happened, and Esther thought the plan might have failed, when a single crack of a Windmoeller reached them.

"Target down," Gunny Chun passed.

"Give me a feed," Esther demanded.

The gunny connected his Miller's feed, recycled fifteen seconds, and the image of a figure in some sort of ghillie appeared, a breathing system over his mouth and nose and hunched low as he ran along one of the terrain ripples Gunny Medicine Crow had spotted.

She hit that on the nail head!

The sniper had his head turned in the direction from which the rest of the Marines were advancing. Gunny Chun wasn't in that direction, of course. He had flanked the position.

The gunny fired just as the man turned to him, as if he'd realized his mistake, but it was too late. He'd just started to dive away when the gunny's round took him in the chest. He fell, tried to rise, then collapsed to lie still on the dirt

"Any sign of anyone else?" Esther asked him.

"That's a negative. It was just him."

Marine snipers always worked in pairs, but memitims often worked alone. Esther didn't know if that was a Brotherhood sniper or not, but she needed to find out.

"We need to recover the body," she passed. "We've got to find out who he is. Staff Sergeant Rapa, you and Sergeant Delay are the closest. You're up."

Esther pulled out her binos and began glassing the face of the rise. They weren't as good as the gunny's Miller, but the more eyes, the better. But as the two Marines reached the base of the rise, nothing had been seen. There was no cover on the front slope, so Rapa and Delay stood up in plain view. Still, nothing happened, and Esther's tension backed down a hair.

And as with the idiosyncrasies of the gods of war, that was when the shots were fired.

Esther rose slightly to see, but both Marines were very much alive and scrambling for cover. She dropped the binos to check the display, and took a gut shot as she saw Gunny Chun and Sergeant Rikoman's avatars gray out.

"No!" Gunny Medicine Crow shouted out.

"Who saw anything?" Esther asked as she tried to pull up the Eagle Eye again, the bile rising in her throat.

She queried the AI, but nothing was popping up.

"Captain, right now, put everything you have on that spot with the M99. Everything!" the gunny told her.

Esther paused a second, identifying just what spot the gunny was indicating. She wanted to ask why, but in combat, Marines had to react. She trusted the gunny, and that was enough.

She didn't have a shot while prone, so she rose to one knee and started "throwing darts." With 4,000 of them, that was some pretty hefty firepower.

With her peripheral vision, she saw the gunny take off like a jackrabbit. She ignored her, just watching pieces of fungus explode as the hypervelocity darts struck. She was feeling a perverse joy in it, and she could feel the power flowing through her veins. Surely nobody could stand up to that onslaught.

Somebody could, though. Just as the gunny came back into view, less than 100 meters from her target, a mule kick hit Esther in the hip. She dropped her M99 and fell to the ground.

I've been shot, she told herself, amazed.

And then everything started tunneling in.

Chapter 23

"Captain, are you all-right?" Gunny Medicine Crow was passing on the P2P, something that took her a few moments to realize.

"I. . . I think I'm hit."

Am I hit?

"Stay down. Don't become a target," the gunny passed.

OK. That sounds reasonable.

Esther still wasn't quite sure what had happened, so she picked up her M99 and started to take stock of herself. Her ass and hip were burning, and it wasn't until she caught the tiniest whiff of something nasty that she started into mini-panic mode. Twisting her body didn't do jack in finding out what had happened, so she felt around. Her fart-catcher was askew, almost on her hip, and her questing fingers caught a hole in it.

It fell into place. Somehow, despite kneeling and facing the enemy sniper, a round had caught the edge of the fart-catcher, driving it into her ass and hip. And now, the planet's atmosphere was beginning to seep in. Something was still keeping most of it out, but with any movement, that could open the floodgates, and she'd be dead, killed by her own HED. She'd be resurrected, but that wasn't anything she wanted to go through.

What now?

She quickly sat down, hoping the ground would block more poison from entering her HED. Her nose started itching, whether from her thinking about the atmosphere or that enough hydrogen cyanide had reached her, she didn't know, but she knew she'd better not sneeze.

A shot sounded out from in front of her. She wasn't positive, but she thought it was a Windmoeller.

I hope she got him.

But there was no "Target down" passed. She wanted to call the gunny for an update, but if she was going sniper-on-sniper, she didn't need any distraction.

She pulled up the gunny on her face shield display, but unlike a regular combat helmet where as a commander, she could pull feeds, all HEDs required a push, and the gunny wasn't sending. Esther couldn't monitor what was happening.

Or could she?

The Eagle Eye's visual capabilities were limited, but she had two more Dragonflies. Maybe they could even help the gunny. Quickly, she directed both to the area.

Another shot rang out, something deeper than a Windmoeller, and Esther switched back to the main combat display. The gunny's avatar remained a bright blue, and Esther let out a sigh of relief.

Her hip was burning more. Esther wasn't sure why, but she feared that the atmosphere that had gotten inside her HED was just sitting there, reacting with her skin. The design of the HED 2, where the polymer skin hugged the body, had kept most of whatever had leaked in trapped around her hip, and with her sitting on the hole, at least no more was coming in.

She pushed those thoughts out of her mind. She checked the progress of the dragonflies. Number one should be over the gunny in fifteen minutes.

"Staff Sergeant Rapa, do you have eyes on Gunny Medicine Crow?" she asked on the P2P.

"That's a negative. She told Tenner and me to move into position where we can cover her, and we're on the move now."

"Is there anything else we can do?"

"More people might interfere with her, Skipper. I'd suggest letting her handle this."

Esther had gotten the impression that there might be something going on between the two of them, but Rapa sounded pretty calm and collected. And he was probably right. If there were yet a third sniper, anyone rushing forward to help her would be toast.

And so what am I doing just sitting here? she asked herself.

She was pretty exposed, but she didn't want to get down on her belly. She reached back and under her to touch the hole, and her fingers played along the edges of the duct tape Rapa had used to secure it. Her fingers played with the edge, and then it hit her. Carefully twisting around, she could just about see the bullet hole. But Rapa had gone crazy with the duct tape, and it wrapped all the way around her waist.

Esther reached down and slowly pulled on the edge of the tape. She released six or seven centimeters, then tore off a strip. Rolling over and reaching to the fart-catcher, she placed the strip over the hole and pressed it down. Ideally, she'd have had the power off to transfer the tape, but it didn't seem to matter. It stuck fast, just as duct tape had been doing for centuries. It had worked to get NASA astronauts back from the moon during the 20th Century, and it worked just as well on Kepler 9813-B now.

She slowly sat up and leaned forward, exposing the fart-catcher, and her suit registered at 100%. She wasn't about to run the hurdles, but it should last until she could get back to the station.

"Target down," the gunny passed over the circuit, bringing Esther back to the mission.

Esther looked up confused. She hadn't heard the report of a round being fired.

The dragonfly was almost within range. Esther directed it to focus in on the gunny. Within moments, Esther could see her, standing over the body of what she assumed to be the enemy sniper. In her hand, was her M99, not her Windmoeller, which would explain why Esther hadn't heard the firing but opened up many more questions.

The gunny had some serious explaining to do, but that would have to wait. Esther had five more Marines down, and they needed immediate attention.

Screw the *Porto*, she told herself. They were going to send down a shuttle now, she vowed, or Commander Chacon would live to regret it.

Chapter 24

Chacon had not sent a shuttle for two days, but not for want of trying. He'd been ordered to stand down. So, the Marines had hauled their dead and wounded back to the station so Dr. Williams could get them into stasis as soon as possible. Esther sent six of her remaining Marines to pick up the dead enemy snipers. With the delay and the effects of the atmosphere, Esther didn't think much could be done with them, but the Intel types would want them DNA-matched, not that Esther thought that would reveal anything. The two snipers, one woman and one man, were probably so deep into the shadows that even their handlers didn't know who they were anymore.

The female sniper had been the one taken out by Gunny Medicine Crow, and Esther was still amazed at how the gunny achieved that. The enemy sniper had the positioning on her, and she had her array of sensors, but the gunny used them against her. Using her fart-catcher, her knife, and some tubing, she set up a dummy firing position, actually blowing out through the tube to make a CO_2 bloom. The other sniper fell for the trick, exposed herself, and the gunny took her out with her M99, the same as any infantry Marine would have done.

It had been a remarkable feat, one that surely needed to be taught in sniper school, but the way things were evolving, Esther was sure no mention of it would be made—ever. This mission was going to be highly classified and buried.

At least they were leaving. At the same time that Esther and Medicine Crow had been waiting for Gunny Chun to get into position, the giant multi-galactic corporation Mei Shan had bought out Allied Biologicals' share in the bio-rights to the planet. The Mei Shan Group was headquartered on the independent (and tax haven) world of Du Pierre 4, but Mei Shan Plastics, Inc, was incorporated on Hiapo, and therefore as a Federation company, qualified under

Federation law for the purchase—this despite the fact that the company had nothing to do with biological research as far as she could tell. As far as Esther was concerned, the buyout changed nothing, but she'd received her orders as well: stand down. Somehow, Mei Shan's purchase evidently removed the threat of the still-lurking Brotherhood ship.

For the civilians, this was a victory, and they were in celebratory mood. They were happy to be leaving the planet, and they'd been told to expect some hefty bonuses. For the Marines and troopers, the eleven bodies stacked neatly against the bulkhead dampened any enthusiasm.

The *Porto's* shuttle had finally been released, and along with the ship's surgeon, the popsicles were being readied. The troopers and the enemy snipers were going to the Mei Shan ship which had just arrived in system, but by unspoken demand, the Marines were going to the Navy ship. The brotherhood between the Marines and the Navy created a trust that wasn't always there with other organizations, and the Marines always preferred Navy medicine.

With the buyout, secrecy was no longer a factor, and the Marines expected to be recalled soon. Mei Shan had their own security teams, so the IS Team was being lifted off today, and the Marines, while still at the station, were somewhat redundant. And the Marines were down to eight effectives. Esther, along with Staff Sergeant Brooke, were two of those effectives.

Esther was still limping. Between the bruise of the impact and the burns from the atmosphere, her hip around to just above her ass was a mess, one that the ship's surgeon said a day in sickbay with minor regen, and she'd be almost good as new. But as long as there were Marines on the planet, this is where she'd be, too.

The eight Marines were standing by to take out the popsicles. Dr. Williams gave six of them fairly good prognoses. Riko could possibly be resurrected in the *Porto's* sick bay. He'd been shot in the side, not doing much damage but destroying the integrity of his HED 2, so the suit had shut him down as per protocol. It was well within the ship's medical capabilities to zap his heart back and heal the relatively minor wound. The rest would probably go back to one of the Naval hospitals before being resurrected. Dutch faced a long and painful regen, but he should be able to make it. Spig and Farouk were the only two confirmed fatalities, and Mobutono was borderline. All told, Dr. Williams said the Marines and the IS Team were pretty lucky to escape as lightly as they did, but Esther thought it had been a pyrrhic victory. Two enemy snipers had taken on the Marines and did far more damage than they should have before being killed themselves. Were it not for Gunny Medicine Crow's intuition first and then action second, Esther thought more of her Marines might have been taken out.

"OK, we're ready for them," a petty officer said, coming into the station.

"That's us," Staff Sergeant Rapa said, powering up his HED.

Veer and Williams helped the Marines and troopers take out the popsicles. Each of them was put in a cradle with old-fashioned straps securing them. The ship's surgeon made his readings, then gave thumbs up. They were ready to go.

Not everything was ready, though. As they filed off the shuttle, Staff Sergeant Francisco and Corporal Hamilton came back onboard, pushing Gunny Medicine Crow's Palomino.

"Hey, what're you doing with Isá?" she asked, watching the bike disappear into the cargo bay.

"Orders," Rapa said. "The Intel types want to get their hands on it."

He lies well, Esther noted and filed that fact away for future reference.

The bike was not going to Intel. Staff Sergeant Rapa had approached her the night before about it. The gunny had taken a liking to the bike. Who wouldn't? But she had gone further than most, for reasons Rapa had tried to explain but still eluded her. But the bottom line was that he wanted to take the bike back before the new Mei Shan landlords claimed it.

Esther knew what he was suggesting was illegal. It could even be career-threatening, both for Rapa as the mastermind and for her as the officer-in-charge. But she didn't hesitate. Medicine Crow had gone above and beyond, but she would never be recognized for it. None of them would. If they were all going to be screwed, it would be nice to screw over someone else in this mess.

She wasn't sure how he was going to get the bike all the way back to Earth where Medicine Crow was from, but she wasn't going to ask. The SNCO mafia could get almost anything they wanted done.

They all stopped at the airlock, eight Marines, five FCDC troopers, and two civilians, bonded by their experiences. The shuttle slowly rose before speeding up. They watched until it disappeared from sight.

"I don't know how much longer we're going to be here," Esther said, initiating the airlock sequence. "But we might as well make the best of it."

FS PORTOLUMA BAY

Chapter 25

"Well, sir, I'd best get the team up here, then," Esther said, her voice tight as the anger smoldered inside of her.

Esther knew she could be a hard-ass, but she didn't consider herself an angry person. This mission, though, had seemed to put her in a permanent state of anger, and it had been difficult for her to avoid lashing out as Lieutenant Commander Chacon briefed her. The only thing that held her back was the knowledge that the man had no control over the situation, either.

Esther had figured that something was up five days after the Mei Shan team's arrival. They'd invaded the station amidst palpable excitement and had not only repaired the lab, but two days later, construction crews arrived to start an expansion of the facilities. That construction effort came to a screeching halt three days later after one of the corporate bigwigs came down to the station and locked himself and his retinue in the lab with the scientists for five hours. When he came out, he was not looking happy. Two hours later, the construction crew was picked up and lifted off-planet.

With the security turnover with the Mei Shan team completed, the Marines had simply sat around, watching serioholos on the new projectors the Mei Shan crews had brought with them. Once a day, Esther had asked when they would be taken off the planet.

For Esther, that occurred on the ninth day. Leaving Gunny Medicine Crow in charge, she was shuttled to the *Porto* where she'd cooled her heels for a day until the captain had briefed her.

She left the captain's stateroom to the comms shack and had the sailor on watch connect her to the station. One of the Mei Shan techs answered, and she had to wait while he got the Gunny.

"This is Gunnery Sergeant Medicine Crow," the gunny said as she took the mic.

"Gunny, you've got 90 minutes to pack up and get ready to leave," Esther told her without preamble.

"Ninety? That's not enough time, ma'am. The weapons are still in the racks."

"I had to fight to get that. They wanted an hour."

"What's up, ma'am?" the gunny asked.

"I'll tell you when you get up here. Go to it."

She cut the connection, then went back to the small stateroom she'd been assigned as the senior Marine onboard. It was tiny, with a rack that pulled down from the bulkhead, but she was glad that she wasn't sharing it with anyone else. She was not in the socializing mood. She pulled down the rack and got on, not even bothering to take off her boots.

She must have drifted off, because a gentle rapping outside her hatch woke her.

"Who is it?" she asked, her mouth dry and nasty.

"It's Gunny, Skipper. We just arrived."

Esther stood up and opened the hatch. The gunny was still in her HED poly skins, and she had to be dying to get out of them.

"Um . . . go get cleaned up and get some chow in you. Let me check with Commander Chacon, but plan on meeting in the wardroom at, say, 2000."

"Roger that, ma'am."

Speaking of eating . . . Esther thought as the gunny left.

The *Porto's* wardroom was small and had only one sitting, and that sitting should have ended about ten minutes prior. But the fabricator was available around the clock. Esther had only eaten twice on board, and she was hungry. She had some time to kill, so after confirming the meeting with the commander, she headed on down and dialed up some beef stew and a jackfruit smoothie. She sat down and buried herself in the food, trying to focus on the food and calm down.

It wasn't working. She was still angry when she went back to her stateroom, and that hadn't ended when she picked up Commander Chacon. Moving down the passage, she tried the breathing exercises her brother Noah started her doing back when they were teens. She wasn't sure if it did any good, but she hoped she looked calm, at least, as she and the commander entered the wardroom where her Marines waited.

Commander Chacon motioned for her to take the lead. Esther had thought he would do the brief as he was more familiar with the situation, but she nodded, and moved to the front of the small group.

"That was not the easiest mission I've had," she started. "And I'm sure you can all say the same thing. We've lost one of us for sure, and that could end up being two. Seven more are going into regen—well, maybe not Sergeant Rikoman, but you know what I mean.

"But no matter what, we upheld the honor of the Corps. We got hit, but we hit back.

"That's not why I called you here, though. We'll write our after-action reports. I'll conduct your exit interviews. But that will start after we get a good Navy meal and some sleep in a real rack. Right now, I wanted to let you know just what the heck has happened."

Almost as one, seven Marines leaned forward to hear what she had to say.

Esther took a deep breath, looked at the ship's skipper, and then turned back to the Marines.

"As you know, Mei Shan bought the bio-rights to whatever Allied Biologicals had on the planet. How that worked, I don't know, and it's not important. What is important is that the planet is a bust. That is, what is on it is a bust. There is no known biological gold mine."

The Marines broke out into quiet murmurs at that, looking at each other in confusion, and Esther held out both hand, palms down, to quiet them.

"Whether there was ever any potential, we don't know yet. What is pretty clear, though, is that Allied Biologicals knew pretty early on that the line of research was a dead end. That might have been after the initial word had been leaked, or it could have been a scam from the beginning."

"Scam?" Sergeant Delay asked.

"Yes, a scam. We are now sure that from the time we arrived, the planet was a dry well. There was scientific interest, both as a ribbon world and because of its life forms, but nothing there is of benefit to man."

"No medical miracle?" the gunny asked. "No cure for the Brick?"

"None at all. Which should have been obvious. Have we ever discovered organics on any planet that we can make use of? The capys can eat earth products, but have we found anything we could use? We were all pulled in by the promise, an empty promise."

"And that's what all the arguing was about. Tantou, and I bet Polonov, they knew all along. But the others, they weren't in the loop, and when their experiments were going south, they started to see the light," Staff Sergeant Rapa said, sounding disgusted.

"Yes, it seems that way. And Allied Biologicals needed to keep the facade going."

"Until they could sell the rights!" the gunny exclaimed as the impact hit her.

"You got it in one, Gunny. We're sure that's exactly what happened."

"What about everybody else?" the gunny asked. "Why were we getting hit if what was there was worthless?"

"That probably wasn't known initially. It looks like it was coming out, though. The station we took? Their research had pretty much uncovered it."

"Is it true that AB pushed that raid?" Rapa asked in disgust.

"Yes," Lieutenant Commander Chacon said. "Too late, though."

"What about the attacks on us?" the gunny asked, seemingly pushing for something.

Esther looked at the commander to make sure she could give out more.

"Sources indicate that the indirect fire attacks were made at the behest of Allied Biologicals. They wanted to push a sense of urgency into the bidding process."

"If others are desperate enough to hit Marines and FCDC, then whatever was being guarded had to be pretty valuable," Gunny Medicine Crow said, the bitterness evident in her voice.

"What about the Brotherhood? Were they here?" Staff Sergeant Rapa asked.

"Almost certainly," Esther answered.

"Were those memitim that the two gunnies zeroed?" he persisted.

"Probably. We'll never know for sure, though."

"So, we get into a sniper match with Brotherhood memitim, and what, we just ignore it?" the gunny asked.

"They won't admit it, and to be frank, neither will the Federation. You won't mention it again, once we leave this wardroom."

"That's bullshit, ma'am," Sergeant Delay said. "They killed Spig. Dead. No resurrection."

"That's right, they did. And Gunny Medicine Crow killed one of them. Dead. No resurrection.

"Look, I know you're all upset. The Brotherhood is never going to come clean on this. They don't want anyone to know they were taken in. And the Federation isn't going to force the issue."

"Why not, ma'am?" the sergeant asked.

"Because it's not worth a war. No single Marine is. Not Spig, not anyone else. No, according to the records, Spig was killed in the line of duty in action against criminal elements."

"So, what's going to happen? I mean to AB? Mei Shan, they're one of the biggest corporations in the world," Staff Sergeant Francisco asked. "They're not going to stand by and let some two-bit company take them like that."

"They probably will. Whatever they paid for the rights, that's peanuts compared to the damage they'd suffer if it were known that they'd allowed themselves to be taken. If I had to guess, I'd say they'll keep the research station open, always on the brink of making a breakthrough. Eventually, it can be closed down on a cost-benefit basis."

She looked at the Marines as they took it all in. Most looked royally pissed—just as she felt. There wasn't much else to say. Oh, there probably was, but Esther certainly didn't know everything about the situation.

"Sir, do you have anything?" she asked Lieutenant Commander Chacon.

"No, I think you covered it."

"OK, well, everybody settle in. Grab some chow and get some rest. I'll contact you tomorrow when I find out what's next."

"May I speak with you privately, ma'am?" the gunny asked as the rest of the Marines filed out of the wardroom.

Esther nodded, and the two Marines returned to her stateroom. Esther closed the hatch, then pointed to the fold-down stool in its slot in the bulkhead. The gunny remained standing.

"Captain, all of this is so much bullshit, I don't know where to start."

"You think I don't know that, Gunny? You don't think I'm royally pissed?"

"I killed for them, ma'am. I killed three people, not to protect the Federation, but so the Allied Biological CEO can buy a blue Lambo to match his red one. In my book, that's murder. You don't have that on your hands, ma'am, with all due respect."

What the . . . just who the hell do you think you are, Gunny?

Esther pushed back on the volcano that threatened to erupt and said instead, "Because you pulled the trigger, you think that makes you more liable? I'm the one who ordered you into the fight. I'm the one who ordered Marines to kill and die. I'm sorry Gunnery Sergeant, but you don't have a flying fuck of an idea on how heavily that weighs on a commander's shoulders. You were obeying orders. I *gave* them!"

The gunny didn't seem to understand she was treading on thin ice as she said, "You should know, of all people. Your father led the Evolution, so we could escape the yoke of corporations, yet now you seem to be surrendering to them. How can you do that, you of all people?"

Esther was gobsmacked. She slowly stood up to tower over the shorter Marine, her fuze exploding.

All of the last few days spewed forth with "How dare you, Gunnery Sergeant! You don't know the first thing about my father, what he believed in, what he fought for, what he died for! He believed in the Federation, all of it. And that includes the corporations. He did what he did to save the Federation, and some of what he did was horrible. He killed 11,000 people on Watershed. Men, women and children. How the fucking hell do you think he felt about that? He was devastated, but without a doubt, he'd sacrifice another 11,000 in a bleeding second if that was what it would take to save the Federation. Eleven-thousand more innocent souls.

"Let me tell you this, Gunnery Sergeant! If you try and bring my father into this to shame me because you don't have a clue as to what sacrifice means, I will fucking crush you like a cockroach," she said, her nostrils flaring.

The gunny didn't seem cowed in the least. She leaned her head back to look Esther in the eyes.

"With all due respect, ma'am, I've 22 years in, so I've got my validation. I can resign today, and there's nothing you can do about it. You can write me up, you can court martial me, but when I'm 70, I get my retirement one way or the other."

Esther stared at the smaller women. She had so many things she wanted to say to put her in her place, but she was a captain in the Marine Corps, not some hooligan. If the gunny was willing to accept a validation instead of a full retirement and not receive pay until she was 70, then who was she to stand in her way? She took two long, calming breaths and gained control of herself.

"If that is your wish, Gunnery Sergeant, so be it. Head down to personnel and fill out your resignation. I'll approve it and forward it out today.

"You're dismissed."

Without another word, the gunny came to a position of attention, performed an about face, then marched out.

Esther started at the empty hatchway.

How the hell did it come to this?

Esther had never felt a significant connection with the Gunny. That wasn't very surprising. Esther tended to keep people at bay, preferring a professional relationship, and from what she'd seen, both in the gunny's records and in person, she was much the same. But Esther respected her, and after their mission together, she'd come away thoroughly impressed. Gunny Medicine Crow was an invaluable asset to the Corps, and if she left, it would make the Corps just a little bit weaker, and little less capable.

Maybe she's just blowing off steam, and tomorrow, this will all be ignored. I'm willing to forget it happened.

Deep in her heart, however, she was pretty sure that come morning, the gunny's resignation would be on her desk for signature.

TARAWA

Chapter 26

Esther hit send and closed the secure PA. She hadn't written anything new there that she hadn't said during her debrief, but procedures had to be followed. This had only been the Marine Corps debrief; she'd be going through it all over again once she got back to Mars. Her next set of briefs wouldn't be quite as detailed. It wasn't that she would be holding back anything vital to the Second and Fourth ministries—but although she worked for the Chairman, she was still a Marine, and Marine-related issues stayed in house.

Not that she'd been totally open with the Corps, though. She reached down to her cargo pocket, feeling the resignation letter Gunny Medicine Crow had given to her while aboard the *Porto*. She'd decided not to turn it in. If the gunny was serious about resigning, she could still do that when she got back to her regular billet at Sniper School.

She checked the time, then grimaced. Of course, she missed chow. Just as well, though. She'd be leaving in the morning to return to Mars, and the thought of New York's Old Fashioned Pizzeria's pizza had been bubbling around in her mind all day. Maybe she could head on out for half a pie, then go to the Globe and Laurel for a transfusion of Marine Corps history. Station One might be the largest military installation in the Federation, but the Marine Corps footprint there was minimal at best, and down on the surface of Mars, it was almost non-existent.

She stood up and decided to go back to the Q and change before heading out into the ville, but as she walked back, a voice called out, "Is that you, Lysander?"

Esther turned around to see Falcon Upshick, someone she hadn't seen since NOTC.

"Falcon, as I live and breathe. I'd have thought you'd be in the brig by now."

"They just haven't caught me yet," he said with a deep laugh. "But what about you? I heard you've got some desk job on Mars?"

"Yeah, payback for having fun in Recon."

"I read about Elysium in the *Marine Corps Times*," he said, suddenly serious. He pointed to her chest and asked, "Is that the . . ."

"The Star of Nikólaos. Yes."

"Pretty gaudy, huh?"

"You should see the medal itself."

Esther had been awarded the Star by the Elysium government after the fight on Mount Zeus. As a foreign award, it has a lower precedence than any of her Federation medals, but it was quite rare for a Marine to have one. On the top of her ribbon bar was her Navy Cross with a gold star in lieu of a second award, and that was even rarer, but not nearly so exotic.

"I did. The *Times* had a holo of the ceremony. But what are you doing here?"

"Oh, just passing through. I'm going back in the morning."

"In the morning? So soon? Well, then, you've got to come to the club. A bunch of us are getting together," he said, slipping his arm through hers and pulling lightly towards the O-Club.

Esther hesitated, the pizza calling her, but the idea of socializing with other Marines was tempting. She relented and let him lead her off as he started waxing rhapsodic about his rifle company. She felt only the tiniest twinge of jealousy which she quickly subverted.

Falcon led her into the ancient club, and as always, Esther could feel the thousands upon thousands of officers who'd walked through the front doors. Growing up in the shadow of the club, it had always taken on an almost church-like air, something she'd never shaken.

Not that it was solemn. As they entered the Chase Regan Room, shouts of "Falcon" rang out. Everyone probably knew who she was, at least by reputation, but as a classmate, Falcon had the honors of introducing her to the officers of Second Battalion, First

Marines. Someone shoved a beer in her hands, and Esther felt the stress of the mission on Kepler 9813-B just slough away. The other officers welcomed her as if she was part of the battalion, and no one bugged her about her Navy Crosses or told her how they'd served with her father. She was just a Marine, like any other. And when she offered to buy the next round for the battalion, the cheers almost made her choke up.

Come on, Lysander! Don't be maudlin! she told herself, but she accepted the toast they gave her with the beer she bought them.

The battalion was there for a hail and farewell, where goodbyes were made to those leaving and new officers were officially welcomed aboard. Esther personally only knew Falcon, but she knew Marines, and when the Ops O was getting his farewell, the XO, who she found out was the somewhat renowned (or infamous, depending on who was telling the story) Marine Major Timothy William McKenna, shared a story about him getting his clothes stolen at the hot springs on Theo's World and somehow making it back sight unseen to the camp stark naked, she laughed with the rest of them. The story, told with much humor, was simply so Marine.

After the official hail and farewell, the partitions in the rooms were recessed, opening it up to the bar proper. A squadron had just finished its own hail and farewell, and it turned out that both the battalion and the squadron XOs were Academy classmates. Both units started mixing with about ten of them joining the two majors, who were somewhat two sheets to the wind by then, in singing songs at the top of their voices.

Esther had switched to cider and sat back at a table with Falcon and three of his lieutenants, simply drinking in the scene. She hadn't realized how much she missed this type of camaraderie until just now, and she really didn't want to go back to her desk on Mars, waiting for someone to break her glass.

"Can I get you another?" Second Lieutenant Velma George asked, her eyes eager.

The whip-thin lieutenant had sat with her for the last fifteen minutes, saying nothing, but watching Esther intently. She could see the hero-worship in the young woman's eyes, and for once, it didn't bother her.

"No," she said, "but I'll buy if you fly."

The lieutenant's eyes lit up and she almost jumped at the chance to serve the reasonably famous Esther Lysander.

Right, I'm so freaking famous. Get real, Lysander, Esther thought reminding herself that she was just one more Marine, no more, no less.

"Take him, major!" voices rang out.

Over by the bar, the two XO's were squaring off with other Marines making a ring with their bodies.

"Oh, this isn't going to be pretty," another of the lieutenants said. When Esther looked up at him with a questioning look, he added, "Major McKenna was sixth in the Federation in wrestling, ma'am. Back when he was at the Academy."

That caught her attention. She'd been a Fourth Team All-Federation volleyball player and a Second Team All-Planet Etherball player while at the University of Michigan, and she still loved university-level sports.

It was over almost before it began. Major McKenna rushed the squadron XO, grabbed him around the chest, and with a textbook soufflé, slammed the man hard onto the deck to the collective groans of the watchers.

"Revenge!" one of the airedales shouted, and in a moment, the pilots were jumping on the grunts.

There were no fists being swung, but that didn't mean there was no damage being done. One of the airedale captains flipped one of the battalion captains, his feet crashing down on Esther's table, scattering their drinks and snapping a good meter off the edge of the tabletop.

"Come on, ma'am!" the lieutenant who'd told her the XO had been a wrestler shouted.

Without hesitation, Esther jumped to her feet, ignoring the cider that had spilled onto her Charlies blouse. She wasn't a member of the battalion, but they'd welcomed her. Besides, airedales could never be allowed to beat grunts, not in the universe according to Esther.

She grabbed a lieutenant by the shoulder, spun him around, and with a deft heel trip, sent the surprised young man down on his ass. Over by the bar, Major McKenna, his blouse torn, and three more officers, were facing an advancing horde of pilots. Esther started to wade in when someone grabbed her from behind. Whoever it was was ungodly strong, much stronger than she was. She tried to stomp on the man's feet, but he was laughing as he danced back and forth, hopping each foot out of the way of her strikes.

Esther tried to pull something out of her MCAP training, but whoever was holding her had the same training, and he was simply overpowering her—until he wasn't. Someone had pulled him off of her. Esther didn't even turn but lunged forward to grab one of the airedales by the collar and yanking him back.

"The MP's have been called and will be here immediately. Stop what you are doing and await their arrival," an amplified voice reverberated throughout the club.

Marines froze where they were, making an odd tableau. Slowly, each of them started to straighten up.

"Run away!" someone shouted.

Major McKenna pushed through the pilots in front of him, picked up the squadron XO, and together, they started to run to the entrance, immediately followed by the mass of officers. As the two majors reached the doors, they turned and in unison, shouted, "Bulk Fuel rules" before wheeling back around and out of the Club.

Esther had to vault a couple of broken chairs, but she found herself in a group of Marines and a chaplain, all laughing as they hooted and shouted "Bulk Fuel!"

Esther laughed at the weak attempt at subterfuge. Bulk Fuels was the logistics company, mostly manned by civilians, that purchased and distributed liquid fuels. With only a major and a lieutenant as officers, she could imagine the poor major being called on the carpet by the commanding general for wrecking the club.

Out on the grass, she swung to head to the BOQ when a squadron captain grabbed her by the upper arm and said, "Come on. Bryant's got a ute."

A rational person would simply say no and return to her room and try to avoid trouble. But Marines were never known for their rationality. The other captain said Bryant, whoever that was, had a utility hover, and that was good enough for her.

She took a quick glance for Falcon, but when she didn't see him, followed the rest, and within moments, nine of them were crammed into a Swoosh utility hover designed for four.

"Where're we going?" someone crammed under Esther asked as Bryant started up his Swoosh.

"To S-Ville, of course. There's still more drinking that's got to be done, and we're the ones to do it!"

That sounded copacetic to her. Esther pushed the knee that was digging into her back and settled in for what looked to be a long night without sleep.

JULIETTE PRIME

Chapter 27

Esther waited in the anteroom. A single, well-dressed young man with a decided air of danger stood silently by the door, hands folded in front of him in what might look like a relaxed posture, but one from which Esther knew he could spring into action. She tried to ignore him, which was pretty difficult. Esther was middling confident as to her hand-to-hand capabilities, but she instinctively knew that with her guard/guide, she was way out of her league.

Lucky for me I'm here on official business, she told herself as she couldn't keep from glancing up at him again.

After her Kepler 9813-B interlude serving with Marines again, it was back to her routine, divorced from the Corps. This was her fifth courier mission, a "mule mission," as they called it back on Mars. These were boring, mundane missions that Esther didn't understand. She was pretty sure all she'd carried to the Grand Meister were documents and a molecular drive. She couldn't be sure, as while she was cleared to carry the "bindle," she was not cleared to know what it was she was carrying.

With hadron messaging, the only possible way for someone to intercept a message or document would be if they had stolen one of the other repeaters in the nest. There were no transmissions that could be intercepted, so if all the repeaters were kept in secure locations, messages and documents would be safe from prying eyes. And as Major Lent had mentioned over lunch the week before, couriers were not as secure. The bindles were locked to the courier's left arm, but a simple hack with a machete, and someone with ill intentions could at least take possession of one. Whether they could open the case without detonating the interior charge was another matter, but at least there was the possibility, no matter how slight, of that.

She idly twirled the snake around, letting it rise, then catching the "head" as it fell. She dropped it, then repeated the process. The "tail" of the snake was locked into the bracelet around her wrist; the head was now free, waiting for the return of the bindle, which she'd given to the Grand Meister's lackey.

The first time she'd been a courier, she'd felt a little thrill of excitement back in Brussels as the bindle was attached to her wrist and the bio-lock programmed into the release. This was more like all the spy flicks she'd seen over the years. It hadn't taken long to realize that she'd never done anything so boring in her life. She was not allowed to take her personal PA, only a shielded diplomatic PA. She was not allowed into the ship's messes—food was brought to her berth. She was stuck with the basic entertainment channels in her berth and physical books.

Her second mule mission had been to New Vegas—why there, she couldn't even come up with a reason after letting her imagination run rampant—and she hadn't been able to sample the famous nightlife. She'd been driven in a blacked out-hover, waited for 12 long hours in a secure room much like she was in now, then driven back to catch another ship back to Earth.

Now she was sitting in Juliette Prime, the first and still central station in the group. At least this made a little more sense. The Juliette Group was ostensibly neutral, but rumors had run rampant that her father's escape from Juliette 2 during the initial stages of the Evolution had been facilitated by Glenda Henricks-Pata, the Station 2 meister. There had been a degree of a "special relationship" between the Juliettes and the Federation ever since.

Esther first tour had been with First Battalion. Sixteenth Marines onboard Wayfarer Station, which couldn't hold a candle to Juliette Prime, at least according to reports. She'd really like to play tourist, even for a few hours, but she knew that wasn't going to happen.

And she was right. The door to the room opened, and a nervous-looking middle-aged man, his too-thin face compressed into a grimace as he came in and gingerly handed the bindle to her.

Esther had opened it for the same man when she'd arrived. Once opened, the bindle was safe from its little destructive surprises. She'd instructed the still unnamed man on how to seal it when finished, and she had to assure him several times that sealing it could not activate any of the security measures. And once sealed again, not even Esther could open it, so if the Grand Meister wanted anything sent back to the Chairman, the bindle had to be left open until whatever was put inside.

The man watched in almost morbid fascination as Esther connected the snakehead to the bindle's connector ball. Within moments, it had melded itself into the ball, molecularly bonding with it. Until Esther was back in Brussels, the bindle might as well be part of her body.

"Well, Mz. Patterson, thank you for delivering your package to the Grand Meister. Mr. de Gruit will now escort you to your ride back. Have a safe journey."

He nodded and left while her guard held the door open for her.

Nice to have a name, at least, she thought as she left the room.

Mr. de Gruit led her down a long, windowless passage. A door blocked the end.

He leaned in for a retinal scan, and as the door opened, said, "If you please, Mz. Patterson," in a surprisingly soft and almost effeminate voice that totally clashed with his deadly air.

Esther almost laughed out loud, but she stepped into the back seat of the waiting two-man hover. De Gruit held open the door before walking to the other side and getting in, sitting beside her. He didn't voice any obvious instructions, but the hover rose and took off.

"So, have you been a Julietter all your life?," she asked, wondering if he'd respond.

"Born and raised," he said in the same soft voice. "I love it here."

Esther had thought he might not answer. The "quiet" and "dangerous" pairing was somewhat of a Hollybolly trope, after all. Evidently, de Gruit was not familiar with the trope, because he opened up about his life on Juliette Prime. His eyes were constantly moving, constantly taking in the surrounding area, but he chatted as if they were old friends.

Where was this chatterbox while I waited for 12 hours in the room? she wondered. *I could have used the company. Maybe I just had to ask a question to get him going.*

Juliette Prime was a spiral station, with terminals jutting out from the central habitat. The tiny hover skipped past security at the base of one of the terminals and proceeded to the end.

"Have a wonderful trip, Anna," Tater de Gruit said, holding open the door.

"Thanks. I intend to, Tater," she said.

She'd felt Tater had been somewhat menacing back while she'd waited. Now, in 15 short minutes, it was like they were old friends. He still was a dangerous man, she knew, but at the same time, he was a "good guy."

Tater escorted her to the gate, swiped his card, and let her into the gantry. The ticket agents didn't give either of them a second glance. Esther turned once to wave at him, then continued on to the ship's main hatch.

The next yeoman in a line of them barely glanced at her readout, scanned her ticket, then said, "If you'll follow me, I'll take you to your stateroom.

Pretty fancy, she thought. *A live escort?*

Couriers could be assigned to any kind of craft, from military to freighters to liners, but even most liners had guided follow-mes to guide passengers to their berthing. This liner was obviously a step up, and as she followed her guide, she quickly realized that this was more than a single step up in class. This was a luxury liner, with emphasis on the "luxury."

"And to your right, Madam, is the Grand Ballroom. The Welcome Aboard reception will start at 1600, ship's time. That's 4:00 PM. Just query your PA, which will automatically synch to ship's time to ensure you don't miss any of the ship's activities."

The passage skirted the ballroom, separated by plastiglass. A decent-sized stage graced the opposite side of the ballroom, and at the far end was a bar that put most other bars she'd seen to shame.

At least a hundred people were already there, looking like they were getting an early start to the reception.

Not for me, though, Esther told herself with only a slight hint of self-pity. *Looks pretty copacetic to me, I'd have to say.*

Farther aft and up a deck, her guide keyed open her stateroom. He asked Esther to scan her eyes, assuring her that only the cleaning staff would have access to her room, and then only if she requested service.

The stateroom was not obnoxiously luxurious, but it bespoke quality. The far side, under a faux window, which now showed the view from the ship towards the central station, was a queen-sized bed, her small valise centered perfectly on it. There was a small sitting area with a couch and a desk, then a small, but complete head with a sonic shower and what looked to be a real water-tub.

"If you need anything else, simply ask your stateroom. Someone will attend to your needs. And thank you for choosing Ambrosia Lines."

He gave the briefest of glances at her bindle. He had to know she was a courier even if not for whom she worked, and so he knew she had no choice as to which ship she took back to Earth, but still forms had to be followed. Esther was tempted to tip him from her own funds, but he undoubtedly made more than she did, and she knew the travel office would take care of it, so she thanked him and closed the door behind him.

Now what?

Esther was in a pretty good mood. Mule duty was a pain, but her surprising conversation with Tater de Gruit on the way over, then the opulence of her ship had a way of making her forget that. She wasn't going to be able to explore the ship, but it could be worse.

She hesitated. She was hungry, but that bathtub was calling her name. She asked the room to run her water at 44 degrees, then started the process of taking off her clothes. The tricky part was to get the three layers of tops off, but they were designed to get around her bindle, even if it took some effort. Within a few moments, she was luxuriating in the bath, her left arm over the edge and out of harm's way.

Not that bath water could harm it, she acknowledged to herself. *A meson beam couldn't scratch it.*

Still, she didn't bring it into the tub with her.

The tub kept the water temperature steady, and Esther felt her muscles slowly relax. She didn't bother to get out when the announcement was made that the ship was undocking. With all the dampeners on the ship, she never even felt it pull out and start the first of two legs of the journey to Earth.

Her skin wrinkled like a prune, she finally got out of the tub. She walked, dripping, over to the bed and started to open her valise to get changed, then thought better of it. She opened the closet, and sure enough, there was a robe and a set of loose pajamas. She wasn't going to be on the ship long, but she might as well be comfortable. She managed to put on the pajamas, and she immediately knew she'd made the right choice. They were marvelous, some fine-spun synthetic that felt great against her skin. She dumped the valise, unopened, in the closet, and lay down on the bed.

The "window" showed a view of space. Juliette Station was no longer in sight, and stars filled the screen. Sailors and Marines referred to space as "the black," but this was anything but. She thought the view had to have been enhanced for the passengers.

She asked the room to pull up the menu, and immediately the flat-screen on the bulkhead lit up. Food on the ship was provided as part of the ticket price, along with house pours. Other booze required payment, which while the prices gave her pause, didn't really affect her. She was dry for the trip. She ordered a ribeye steak, sunrise potatoes, and montez beans, then started scanning the entertainment menu to find a good flick to start off the trip.

****

Esther turned off the screen, a lump in her throat, tears forming in her eyes. It was stupid, she knew. Suki Hodges was the figment of some writer's imagination, not a real person. She wasn't the mother of two that she'd given up for adoption, she didn't have the Plaxico

Virus, and she didn't finally succumb to the virus with her long-lost kids and her old flame at her side. Still, the story was both sad and happy, all at the same time.

She wiped her eyes with the corner of her 5,000-thread count Albergis cotton sheet (she knew that because of the placard the ship's staff had left on the headboard) and leaned back on her pillow. There were four more flicks in her queue, but she needed time to digest Suki's story.

Her empty plate sat on the night-table, empty. The steak had been delicious, a Big Black. She had to remember to let Noah know she'd tried it. He was partial to Higgensworth (he always made sure to state the full name of "Higgensworth of Parker Manor"), but Big Black, a 50-year old strain of a Black Angus named Big Black 43 (something else she'd learned from the placard that came with the meal—evidently Ambrosia Lines didn't just want to offer luxury, but make sure everyone knew it was luxury) was also one of the foodie strains that everyone was supposed to eat at least once in their lives. She contemplated ordering up a dessert, but she was still full.

"Room, what time is it at Station One, Mars?"

"It is 23:31:50 at Station One, Mars, Sol," the room's AI informed her.

With her own PA, she could keep track of simple things like that, but without it, she was a little lost.

Esther liked to synch her time when traveling as early as possible. She'd never gotten into Juliette Prime time, which for some reason, was different from GMT, unlike most stations in human space. Still, she should be getting some sleep. She blanked out her window screen, then dimmed the lights.

Sleep wasn't coming though. Her thoughts flitted from Suki to viruses to the Brick, never going deep, but bouncing back and forth. She wondered what would Tater de Gruit say if she came back one day, but as herself, Esther Lysander. She thought about Noah and Miriam, hoping things were OK between them. She thought of just about everything, and that kept her awake.

She could take a zinger, and that would ease her into sleep, but Esther wasn't a big fan of the hormone supplement. Most people swore by it, but she didn't like the feeling of giving up control.

But you'll drink five ciders, Lysander.

Alcohol had far more effect on a body than a zinger, but still, she refrained. Sleep would come.

Her mind was drifting when she heard the tiniest of whispers at her door. She had to pull herself up from sleep's reach. She'd put the Do Not Disturb on the door, but whoever was trying to get in evidently didn't see it for some reason. She was about to call out to tell them not to bother, that the door was locked when with a soft hiss, it opened a crack.

Esther froze as a shaft of light from the passage briefly lit up a portion of the room, blocked momentarily by the unmistakable bulk of a body slipping in. The door closed, and Esther could feel the presence of someone in the darkness.

She tried to keep her breathing steady. This wasn't housekeeping. Someone was in the stateroom do her harm.

Couriers did get hit on occasion, which is why she, Major Urritia, and several of the other Marines felt that human couriers were not the most secure form of communications. Most couriers who were hit, though, were commercial couriers who were transporting goods of value. Esther didn't know of a government courier who'd been hit recently.

It looks like it's happening now, though, Lysander. Get yourself ready.

Her stomach fluttered in nervous anticipation as she considered her options. This wouldn't be some street thug looking to brawl but a professional. She wasn't a pushover, but neither was she a hand-to-hand expert. She had to find an advantage.

Slowly, on little kitten's paws, the body moved across the open space. Esther kept her eyes closed, figuring the intruder had on NVGs. With her mouth open, she had to concentrate on keeping her breathing steady, the very picture of a woman in dreamland. She waited, listening for the tiniest of sounds until she was sure the intruder was standing beside her. She heard the barest whisk, perhaps of a blade being drawn.

"Window, daylight!" she shouted, rolling forward just as something thunked into her bed where she'd been laying.

A tuxedoed man stood beside the bed, a blade of some kind stuck right through all 5000 threads and into the biofoam mattress. He reared back, abandoning the blade, hands reaching to tear off the small NVGs he wore.

Esther didn't hesitate. She continued her roll off the bed, and with a lunge, jumped on the man's back, flipping the bindle's snake over his head and around his neck. She pulled tight, knee in the man's back, straining for all she was worth.

The man was a beast. He reached back, hands grabbing the top of her head with incredible power. If he could get those paws on her face, Esther knew she would be lost. Panic gave her strength. She kicked the back of his knee and pulled him over, taking the opportunity to make another loop around his neck before he could react. He tried to body slam her with his back, and as she felt his hands reaching for her, she simply got small.

Hugging his back, pushing her head into him, she suffered several blows, and a chunk of her hair was pulled out as she tightened the noose with all her might. He almost got loose when he half-rose and threw her into the corner of the night-table, but she desperately managed to hang on. His struggles got weaker, but she didn't let up. Even when he stopped moving, she held on, pulling with every ounce of her strength.

Finally, she released the pressure, ready to reapply the noose at the first hint that he was still conscious. He made a rattle from deep within his throat, but he didn't move.

"Room, lights," she said, barely getting out the order through her gasping breaths.

Turning the window into a daylight view didn't flood the room with unbearable light, but the man, with his NVGs on, would have been momentarily blinded. That had given her the opportunity. And now, under full room light and looking at the man, looking at the chunk of her scalp he'd torn off that was now laying on the deck, she knew she'd needed that opportunity. He was corded with muscle.

Esther pushed the body off of her, then felt his carotid. His pulse was feeble, but he was alive. She contemplated rectifying that situation, but the Federation would want to know who he was and why he'd targeted her.

She couldn't let him recover, though, so she pulled the blade out of her bed. She could see the blade, which looked to be made of some densely-packed wood or synthetic wood, had been hidden inside an ornate walking stick, a recent affectation of some of the uber-wealthy. The bejeweled handle of the walking stick didn't make for a convenient sword hilt, but the blade was sharp, and she quickly cut some strips of the sheet. She used them to tie his legs and arms, then asked the room to deliver some duct tape.

Whatever she ordered, food or otherwise, would be noted by the ship's crew, but if they thought that her asking for the tape was odd, that didn't interfere with their customer service. A few moments later, a small chime announced its arrival.

Holding the sword pointing at the man, she reached inside the dumbwaiter and pulled out the tape. From outward appearances, the tape wasn't much different than when it was developed centuries ago, but it had been improved over time. Easy to pull off the roll, it was all but impossible to break once applied. Esther ran the tape up along his legs, encircling him like a maypole. Then, with his hands behind him, she did the same with his arms. He was just coming to when she shoved him up against the bulkhead and ran the tape across his neck, each end fixed on the bulkhead itself. His eyes opened just in time to see her apply the last piece to his mouth. She jumped back and picked up the sword, pointing it at his chest.

He immediately tried to pull forward, but the tape across his throat convinced him this was a bad idea. There was a flash of anger in his eyes as he glared at her, and she could see his muscles bulge as he tried to pull against the tape.

Esther was running full throttle, her heart pounding, but seeing him, in what she assumed was a very expensive black and silver tux, complete with a bio-metallic silver rose boutonniere that had somehow stayed in place during their fight, made her want to laugh with relief. This was a professional, and now he was trussed up like a medieval pig ready for the spit.

She felt something seeping out her smashed nose, and she slowly lifted her tongue to taste the blood. She wasn't sure when she'd hit her nose so hard, but she was pretty sure it was broken.

The fire in the man's eyes faded when he saw her touch her tongue to the blood. It didn't turn into fear or despair, but more like resignation. She figured that he knew if she hadn't killed him yet, she wasn't going to.

"Room, ignore any voice other than mine until I debark," she said.

She didn't think her prisoner could free his mouth, but she wanted to be safe.

"Understood, Mz. Patterson, and logged in."

The man almost snorted disbelief above the tape covering his mouth.

So, he knows who I really am? Or just that I'm not Anne Patterson?

Esther could call ship's security. They'd be more than accommodating, arresting her attacker, upgrading her to a suite, and probably offering her all sorts of lucrative compensation. That wouldn't do Esther Lysander any good, and it wouldn't do the Federation any good, either. Ambrosia Lines was registered in Manna Lipo, and it was licensed to operate within Federation Space, of course. But at the moment, the ship was in deep space, out of Federation jurisdiction. If the ship took custody of her prisoner, the Federation would never get its hands on him. And that wasn't good enough for her. Even if she didn't have a duty as a Marine, she wanted to know why he'd been sent to take her bindle.

Almost getting killed had a way of making it personal.

Once they docked at Glenn Station, the Federation security forces would board the ship, if they had to, to take custody of the man.

Esther leaned the walking-stick sword up against the side of the bed, then took a tissue, rolled it up, and stuck it in her right nostril, from which most of the blood had flowed. It was pulsating with pain now, in counterpoint to her throbbing head where her attacker had pulled out a chunk of scalp, but she wasn't going to give the man any degree of satisfaction.

Standing there, she surveyed the stateroom. It was a mess. She took five minutes cleaning up, aware of her prisoner's eyes following her every move. There wasn't much she could do about the damage, however.

There was one more thing she had to do, though. She grabbed a towel from the head, then lifting her prisoner's legs, slid it the best she could under his butt. Mr. Tuxedo was not going to be released for piss breaks, so when he did let go, she wanted something to sop it up.

"Room, menu, please."

Her mouth was dry, and there was blood in the back of her throat. She really needed something to cut through that, and she ordered a pomegranate juice. At the last second, she ordered a pasta that she didn't recognize, only that it had "triple garlic."

She said nothing to the man as she waited for the food. A soft chime sounded four or five minutes later, and she reached into the dumbwaiter to pull out her food and drink. The smell of garlic instantly filled the stateroom. She carried the plate over to her bed, then made a show of eating it. She hoped her message was clear. Mr. Tuxedo wasn't getting anything to eat until the Glenn Station police had him in their hands.

Surprisingly, and maybe more from relief than anything else at simply still being alive, the pasta was pretty good, and the pomegranate juice was refreshing. Her hands were barely trembling as she put the plate back into the dumbwaiter.

"Room, I want to watch 'Suki's Children,'" she ordered.

The reviews of the sequel were not as kind as they were to the original she had watched earlier, but they were going to be there in the stateroom for a while, so there was time to spare. And if it wasn't that good, at least her prisoner, who was taped to the bulkhead and directly facing the display screen, would have to suffer through every moment of it. He couldn't turn away.

A perverse part of her hoped the flick sucked.

MARS

Chapter 28

Esther hit the center of the battle-eye, and locked onto the major, it sent the small, 40-gram squash ball out at him at 135 KPH.

"Shit, Lysander! That's the fourth time," Lent said, rubbing his chest where the ball had nailed him. "I should never have agreed to battle squash."

"Battle squash," or any of the "battle" court games, was simply a modification of the existing game, one favored by Marines, troopers, and drunks. A simple target, called the "battle-eye," was fixed anywhere on the forecourt wall. If a player hit the red center of the battle-eye with a ball, shuttlecock, or whatever, the target's AI tracked down the opposing player and fired the ball right back at him or her. A player could possibly dodge out of the way, but not often. To make things more interesting, if the player hit the blue ring outside the center bullseye, the same thing happened, but the player *hitting* the ball was targeted. The blue ring kept players from targeting the battle-eye continuously, only attempting when a good opportunity presented itself.

"My serve," Esther said, picking up the ball.

She was being a little rough on the major, she knew, so she fed him an easy return, and sure enough, he pounced on it—and hit the blue "ego ring." He didn't have enough time even to attempt to dodge when the battle eye nailed him in the chest again.

"Son-of-a-bitch," the major muttered, rubbing the spot. "What's with you today? Anything to do with your new hairstyle?"

After getting her debrief, Esther had reported to the government clinic in Brussels before catching a hop back to Mars. She hadn't been damaged enough for regen, so a nano-boost had been enough to close off her wound. But nanos didn't grow hair, so unless she gave in and shaved everything or spend the big credits needed for an acceleration at a salon, she was going to look more than a little shaggy. And maybe that had put her in a bad mood, one she was taking out on the major.

"All the rage in Brussels, sir. Haven't you heard?"

"What I did hear was that you caught yourself a fish on your mule mission," he said, looking out of the corner of his eyes at her.

Esther shrugged. Their missions were supposed to be secret, even from each other, but secrets were hard to keep.

"I can neither confirm nor deny, sir," she said, the rote answer.

"Kind of hard to deny something interesting happened. Ambrosia Line issued a blanket apology for failing to keep passengers safe while at the same time protested the Glenn Station police for boarding one of their ships."

"You know how it is, sir, with those commercial lines."

"Yes, I do. I've been on the *Ambrosia Cloud* twice myself. Helluva nice ship, huh?"

"Yes, sir," she said with a smile, giving in. "Helluva nice ship—for all we get to see of her."

She didn't know why she was being so aggressive with the major. Her nose felt fine, and her scalp was only slightly sore. The trip to Earth hadn't been that bad. She reached a truce with her prisoner, taking off the tape over his mouth and even letting him pick a flick to watch, a horrendously sophomoric teen comedy. Pretty gracious of her, she'd thought, for someone who'd tried to kill her.

She'd actually been thanked during her debrief, something that had never happened to her before. Most of all, she was alive when she should have been killed. So, she wasn't sure why the pent-up emotion, and why she was trying to kill the good major with death-by-squash-ball.

"If you want to take off the battle-eye, sir, I'm down with that."

"What, and let you get off scot-free, your tender skin unbruised? *Au contraire, mon capitaine.* Serve it up."

You can always tell a Marine, she thought to herself. *You just can't tell them much. Ba-dum-dum!*

She was killing him, but Marine pride wouldn't let him back down.

"Your choice, major, and your body," she said, sending a wicked serve into the corner of the court—which he somehow reached and sent right back at the battle-eye.

She'd have thought the slower man would never have reached the ball, much less hit the battle-eye, so when the red center flashed with a hit, she hadn't even tried to dodge by the time the ball smacked her in the shoulder.

Esther didn't know what was worse: the pain in her shoulder or the surprised, but satisfied smile on the major's face.

"Your serve, Major," she said grimly, getting in position.

Game on!

Chapter 29

"Hi, Helen-Lee. Is he ready for me?"

"Go right on in."

Without a Break-the-Glass for almost a month, Esther had been bored out of her skull. She'd even welcome another mule mission, just to get off Mars and away from her reports. And this would be her 20th mission. Back during Earth's WWII, bomber pilots would stencil images of bombs on the fuselages of their planes, and Esther had cut out a crude stencil of a cartoonish spy head and shoulder, and after getting the message, she'd gone ahead and put up another spy on the wall, completing the fourth row of five. She didn't know how many more she'd have before getting her next set of orders, but a nice round 25 had a solid ring to it. She was probably breaking some sort of security regulation by doing it, but given her artistic skill, or lack thereof, she had to admit that no one would probably recognize the figure as a spy. A woodchuck, possibly, or even a pig, but not a spy.

"Yes, sir," she said as Mr. Byzantine looked up upon her entry.

"Captain, as you can surmise, I've got your next mission," he said, pulling out his PA. "You'll be working with the Third Ministry."

"The Third, sir?" Esther asked, surprised.

The Third Ministry handled public works, education, and health within the Federation and, under the auspices of the Second Ministry, to other governments. The Marine Corps had very little to do with the Third Ministry. The Navy Seabees worked in conjunction with them quite often and had a fairly robust liaison effort, but not the Marines.

"Yes, the Third," he said, motioning to her PA.

She took it out, and they tapped, sending the secure file over to her.

"You and one other will be accompanying an FAID medical team to Lorton-Delos AD. There's been an outbreak of a yet-unknown virus on the planet, and the Chairman has offered Federation expertise to help identify and create an anti-virus and vaccine, an offer which the CEO of Delos AD has accepted for the planetary administrator."

Esther scrolled through the background material. She knew what Delos AD was, of course. One of the 50 largest corporations in human space, its reach was significant. The brief gave her some background on the planet. Lorton-Delos AD had been first surveyed and claimed by a Cecelia Lorton, a noted pax-anarchist of her time. Evidently, she was not so adverse to big business as to refuse Delos' offer to help finance the terraforming, however. As with many of Delos' projects, it was done on the cheap, and there were many delays, but the planet was opened to immigration almost 20 years prior.

The planet was an autonomous associate member of the Federation, which was not uncommon for planets terraformed by Federation corporations or other planets. Without the tax burden of full member planets, the huge terraforming investment could be recouped earlier while still under the treaty-protection of the central government. And technically sovereign, they could follow whatever laws and regulations they themselves made.

FCDC troops were only allowed to operate on Federation planets if invited, but with the associate status, Esther thought that if FAID needed security of some sort beyond their own teams, the troopers could fill that role. They wouldn't need a Marine presence, not that two Marines could really offer much in the way of security. That made Esther's assignment even more puzzling to her.

"Sir, why me?" she asked.

"You've made a name for yourself with the director," Mr. Byzantine said.

"I have? How?"

"Copia 2. I shouldn't have to tell you that, Captain."

"But I was Robin McShay on that mission," she protested.

The condescending look on Byzantine's face was all he needed to do to convey his opinion on that statement.

OK, maybe I'm being naive. I guess ministers can find out what they want to. Still, I was supposed to be anonymous.

"As I was saying, you've been specifically requested by the Director, and from him, through the Third Minister. And so it goes."

Yes, so it goes.

Esther officially worked for the Chairman, but as she'd discovered, she, and the others like her, were simply Break-the-Glass tools for any of the ministries. They were all convenient resources to be used.

"You've got four hours to acquaint yourself with the overall mission, draw your gear, then report to your shuttle. I suggest you get started."

Esther realized she was being dismissed. Mr. Byzantine had zero social graces, but she'd long accepted that. She nodded, stood, and left his office.

She'd hoped for something a little more exciting, but it was what it was. FAID did some good things, she knew, good for the Federation and good for humanity. A semi-independent agency within the Third Ministry, it was the arm that focused outside the Federation boundaries. It covered many of the same broad areas as the Third Ministry covered within the Federation such as health, education, and infrastructure, but as it also covered more diverse areas such as agriculture and nation-building, there was significant cross-pollination with Second, Third, and Fifth Ministry personnel.

What they did not do was take sides in conflicts, and they were never armed as a matter of policy. So, while Esther gave grudging respect for what they did, they were not warriors, and so she was pretty sure this mission would be as boring as most of hers had been.

EARTH

Chapter 30

Director Nunez-Akhmetov was a short, florid-faced man who was already striding out from around his desk, hand out to shake by the time Esther had passed through the door and into the office.

"Welcome, welcome, Captain Lysander," the director said, taking her hand with a firm, but not bone-crushing grip.

Initially, Esther was going to have an alias for the mission, but the director had requested that she serve under her real name. Despite pushback from the security goons in Fourth, she was there as herself. As he shook her hand, she could tell he was excited to be meeting her, and she half-expected him to launch into a story about when he met her father at some point in his career.

"Thank you for making the trip to Brussels to see us, Captain, especially on such short notice. But I thought it would be good for all of us to meet up here, first."

Like I could ignore a Director? That's only one step below a minister.

"No problem, sir. I'm here at your service."

"Good, very good," he said, finally letting go of her hand. "Yes, very good. Well, let me introduce you to the leadership of our little project," he continued, taking her arm in his as if they were a married couple going on a stroll through the park, and turning her around to where three people sat, one of them being another Marine.

"Captain, this is Dr. Bao Bingwen, our project head."

"Please to meet you, Dr. Bingwen," Esther said, hand out to shake with the tall man with just the right touch of gray at the temples to give him gravitas.

"Oh, I'm a traditionalist, Captain. I'm Doctor Bao. Bingwen is my given name," he said with a high-pitched, but infectious laugh, which totally wiped out that gravitas. "But after saying all of that, please call me Bing, if you would. We don't stand much on pomp here."

"Uh . . . sure . . . Bing," she said. "And you can call me Esther, if you want," she added, knowing it had been expected.

"And this young woman here is Security Specialist Three Michelle Jeanmard," the director said, giving her a nudge to move in front of the security specialist.

"Young" was relative. The woman probably had five years on Esther. On the trip over from Mars, she'd looked up as much as she could about FAID, and the security specialists were in-house FAID personnel, tasked with both passive and active security. Esther got the idea that they were something like jumped up jimmylegs hired to check IDs and walk empty buildings at night.

"Captain Lysander, I'll be looking forward to sitting with you to discuss our procedures on the way out, if you please."

I guess there're no first names with her, Esther thought, a bit relieved.

After so many years in the Corps, she was comfortable with defined levels of command and responsibility, and first names, along with the implied familiarity, could blur the lines. Dr. Bao, no, Bing, was the project manager, but Esther still wasn't quite sure as to where she fell in with regards to command and control of the "project," as they termed the mission.

"And do you know Captain Aylsworth?" the director asked. "James Aylsworth?"

"I'm afraid not," she said, reaching out a hand.

Captain? Isn't he a little young for that?

Esther was only 29 herself, but the Marine captain standing in front of her looked to be barely out of his teens.

"Captain, please to meet you. Jim Aylsworth," the captain said, taking her hand.

"Esther Lysander."

"Well, with introductions out of the way, let's sit at the conference table," the director said, once again, taking Esther by the forearm and leading her to . . . the conference table?

In front of a plush-looking orange couch was an oddly-shaped low table. A number of mismatched chairs surrounding the other three sides. As she got closer, she could see it was made from highly polished wood, but not from a nice circle or rectangle. It looked like someone had taken a slice out of one of the twisted bristlecone pines that grew in the American southwest. Those trees were protected, so she knew it couldn't have been made from that, but she couldn't think of anything else that would have such an irregular shape.

She took the proffered seat and sunk down deep. This was like going to some chic house for tea or drinks, not a meeting with a director-level bureaucrat. The others were nonplussed, though, as the director asked if anyone wanted a drink. She asked for a tea, and as he found out what the others wanted, she looked around the office. Almost every square centimeter was covered with plaques, pics, and loop camcordings. She swept her eyes across them, and one caught her attention. Focusing on it, she almost laughed. She knew the director wanted to talk about her father, and there, in a flat pic, was a younger Dr. Nunez-Akhmetov in some sort of field clothing. Standing next to him, his arms around the director, was her father. She wasn't close enough to see it well, but it looked like it was taken when her father was a major general.

"Well, while we wait for our drinks, time is short, so let's get this going. I know you have better things to be doing, but I think it's important to set the tone for this project.

"First, from a humanity prospect, I don't need to tell you how vital it is that you isolate the virus and manufacture an anti-viral and vaccine.

"Captain Lysander, you have been briefed on what you face, right?"

"Yes, sir."

What she didn't know was why she was there. Yes, she saved two FAID workers on Copia 2, but that didn't qualify her for this mission. She wasn't a doctor. And at the moment, of the four people being briefed at the director's conference table, only one of them was a doctor. The other three, herself included, seemed to be more security-oriented.

"OK, good. Above all, we need to save lives. Too many have been lost already, and Bing, you've got a good team with you, some high-powered people. Dr. Housa's team is already working on the DNA scans, and we'll keep you updated on everything that happens back here, but you're going to be at ground zero, so it's probably going to fall on you.

"For you three, most of this has already been discussed with the medical team, but I wanted you to be fully on board with what's at stake."

Which explains this meeting. The science-types already met and are doing whatever science-types do before a mission—I mean, a project.

"What I want to talk to the four of you is ground zero itself. None of you have been on a project like this before."

The director wasn't asking a question. He knew that already.

"And it is imperative to remember that these are real people you are dealing with. They're afraid, and rightly so. For every extra hour it takes you, more of them will die, and from all accounts, die horribly, their bodies turning into liquid as they watch.

Liquid? Esther wondered, her stomach fluttering. *What have I got myself into?*

She'd been so concerned about learning FAID's modus operandi that she'd pretty much ignored the reason for the mission. She was going to rectify that the first free moment she had.

"The situation on the ground will be dangerous, and not just because of the Schleizen Virus."

Who's Schleizen, Esther wondered, but didn't voice the question aloud.

"The people will praise your arrival, but the longer it takes, the more they'll panic, and the more they'll resent you. Very, very quickly, you'll fall from being guardian angels to become the perpetrators of their suffering. They will accuse you of having a cure, but that you won't use it for nefarious reasons. Even your local security will fall into the trap, and either run away or join the crowd."

He was quiet for a moment, lost in his thoughts, until he softly said, "On Manteo's Grace, back before the Evolution," he said, giving Esther the tiniest of glances, "I was part of a project. The population of one of the towns was suffering from rampant heavy metal poisoning, and the treatment they were given exacerbated the situation. We had 11 filtering stations set up, but treatments were taking an hour simply to stabilize the patients. Meanwhile, people were dying.

"Quickly, we were accused of withholding treatment of the rest. The unrest built up, and the dam broke. Our local security fled before the flood.

"Children were ripped off the machines and trampled into the ground. We tried to stop them, but we were beaten down as well. Four of us died, four out of a ten-man team. Several of those who were torn from the machines died."

"What happened to the people?" Esther asked, her voice hushed.

"They died. Or most of them did. A local police chief stormed the crowd and pulled us out, but our equipment was destroyed. We were extracted off the planet. From what the planetary government told us, more than 92% of the population of the town died, quarantined from the rest of the planet."

"Quarantined? For heavy metal poisoning?" Bing asked.

"It wasn't just the sick people who panicked, Bing. Everyone panics."

All four of them sat lost in their thoughts for a moment. Esther knew why she was there now, but it was a mistake. Maybe Specialist Jeanmard had training in crowd control, but not Aylsworth and her. They were Marines, taught to kill the enemies of the Federation. They were not a police force.

The director should have requested an FCDC team. That was their bailiwick. But for whatever reason, he wanted Marines. Esther was pretty sure that he wanted one particular Marine, Captain Esther Lysander. As much as he was quirky, as much as he was personable, he was still a politician. No one reached the director level without being a politician. Even now, he was probably wondering how he could use her identity, even after the fact, to bolster his agency.

Esther didn't think the director had any malfeasance in his intensions. She'd just met him, but she was sure he was a well-meaning and honorable man. But there were limited resources for the central government, and FAID would be competing with other agencies for those resources. He was simply trying to do what he could to better place the agency.

But he was wrong. Despite going through a tough situation in his earlier service, he didn't seem to understand that there was a reason the Marines and the FCDC were different. They had different skill sets. And by thinking about the agency as a whole, he was making a mistake. It could jeopardize the mission if it all went to shit like his project on Manteo's Grace.

Hopefully, it wouldn't get to be anything like that. They were there to help the people, after all. And with all the resources available to them, they'd be able to chart the virus' genome and start manufacturing vaccines within a couple of days.

But if it came to that, Esther planned on being ready for whatever was thrown at her.

FSNS BAY OF BENGAL

Chapter 31

"I've got to ask you, how old are you?" Esther asked Jim as they sat in the small lounge while waiting for the second seating in the mess.

She'd told herself she wasn't going to ask, but only ten hours into their transit, she couldn't hold back. The roll of his eyes told her he'd been asked that before, and he wasn't too happy about it.

"I'm 23," he said in a resigned voice.

"Twenty-freaking-three? How the hell are you a captain?"

"I graduated from Tori when I was 16," he said.

"You? You graduated from Tori Institute of Technology when you were 16?"

TIT was one of the best-known—and hardest to gain entry—universities in the Federation. Graduates were actively recruited for extremely high-paying and prestigious jobs. And he graduated at an age when most people were still in Secondary.

"Yeah," he said, as if it was nothing.

"Um . . . I don't know what to say. But you went into the Marines?"

He shrugged and said, "It seemed like a good idea at the time."

"OK, so assuming you got a waiver and came in at 17, that was six years ago. How are you a captain?"

"I did one year enlisted, then was offered a commission. And I just put on my railroad tracks four months ago."

Esther furrowed her brows in thought. Something wasn't right. Then she keyed on a what he'd just said, that he was "offered" a commission.

"Your commission, was that a foregone conclusion?"

He smiled and said, "You might say that."

"And it had something to do with your studies?"

She didn't need an answer. She saw it in his eyes.

"I'm not even going to ask," she said. "And so, you haven't really been in the fleet, have you?"

His eyes flashed in anger, and he blurted out, "Of course I have. I was with 3/9 as a PFC, and I did three years with 1/13 as a lieutenant."

"One-thirteen? Were you on Gilead?" she asked.

First Battalion, Thirteenth Marines, had fought a very tough, six-month campaign on Gilead, suffering the most casualties of any unit since the Evolution.

"Yes, I was."

"OK, you and I are going sit down so you can tell me about it sometime. I want to hear it from the ground truth. But you aren't with a unit now, right?"

"I'm APOC."

"Commandant or Chairman?"

"Commandant, currently detached to the Third Ministry."

"And that has to do with your studies, I'm assuming. I'm APOC, too. Chairman."

"Makes sense. You've fallen off the map," he said.

"Oh, so you're following where I'm at in the Corps."

"Not really. You're fairly well-known, and when I saw we were going to be in this together, I looked you up. Not that there's been much of anything for almost two years."

"Don't I know it," she said.

"Ah, our guests," a Navy lieutenant said as he entered the wardroom and took a seat with him. "I trust the *BB's* hospitality suits your needs? I'm Geral Kleinfelter, cargo officer for this fine ship."

Esther didn't know if he was joking or not about "this fine ship." The *Bay of Bengal* had been a full ship-of-the-line when it was built over a hundred years ago, but it had long been transferred to the Federation's maritime force. Most of the officers were Navy, but a good portion of the crew was contracted civilians. The ship looked to run well enough, but it was not a modern warship, and she was feeling her age.

"Esther Lysander," she said, shaking his hand.

"Jim Aylsworth. And yes, everything's fine, thanks."

"It'll be a short hop before we drop you and your charges off. That will be our first stop in a nine-month round-the-Federation."

"Nine months? Long time to be away from home," Jim said.

Geral shrugged, then said, "That's the way it is with us."

Esther didn't think he was overly proud of his billet. She didn't know much about the Maritime Service, but as a Naval officer, it probably didn't hold the same prestige as being on a Navy ship-of-the-line. The Navy relied on the Maritime fleet to supply and maintain its ships, but she doubted too many Naval officers wanted to be assigned to them.

"Better than you guys, though. What, only two of you with all those FAID tree huggers? I'd go batshit having to babysit them."

"What do you mean?" Jim asked.

Esther knew that many in the military had a low regard for the civilians in the government as a whole, and Third Ministry in particular. And that held true for FAID as well. She'd heard them called "Fucking A" on more than a few occasions. Winning the hearts and minds didn't always jive with how Marines viewed life, but as General Simone had said to her once, every job FAID created for someone meant one less terrorist, one less enemy the Marines had to fight.

"What do I mean? You know what I mean. They're fucking peace-aholics, no guts to them."

Kristian Dymond had some guts on Copia 2, Esther thought. He'd reacted quickly when Esther had made her move on Copia 2, even if Tokiyashi-Jules hadn't.

"They go to into some pretty hairy situations, and without arms to defend themselves," Jim said, a little bit of steel in his voice.

"Well, maybe. But that's because they think everything's kumbaya, and you can do anything if you just love the enemy to death. They're too stupid to know when there's danger, and they're a big waste of the taxes I pay. And speaking of the devil," he continued nodding towards Doctors Bao and Humbert, who'd just poked their heads in the hatch.

"Is this where we're supposed to eat?" Bing asked.

"Yes, yes, yes, come on in," Geral said as if he hadn't just been disparaging the entire FAID. "We've still got another six or seven minutes, but come take a seat here."

Esther didn't like duplicity, and so the good Lieutenant Kleinfelter did not impress her. Luckily, they wouldn't be on the ship long. She looked over to Jim, and if Kleinfelter had caught the glare the young captain was giving him, he would have pissed his pants in fear.

It seemed as if her fellow Marine had a bit of vinegar in him.

LORTON-DELOS AD

Chapter 32

"And here we are," Heidi Boonprasong said as the bright purple Open Arms hover pulled into the compound.

Esther, in the back seat, was not happy at what she saw. The compound looked to consist of two new Farrell-Lee expeditionary buildings with another still in its crate, waiting to be erected. A ring of simple chain-link fencing, top with memory wire encircled the area. Memory wire was an adequate tool to use in crowd management, but it was on top of chain link that could be cut with a simple set of snippers. If someone wanted to break in, they'd just cut the fence and enter under the wire.

Not that anyone had to break in. The front gate was wide open, and as she watched, a man, woman, and child walked through. Standing in a loose line, another 40 or 50 people stood waiting in front of one of the buildings. Some had on surgical masks, some had on more elaborate mechanical masks, and some had on full environmental suits. More than half, however, were without any sort of protection.

What hit Esther hardest, though, was that five or six were lying flat on the ground, a couple with someone tending them, but three seem to have an invisible boundary surrounding them, keeping the rest of the people a couple of meters away from them. One of them was a little girl, a bright sky-blue blouse making her stand out. An older woman sat beside her, the girl's hand in hers.

"This isn't going to do, Mz. Boonprasong," Bing said from the front seat. "I thought Open Arms was more professional."

At least he sees the security problem.

"We try, Dr. Bao," Heidi told him. "But I'm a logistics specialist. Our whole team is. We were tasked with erecting the

Farrell-Lees, powering them up, and putting up the fence. The people, they just started showing up hours ago."

Open Arms was an NGO based out of the Brotherhood. Heidi and her team were out of Trek 4, a Federation hub in the sector. Esther was only vaguely aware of the work Open Arms did. She'd been surprised, though, that it was the NGO who had met them at the shuttle port, got them through the quarantine checkpoint, and transported them to this compound. They should have been met by the government, not an NGO.

"We've got people lying in the dirt, for God's sake, people who need treatment. Most of those others are just standing there right next to each other, including those who are pretty obviously infected. We need to rectify this at once."

It took Esther a moment to realize that Bing was not complaining about security, but rather the condition of the patients.

Oh, real classy, Lysander. They aren't the enemy—the virus is. Get your head in the game.

"Hoods on," Bing said as the hover pulled up.

The team was already in their PPE's, the Personal Protective Equipment, but without the hoods attached. The hover had positive pressure, and it had been scanned, so it was a safe environment. Out there, though, that was where the virus roamed. Esther immediately pulled the hood over her head and activated the seal. A few moments later, the PPE, having done its integrity test, lit up the small green LED that let her and everyone else know that she was protected. A red flashing light—well, she just hoped she never saw that.

"Unsealing," the driver, whose name Esther never caught, said.

With a whoosh of air, the overpressure rushed out, and Esther opened her door, stepping out. She turned to watch four more passenger hovers and two trucks pull in. One by one, the hovers' doors opened, and the ten medical personnel, six security, and Jim stepped out.

Dr. Gene Humbert, Bing's second in command, immediately went to the trucks, and like a traffic cop in the old flicks, started guiding them to the building for offload while Dr. Veta Ericsson took three of the nurses to start triaging the patients.

Esther felt a little useless. She didn't have a job at the moment, and she didn't know where she could contribute. She'd never seen a Farrell-Lee actually being erected, so she wandered over to the Open Arms team, who were just starting on the third building. The foreman, or who Esther assumed was the foreman, was just finishing laying out the pad with the forms. Two men stood by with the foamcrete dispensers, and when given the signal, started on the far side of the pad, spraying a thin layer of white liquid which almost immediately started foaming up, rising ten or twelve centimeters. As the two men started walking back, Esther strode up alongside the near edge of the form until she reached them. Kneeling, she put her head down to the level of the foamcrete, marveling how smooth and level it was. Each new swath laid down by the workers rose to the level of the already applied section and melded together without a visible seam.

"Go ahead, step on it," the foreman told her.

"Really? Doesn't it have to set?"

"It's set. Takes about ten seconds," he said, then demonstrated it by stepping up on it.

Esther stepped on it as well. It felt perfectly smooth under her feet—and strong.

"What happens if I'm standing there and they foamcrete me?"

The foreman laughed and said, "No, it's safe to use—it's got safety nanos. Can't stick to humans. Oh, it'll trap you in place, sure enough. Most everybody's been 'shackled,' as we call it, at least once. You owe the rest of the crew a round if you let that happen."

"I'd better watch myself then. I don't need to be buying drinks for everyone," she said. "That looks pretty hard. If that was around my feet, I don't think I could pull free."

"Never in a million years. Nah, if that happens, we either got to get the jackhammer or the cat."

"The cat?"

"Oh, sorry. The catalyst. That breaks down all of this when we leave. The ground will be a flattened, but no trace of the pad will remain. Part of the requirements for temps. We've got to take everything with us when we leave."

That made sense to her, but it seemed amazing that all of what looked to be a huge pad of regular plasticrete could simply disappear. What seemed even more amazing is that the two men finished the pad from one, fairly small tank of the foamcrete liquid. Ten minutes after Esther walked up, the pad was ready, and the installation of the Farrell-Lee could commence.

She watched with interest as the five crates were horsed into position. Most of the erection was automatic, but the initial placement was done with old-fashioned brute strength. She stepped in to help, happy to be doing something. Eric—the foreman—checked the positions, then initiated the erection. Esther was looking forward to watching the expeditionary building take shape when Bing walked up to her.

He pulled her aside and quietly said, "Esther, I know this isn't part of your job description. But the entrance, there is simply no excuse for that, and I don't care what Mz. Boonprasong says. There are codes for what we do. I've got the requirements here." He pulled up his PA, which Esther dutifully tapped. "If you can take Michelle and her team, and any of the Open Arms folks you can shanghai, can you honcho building the screening and decon station? No one is to enter or leave the compound without going through protocol. If you can get this up to step 18, then you can ask Gene to install the units. Once it's done, we need it manned around the clock."

Bing was right. This wasn't part of her job description. And from talking to Michelle, it wasn't part of hers, either. The security specialist could man this station Bing wanted with her team, but she wasn't a construction engineer.

But then again, there was nothing in an infantry officer's job about fighting some sort off megavirus, and as Bing had said, the plans were now on her PA. And if FAID was anything like the Marine Corps, she was sure they'd be so explicit as to leave nothing to individual choice.

Most of all, it had to be done. The medical staff had their hands full, and if neither the government nor Open Arms had gotten around to it, someone had to pick up the slack. That someone might as well be her.

Well, she could honcho it. Eric might be able to spare a body, and maybe it was time to get Jim's TIT-educated brain involved. No matter how complicated the plans, he should be able to decipher them—that or turn in his diploma.

****

It took almost eight hours, five hours longer than allowed by *FAID Instruction 1002.2.1, Secure Access and Egress in a Contaminated Environment.* It wasn't that the instructions were that difficult. They were really straight-forward. But most of them didn't understand how to actually do what was being directed.

"Install a Class 2 entrance frame two (2) meters from the display station. Ensure frame is grounded and can withstand 15 N of lateral force at 1.3 meters."

Esther, Jim, and Michelle knew what each of the words meant, and they knew that the intent was to make sure the frame holding the scanners would be sturdy enough to do the job. But none of them were sure how to accomplish any of those individual steps. Eric lent them one of his construction techs, and with continual referencing to the net, they managed to construct the gate station. Dr. Humbert brought over the scanners, display and decon equipment, and finally, they were up and running. Another 50 or 60 people had entered the compound in the meantime, but with the station functioning, Esther closed off the gaps to the side with memory wire.

For all the difficulty of constructing the station, it was almost foolproof to run. People wanting to enter the compound stepped through the scanner, which searched for the virus along with a host of other conditions that would exacerbate the effects of the virus. Those found to be clear were given a warning that they were entering a contaminated area and given the chance to leave. If they insisted on entering, which was usually because they were accompanying someone who had the virus, they were given the wrap-around breathing mask.

For the people who had the virus, they went through a surface contamination, then were sent to Building A receiving, where Dr. Ericsson and her staff conducted more detailed tests.

Esther thought it disheartening to know that the compound was designated as a "contaminated area." They were there to fight the virus, not harbor it. But it made sense. Sick people were coming to them, and sick people brought the virus with them. That was why egress from the compound was more difficult. Every single person leaving had to enter the decon chamber, which was a 1.5-meter-wide by 2.3-meter-tall container that looked like a walk-in cooler. Once inside, the person was bombarded with irradiation, ultrasonic, and chemical washes that should kill any virus on the outside of the body. Next, they went through another scanner. Anyone still contaminated had the virus inside of them, and they were denied egress. They were to be returned to the compound, by force if necessary, by the single police officer the government had sent to stand outside the compound.

Bing had told them that this was set in stone, and after she, Jim, and Michelle had discussed just what he meant, they didn't quite know what they could do if the cop outside the gate couldn't or wouldn't stop anyone from leaving. Officially, the project was not armed, as was FAID policy, but she and Jim had packed along a single case of M99's, something they hadn't yet mentioned to anyone else. Esther and Jim decided that those weapons would only see the light of day if it came to protecting the camp—the director's story about Manteo's Grace had a significant impact on their thinking—but they would not use them to stop people from leaving. A better choice would be to simply gang-rush the person or people and hope their PPE's maintained integrity in any scuffle.

Jim, Michelle, and she watched the first few new patients go through the entry procedures. The three guards on duty seemed to have a handle on it.

Esther had told Michelle to make her own hours. She and Jim would be 12 on and 12 off, not that she thought she'd be anywhere else when she was awake. She'd been somewhat surprised that the FAID team was berthed in a nearby hotel, largely abandoned as people fled the capital. She had assumed that they would stay in the compound, but when she mentioned that, Bing had said that he needed to get people out of their PPEs where they could get a good meal, clean up, and relax.

That made sense to her. Watching person after person die had to mess up even the most hardened of them. Still, she saw the cot placed behind his work station, and she thought the project leader would probably spend most of his time there.

Esther, on the other hand, was hardened. She'd killed before, often. She wasn't going to be bothered by people dying.

"Let's check out Receiving, then the lab. If Bing doesn't have anything for us, you go get some shut-eye," she told Jim.

Together, they walked up to Building A, Receiving. The prone patients were gone, and chairs had been set up for the line of people. Some looked at them with sullen eyes as the two of them walked up, probably resenting the fact that the two of them didn't have the virus while they did, but most looked up at them with hope. They were the mighty Federation, after all, and they must have the cure.

I hope we do, I really do.

Esther and Jim stepped in front of the first man in line and into receiving.

"Please wait . . . oh, it's you two. If you want to see Dr. Ericsson, she's in Treatment and Collecting," Henri Monterey said from where he was interviewing a middle-aged and an obviously frightened woman.

Esther nodded and walked around them, though the door, and to the rear 3/4s of the building. Field tables were laid out, and on almost all of them, people lay. All—except for one—were hooked up to various monitor and pumps, and two of the staff seemed to be watching over them. The one person without the monitors was towards the left rear, and two more FAID staff members were leaning over the table. Esther and Jim walked down the middle of the ward, beds on each side of them.

Some of the patients looked normal, if a little haggard. Others looked worse off. Esther tried not to catch their eyes, which was selfish of her. A smile from her might give them a little boost, but Esther was afraid her look might not be very comforting.

A sense of trepidation began to take over her as she approached. Something told her that all was not well. She recognized Dr. Ericsson first, then, she saw the sky-blue blouse draped over the foot of the bed.

It's the little girl, the one who was lying down, she told herself, almost pausing.

Esther stepped up alongside the doctor, and she recoiled when she saw from what the doctor was collecting samples. The mass of liquefying flesh may have been the girl eight hours prior, but it wasn't her now. The body barely looked human, but from the clenched fists in rigor, Esther knew the girl had not faded away quietly. She had died in mortal agony. Dr. Ericsson was putting the samples, which looked like bloody slugs, into the chamber that Bryce Schmitt was holding.

"OK, that's enough. Get these to Dr. Bao in the lab," she said, then turning to see Esther and Jim. "Oh, can I help you, Captain Lysander?"

Esther looked in horror at the mess on the table, then at the doctor, her bloody scalpel still raised.

Esther had killed humans before with barely a pause. She'd seen her Marines, her friends, blown apart in the most horrendous manners possible. Always, she'd kept her cool. This was different. This wasn't war; this was a horror flick, something that turned on a switch deep within her cortex's limbic system that triggered some primeval fear of the unknown.

With a sharp spasm, her stomach heaved, and she vomited. In her PPE, the gorge splashed across the inside of her hood, then started to flow down between her skin and the fabric of the suit. Almost blinded, she stumbled back, bumping up against something hard, something a small part of her mind that remained rational told her was another patient's bed. She spun around, but the vomit on her hood visor blocked most of her vision.

And someone grabbed her from behind, someone with a firm, steady grip.

"Let me help you. Come with me," Jim's voice registered with her, breaking through her panic.

Esther was horrified—and mortified. She was a Marine Corps captain, the deputy project manager. She was the one who was supposed to keep it together no matter what happened. But she'd been taken out of action by the simple sight of a dead patient. She had to gain control of herself. She took a deep breath, only to choke on the acrid fumes of the vomit.

"Come on, let's get out of here," Jim said, pulling her along.

Esther knew she had to center herself, but it was almost impossible. She had to get out of her PPE, she had to clean up, but most of all she had to get out of this house of horrors.

Chapter 33

Esther folded over the polyoptima sheet around what was left of the body, passing her edge to Penelope who brought it down, activating the seal. She ran the decon sprayer over the body, hopefully killing most of the loose viruses. Within a few short moments, what had been the 52-year-old Miller Washburn was sealed to the outside world and ready for the incinerator.

She moved to the head, and with Penelope at the feet, she said, "One . . . two . . . three!"

Together, they shifted him off of the bed and onto the gurney.

"I'll take it from here," Esther said. "Why don't you take a break?"

Penelope looked around the ward, a frown on her face, but there was no one nearing the end at the moment. With four deaths so far this morning, the afternoon looked to be rough, but for the moment, it looked like there would be a break.

She and Penelope made an odd pair for this task. Penelope was Penelope Smith. Her daughter, Krysandra, was the eight-year-old girl who had died and drawn such a reaction from Esther. After her daughter was incinerated, Penelope just hung around, and no one had the heart to tell her to leave. She started doing little odd jobs, making herself useful, and yesterday, she and Esther had taken a shift clearing the beds of the deceased, freeing the medical team to treat the sick and try to formulate the anti-virus.

As for Esther, this was her penitence. No one asked her to, but she'd been so ashamed of her reaction, she had simply started helping out, sealing the bodies of the dead and taking them to the incinerator. She'd been able to overcome her instinctual fear. What was worse than the bodies was the suffering of those nearing the end. She didn't like what she was doing, but at least she could do it.

"OK, maybe I will. My PPE's cooling isn't circulating well or something."

Esther punched in the destination, then followed the gurney as it made its way out of Ward 2, the "Death House," as the patients referred to it. Ward 2 was a brand-new building, erected when it became clear that they were running out of bed space. Those who were responding to treatment remained in Ward 1—those who were on a downward spiral were moved to Ward 2. It bothered Esther that the only medical people in the Ward were the samples-collecting team, but Bing had explained that their mission was to develop a vaccine and anti-virus, not treat patients. He left Veta Ericsson along with two nurses to treat those in Ward 1, and they'd been joined by a local doc who'd showed up at the gate this morning, but the rest of the team was in the lab working feverishly to find a way to beat the virus.

"Please, can you stay with me?" an elderly woman asked, weakly reaching out a hand to try and stop her as she followed the gurney.

Esther could see the tell-tale signs of the end game. Sores were opening up on her skin as the virus ate away at its host. She didn't look to be in pain, which wasn't that surprising. Each patient was hooked to a portadoc, which was pumping her body with painkillers. The first patients had died horribly until they'd been able to set up the portadocs, but now, the pain only became severe at the very end—and they could choose to forego it and slip into unconsciousness.

"I . . . I have to take Mr. Washburn here out, ma'am."

"Please, can you just stay for a while," the woman whispered, her voice plaintive.

Esther didn't need to stay with the gurney. It had sensed that she'd stopped, and so it stopped as well, but she could send it on its way. The incineration shed, however, was not automated, and Esther had to set it manually.

"Mz. . . . Mz. Delbert," she started, reading the name posted at the foot of the bed.

"Please, call me Hannah," the woman said.

Hannah, like my mother.

"OK, Hannah. Let me take care of Mr. Washburn, and I'll come back to you."

"Promise?"

"Promise."

"Oh, such a sweet girl. I'll be waiting. I'm not going anywhere," she said with a half-cough, half-laugh.

Esther gave her hand a squeeze and started forward, the gurney immediately continuing. As they exited Ward 2, they went through an irradiation ring. Bing had assured her that the virus was passed by contact, and it would be difficult for it to live for long outside of a host, but still, they were taking no chances.

As she stepped into the bright sunlight, she could hear a grumbling from beyond the gate. Crowds had started to gather yesterday. Some were begging for treatment, some seemed to be protesting the presence of the Federation team—which made absolutely no sense to her—and others were seemed to be onlookers, reporters, and vendors looking to make a quick credit. She could see Michelle standing easily just inside the gate, watching the crowd.

Esther shook her head and followed the gurney to the back of the compound where the crematorium had been set up. Set up against the back fence, ten or twelve people stood just outside, watching her. She wondered if they were relatives, waiting to see their loved ones cremated. None of them asked who she was escorting, and she didn't volunteer anything to them.

The gurney trundled up to the door and transferred Mr. Washburn's body onto the tray. Once loaded, the tray receded back into the retort. The actual cremation had to be initiated by a human, so once the doors closed and the ready light flashed green, Esther pushed the start button. Immediately, the inside of the retort was subjected to 2500 degree Celsius blasts. After three minutes, the cremulater ground up the cremains which were then subject to another three minutes of the intense heat.

The flashing red light switch to green, and the door opened. Esther had been amazed that after being subject to such intense heat, the tray came out simply warm to the touch. The cremains were neatly packaged in the middle of the tray. Esther waved the scanner over the package, but as expected, there was no sign of any kind of life, viral or anything else.

RIP, Mr. Washburn.

As she started back to the Ward, Michelle passed, "Captain, can you come to the gate, please? Things are getting a little hotter here."

Compound security was Michelle's responsibility, and Esther really wanted to get to the lounge, as they called the tiny hut where they could sit, take off the hood, and eat something real rather than the tube meals that could be consumed while in the PPE's. Esther wasn't that hungry, but she didn't like to use the gel pads in the PPE's that absorbed body waste when there was a real toilet in the lounge.

But if Michelle wanted her, she needed to find out why. She abandoned the gurney and turned to the gate. She could hear shouting but couldn't quite make out what was being said.

She approached the rear of the decon station where Paul Yetter was standing nervously. Paul was Michelle's second in command, and she relied heavily on him.

"Where's Jeanmard?" she asked him.

"Out there, with Doctor Sengatjuo," he said, pointing beyond the gate.

Esther looked closer, and sure enough, there were three figures in the bright yellow FAID PPE's. Dr. Sengatjuo—Josiah—had his hood back, and she could see he was in earnest conversation with a crowd that had gathered around.

"Why did they go out there?" she asked.

"I told her it was a bad idea, Captain," Paul said. "I've been doing this for nigh on 35 years now, and you get feelings, you know?"

"And she still went?"

"She said she had to be there with the doc."

"Where's our cop?" she asked, searching through the crowd.

"He left as soon as it looked like trouble," Paul said, the tone of his voice evidence enough about what he thought of that.

She shook her head. It disgusted her as well, but there wasn't much she could do about it at the moment.

"Michelle, what the hell are you three doing out there?" Esther passed over the comms.

One of the other two PPE-clad figures raised a hand to her ear, pressing in, and Michelle answered, "It was Sengatjuo. He thought he had to respond to the people. I couldn't let him go out alone."

She was right, Esther knew. But it was stupid. She could tell from the mob as they crowded closer that they were angry, and an angry mob was unpredictable.

"Why are they upset? What are they saying?"

"They want treatment. They want a vaccine. They want, well, I don't quite get it."

"OK, hold on. Let me see what I can do."

She switched to Jim and called him up.

"Jim, can you get over here now?"

She could hear the sleep in his voice as he said, "What? At the compound? Yeah, sure. What's up?"

"We've got more people outside, and they're not happy. Look, leave the PPE. Wear your M24, and come in civvies. I want you to hang back and mingle, get a feel for them, OK?"

The civvies weren't unusual. Even now, under her PPE, Esther was in running tights and a sports bra herself. The PPE's were more comfortable than, say, the Marine EVA suits, but still, the less on underneath meant fewer wrinkles that could be annoying as hell. Not wearing a PPE to and from the compound not as common. Bing didn't wear one, telling Esther he didn't want to excite the locals. Esther thought they were already excited, so she wore hers on the way from the hotel, but she knew that was simply a precaution. Unless they came in contact with an infected person, either by touching or by being sneezed upon, they should be safe, and even then, if they had on the M24 Environmental mask, a simple decon after contact should be enough to keep from getting infected. Enough of the people outside were wearing some sort of mask that Jim wouldn't stand out.

"Sure, I've got it," he said with more assurance as he woke up fully. "I'll be there in five."

It was a ten-minute walk from their hotel to the compound, so to make it in five, he'd have to run, which was a bitch to do with any type of mask on.

She put Jim out of her mind, then called Bing.

"We've got a problem here. Josiah's out there with the protesters, and it's getting tense."

"What? Josiah? I wondered where he went to," Bing said, not sounding too concerned.

"He needs to be called back inside before there's trouble."

"Trouble? There won't be. We're here to help, so trouble would be counterproductive."

She keyed off her voice pick-up and said to Paul, "Dr. Bao says there won't be trouble. That would be counterproductive."

Paul rolled his eyes, then shook his head, saying, "The lab rats don't understand the real universe."

Esther had never been on this type of a mission, but she'd faced crowds before, and she knew what the veteran of these kinds of evolutions meant. Director Nunez-Akhmetov's story about what happened on Manteo's Grace had made an impact on her, even if it hadn't seemed to have the same impact with Bing.

Bing was a great guy, and evidently brilliant, but he'd been given the project due to his lab ability. He'd never been in the field in this type of situation. Josiah had, Veta had, as had two of the nurses, but most of the doctors and techs were neophytes, and Esther was beginning to wonder if that was a mistake. Yes, they needed the best and brightest to defeat the virus, but they also needed people with experience working in the field.

"Bing, I think it is a little worse than that," she said.

"Yes, I know some of the people are upset. But they have to realize that we have limited bed space and resources to treat people. If we can come up with the vaccine and anti-viral, we'll save far more people than if we put our resources into comforting those who are going to die anyway. Josiah knows that. He'll be explaining it to them."

"They won't listen, Bing. Use your head. What would you do if you thought you needed treatment, but someone said 'Sorry, but we're trying to save others, so leave us alone?'"

"Oh, come on, Esther. Aren't you being a bit overdramatic?"

"I don't think I am. And as the head of project security, I have to insist that you tell Josiah to get his ass back inside the compound, now."

There was silence for a moment, then Bing said, "Whatever. I don't have time for this. I still think you're being overly dramatic, but I'll tell Josiah to return. I need him now anyway."

"Thank you, Bing."

She watched, waiting for Josiah to break off, but he kept talking, his hand gesturing as he tried to make a point.

"Esther, I can't reach Josiah," Bing passed to her. "He's not answering. Why don't you tell him to come back inside? Tell him I said so."

All of them had small, behind-the-ear comm sets, tied into both their PAs as well as the comms station that was set up in the lounge. Hood off or not, Josiah should be responding.

"Ah, hell. I'm going out there, Paul," she said as she started for the exit.

"No, Captain, stop. Don't leave."

"I've got to. It's not that bad yet."

"I mean I won't let you, ma'am. To protect them out there. You need to go into decon first."

She looked at him in surprise. Things were hot, and he was going to stop her. Looking at him, his body tensed, she realized he wasn't bluffing. He would stop her. And it hit her. He was right. She had to decon first. Hell, she'd just wrapped up Mr. Washburn and taken his body to the incinerator. If anyone had the risk of being contaminated, it was her, much more than those people out there. She'd gone through the Ward 1 irradiation ring, but still, she could still be a vector for the virus right now.

She was worried about Josiah and Michelle, but Paul was worried about the people of Lorton-Delos AG. At least he was taking his duties seriously.

"You're right, Paul. Thanks. Cycle me through."

She stood in the chamber, arms held out wide, as the wash, hit her, then the irradiation. Coming out on the other side, she nodded at Paul, turned to Josiah, then in afterthought, turned back to Paul.

"You have a super-skunk?"

The FAID team was not armed, which made Esther feel decidedly naked. They were not *openly* armed, to be more precise, but that was hardly better. The case of M99's she and Jim had brought were in the storage shed, something to use only as a last resort. But as a matter of course, the team had several crowd-dispersing tools, not the least being the MC-505. It fired a 40mm grenade, nicknamed a "super-skunk," that sent out a cloud of one of the vilest concoctions known to man. It was bent-over-vomiting-and-crawling-in-the-dirt bad. Once out of the cloud, the symptoms disappeared immediately, but it was a very rare person who could even think straight while in it.

"Sure do. Five rounds at the post at all times."

"OK, I want you to get it. If I call, blanket the area, got it?"

"Roger that, ma'am," he said with a slight smile creasing his face.

"OK, see you in a few—I hope."

Esther had only taken a few steps when the third team member, who she hadn't identified yet, was shoved from behind by someone trying to confront Josiah, who saw it and stepped forward to protest. Almost immediately, a fist from the crowd cold-cocked the doctor, and he went down. The crowd surged forward as Esther broke into a sprint.

"Paul, blanket us!" she shouted as she hit the back of the press of people, knocking several to the ground before they knew she was there.

At least two men, one with a mask, the other without, his face enraged, continued striking downwards, undoubtedly pounding on Josiah. Michelle was holding her own, but barely, and Gaius Wójcik, Esther finally identified the third man , was wildly swinging his fists.

Esther burst through the ring of people and launched herself at the maskless man who was pummeling Josiah when, with a thunk and hiss, the first of the super-skunks hit. The man, who was now bent over, realized he was now a target, and he just managed to stand when Esther hit him low, knocking him off the prone doctor.

Esther rolled over and onto one knee, and her target's face was red with anger as he scrambled to meet her—until the moment the super-skunk's payload hit him. Immediately, the look of anger turned to horror, and he dropped to the ground retching.

Esther was knocked flat when someone hit her from behind, but it was the hit of pushing bodies, not a directed strike. Down low, she took a moment to check Josiah, and her heart fell. His face was hamburger. He coughed a few times as the vapor hit him, but he didn't regain full consciousness.

She sensed more than felt something behind her and turned her head to see a man in an ancient protective mask, his arms held high with a club with which he was about to smash her. Esther tried to slip to the side, but with bodies in the way, she knew it was a lost cause. She raised her right arm in an attempt to ward off the blow when another body flew in front of her, hitting her assailant high in the chest, sending both of them backwards. The club, jolted free, fell to the ground, bouncing once before rapping Esther in the knee.

By now, two more super-skunks had landed, and the vapors were affecting visibility as well. Bodies were still in motion, but now, they were simply trying to escape, to stumble to clear air.

"Michelle!" Esther shouted, spotting her bright yellow PPE. "Help me with Josiah."

"I've got him," Jim said, pushing forward.

It took Esther a moment to realize that Jim was the one who'd saved her ass a moment earlier.

"What about—"

"I ripped off his mask. He's non-effective now, puking, probably. Here, I've got the doc. You and Michelle help Wójcik."

The lab tech was just struggling to his feet, and Esther grabbed him by the upper arm, stumbling over prone bodies and she half-led, half-dragged the bigger man towards the gate. A moment later, Michelle took his other arm, and together, they reached safety, quickly followed by Jim, Josiah slung across his shoulders.

"Decon now," Paul was shouting at Nanci Manuel.

Nanci was waving the five forward, and they crowded into the wash. Esther pushed Wójcik upright, spread her arms, and let out a sigh of relief as the spray coated her body, followed by the irradiation. She'd felt vulnerable out there, but her PPE displayed the steady green of an intact suit.

Fuck, Josiah! What about you?

She turned to see the doctor, who Jim had slid off his shoulders. The spray had washed off some of the blood, and he had four or five deep gashes across his face. His nose was obviously broken as well.

"Mz. Jennard," Nanci shouted out. "I'm getting traces on Doctor Sengatjuo and Captain Aylsworth."

Oh, hell. Jim!

"I've got it, Nanci," Veta said as she rushed over from Ward 1. "Let them in."

Sick people came into the compound as a matter of course, but letting them in required the approval from one of the medical staff.

Veta had a gurney, and as soon as the interior gate opened, Esther helped Jim lay Josiah on it.

"You, come with me," Veta told Jim as she followed the gurney into the ward.

Esther didn't know what to do, so she gave Jim a pat on the shoulder and followed him. She couldn't help but notice the torn knees of his jeans and the bloody scrape the tear revealed. She was pretty sure he'd torn them coming to her aid.

"I want a full zymex irrigation," Veta told Bryce, the nurse on duty as he came rushing out from the ward into triage.

Two civilians were in the waiting area, and they looked on in horror as Veta went to work. She cut off Josiah's PPE with sure, quick movements, pealing him like a grape. Next came the mesh monosuit he was wearing. She ran her hands over Josiah's body, lifting him up on one side to check his back.

"Looks like it's just the face," she said.

Just the face? Isn't that enough?

Veta slapped an impact IV on Josiah's inner thigh, dialing up the anti-viral cocktail the doctors on the team thought might help fight the virus the best. She checked the readout, and then ran her hands over his skull. Esther knew that infection was the primary concern, but Josiah was unconscious, and there had to be a reason for that.

"You OK?" she asked Jim quietly as Veta tended to Josiah.

"I feel fine. No big thing," he said, his voice calm and steady.

"But, what about . . ."

"We'll see."

Bryce pulled up the irrigation console, but Veta took it from him, then said, "See about the captain. Clean and rescan."

"Sir, can you step up here?" Bryce asked. He grabbed and held up the biohazard bag, and added a simply, "Sir?"

Jim took off his shirt, dumped it in the bag, then bent to take off his jeans.

"These are my only pair. I want them back if, you know. . ."

"We'll see. Underwear, too."

Jim dropped them, then hopped up onto the examining table. Esther could see a bloody gash on one leg, and more of an oozing road-rash on the other. Beyond that, he looked fine. But that wasn't the concern.

"I would've worked out first, if I knew I was going to be on display," Jim said with a laugh.

The fact that he was trying to joke was proof enough to Esther that Jim was scared. Hell, she was scared, so she couldn't imagine what he felt like.

Veta had the irrigation console, so Bryce used the field expedient method—a plastic squeeze bottle. He filled it, then squirted a stream on Jim's legs, cleaning out the wounds. It didn't take long. He asked Jim to lie back, then he pulled over the portable sprayers, coating Jim's front.

"Turn," Bryce said.

Jim gave Esther a lopsided smile, then turned to his stomach, and Bryce repeated the process on Jim's back.

"OK, Captain. Now for the scan."

Bryce turned, but Veta already had the multiscan and was affixing the transducer pads to various spots on Josiah's body. She

Jonathan P. Brazee

ran the register, handshaking each transducer to the brains of the scan.

"I'll start on your pads, Captain, if you don't mind," Bryce said quietly.

Jim, though, was transfixed on what was happening to Josiah. As were Esther, the two civilians, and Penelope, who'd come in a few moments earlier.

Veta crossed herself, then started the scan, her eyes locked on the display. Esther was holding her breath, anxious to see the results.

He's OK. It was just a beating, that's all, she tried to convince herself.

With a low ding, the display flickered as data streamed across it. Veta let out a deep breath, closed her eyes, and tilted her head back.

Is that good or bad?

When she opened her eyes, she looked at Esther, then slowly shook her head.

"Bing, it's positive. You need to get over here," Esther heard her say into her throat mic.

"Shit," was all Esther could say.

She reached over and took Jim's hand. He didn't say a word, but he almost crushed her fingers.

Veta gave the multiscan a small push towards Bryce, who took it and wheeled it up to Jim's table. He spent a few moments handshaking the transducer pads."

"You ready, Captain?" he asked Jim.

"Hit it."

The transducers sent a variety of pulses throughout Jim's body, searching for any traces of the virus. Fifteen long seconds later, the ding signaled the scan was over. Jim squeezed harder, and Esther could feel her knuckles grind together.

He was only scraped. That isn't enough to catch the virus.

Bryce quickly scanned the readout, and his face broke out into a huge smile.

"Clean, Captain! All clean!"

Esther had been holding her breath, and when she heard the verdict, she almost collapsed in relief. She leaned forward to hug him, knocking off the pad on his left chest.

"I'm so happy for you," she whispered.

"You're happy? Not as much as I am," he said as he finally let up on her hand.

"When Josiah's scan came back, I thought . . ."

"I know."

"Captain, we've got scrubs in the closet. Just dump the transducers in the bin, and you can get something on. You can get another PPE at supply."

"What about my jeans?"

"I'll scan them, and if they're contaminated, I'll run them through the zip-clave."

"Do you want me to come with you?" Esther asked as Jim swung his legs over the edge of the table.

"What, you don't think I can dress myself? I think I'll manage."

"I know you can," she said before grabbing his upper arm and adding, "Thanks for out there. You saved my ass."

"All in a day's work, madame," he said with a mock half-bow. "Now, if you'll excuse me."

A few moments after Jim disappeared into the ward, Bing strode in. He pulled up the readouts, then shook his head.

"Bring him up," he told Veta.

She fiddled with the dispenser for a moment, and less than ten seconds later, Josiah's eyes fluttered open.

"Wha . . . ?" he mumbled through a smashed mouth.

"Josiah, you've been beaten, pretty badly by the mob," Veta told him, her voice even and almost expressionless.

Josiah reached up to touch his face. Instead of recoiling, he expanded his touch while he explored the extent of the damage.

"Did you run—"

"Yes. You're positive for Schleizen."

He didn't seem to react except for a slight trembling of his lower lip.

"The count?"

"B220/plus."

Esther had no idea what that meant, but it had only been fifteen, maybe 20 minutes since the fight. Certainly, it couldn't be that bad? She knew it took most of their patients 20-30 hours to become visibly sick. But the way the three doctors simply stared at each other was enough to convince Esther that things were bad.

"Well, Josiah, it's your call," Bing said.

"I . . . I think I need to keep working."

"It might be early enough," Veta said.

Josiah looked at Bing, who seemed to think it over.

"I don't know. Maybe with this count, and we don't know what's lodged in your brain." He looked back to the multuscan, put in some numbers, then said, "A140/plus."

"I think that's low enough. I think we need to put you under."

The doctors were speaking among themselves, but Esther understood the dilemma. Right after Krysandra Smith died, and it was obvious that they could not yet keep the infected alive, two of the patients whose disease was the most progressed were put into stasis. This was a common practice in pandemics like this where there wasn't medication yet, or there was, but it hadn't been fully distributed yet. Viruses reacted in strange, often unpredictable ways to stasis, but it was generally a valid course of action.

The Schleizen Virus, however, had a defense mechanism that not only was unexpected, but it also had fatal consequences. To protect the body cells, stasis takes about ten minutes to be implemented on a normal-sized human being. It is not instantaneous. When the stasis field was applied to the two patients and the waves first hit the virus, it almost exploded into a crystalized suit of armor, as Bing described it after the autopsy, with shards pushing out at 90 times the diameter of the initial form. Acting as tiny grenades, the viruses destroyed the cells around it. While one virus doing this would have almost no effect on a body, when trillions did it, the body itself was destroyed. Regen could grow a ruined arm, spine, heart, even. But it could not regenerate a brain, at least one that still housed a living person.

What the doctors were contemplating was whether Josiah's brain had enough viruses in it to kill him as he entered stasis. Esther didn't know how "A140/plus" compared to "B220/plus," or any other reading, for that matter, but it didn't seem possible that in only 20 minutes, enough were there to do any real damage. She agreed with Veta; Josiah should go into stasis.

"How close are we?" Josiah asked Bing.

"If this series is successful? Maybe 12, 15 hours."

"And you need me for that. No slight, but Moshe isn't up to it. I am."

Bing shrugged and then said, "I won't disagree with you. You would be an asset, but Moshe, he can contribute, too."

"No, I need to be there. You need me. The planet needs me. Hell, I need me, and I don't want to put my life in Moshe's hands."

You won't be in Moshe's hands if you're in stasis, Esther thought. *But then again, maybe thousands, tens of thousands of people here are.*

"Can you patch me up, Veta? I seem to have gotten kind of beat up."

Veta leaned forward, running a hand through the bloody mess of his hair. Through the doctor's faceplate, Esther caught the tear that started to slide down her cheek.

"I've got you covered. Give me 30 minutes, and everyone will still know you got your ass kicked, but you should be functional."

"Replication will be completed in . . . 43 minutes," Bing said after checking his PA. "I'd like you back in the lab for the justification."

And just like that, he turned away and left.

Veta gave Josiah a nano-boost, then started applying synthoflesh to close off the wounds. Esther watched for a few moments, but she knew she didn't belong there. Outside, there had been a security incident, and that did fall under her bailiwick. She turned and left the building, heading to where the off-shift of the security team had arrived early and were being briefed by Michelle. Outside the gate, much of the crowd has dispersed, but at least 40 or 50 of them, all in various masks, were milling about.

"I called the locals," Michelle told her, using her term for the police. "I doubt they'll send anyone, but there's not much else we can do."

"Did we catch any of the instigators?" Esther asked.

"Sort of. One was hurt pretty bad, so we brought him in. He's getting treated now."

Esther hadn't seen anyone else come in for treatment, but she'd been focusing first on Jim, then on Josiah, so it was possible.

"But as you know, we can't arrest anybody."

Shit, that's right. That's why we need the police.

Marines didn't have the right to arrest a citizen of the Federation or most other governments. They could detain prisoners, but not arrest, which was a pretty slim, but legally significant, differentiation. But as part of an FAID mission, they couldn't even do that.

"Have the recordings ready for the police if they do come, but other than that, no damage to anything? We're still secure?"

"No damage."

Esther stayed out with Michelle, hoping that the police would come. Jim, in a new PPE, came out to join them.

After another hour, Jim said, "Look, I'm here now, so let me start my shift early. Why don't you go back and get some rest? I'll see you in the morning."

Esther started to protest, but she knew he was right. Nothing was happening—even the flow of new patients had trickled to only a few over the last two hours. She might as well get some rest so she'd be functional. Something kept nagging at her, something she'd missed, but she couldn't pull it up. With a shrug, she agreed.

"I'm glad you're OK," she said softly as she leaned into Jim.

"Me, too. Really glad."

"Bing, I'm checking out. I'll be back after getting some sleep. Call me if you need me."

"OK," Bing answered, barely acknowledging her, obviously deep into the science.

Esther entered the exit decon station, raising her arms, when it hit her.

Hannah!

"Stop!" she yelled at Paul. "I'm going back in!"

The station door opened, and Esther sprinted to Ward 2. She ran down the center aisle, counting beds until she came to Hannah's. It was empty. Esther looked back and forth, trying to spot the old woman.

"Hey, Sun," she yelled at the nurse who came in, followed by the gurney, "where's Hannah. Hannah Delbert?"

Sun shook his head and said, "I took her out thirty minutes ago."

Esther slowly turned around and sat down on Hannah's bed. It was cleaned and ready to go, all traces of the woman gone. Esther had promised her she'd be back, and she had broken that promise.

Esther Lysander was an accomplished Marine. She'd fought in combat and succeeded despite some pretty steep odds. She knew how to kill for the Federation. But she didn't know how to keep a promise to a dying woman.

She slowly leaned back on the bed and cried herself to sleep.

Chapter 34

Dr. Josiah Sengatjuo died 27 hours later. The hoped-for anti-viral coming out of the incubator had not been effective, but he and Bing had made adjustments, and the second trial looked good. It had been too late for Josiah, however. He'd been injected with the treatment, but the damage to his body had progressed too far. Veta said that four or five hours earlier, and he might have been saved.

As one of the first people to receive the Series B treatment, tissue samples were taken before Bing himself incinerated Josiah's remains. The staff stood silently for a few moments before Bing told them to get back to work. The Series B looked good, but the anti-viral and associated vaccine had to be incubated in huge batches to cover the planet's population.

For once, the government got involved. A series of helojets were landing, picking up the anti-viral, and taking off to get it distributed. Esther watched the most recent aircraft lift off the makeshift landing pad, the rotor wash whipping her hair. It felt good to be out of the PPE's. They were far more comfortable than what she'd had to wear on Kepler 9813-B, but that was only relative. Bing insisted that they still wear surgical masks, and she was fine with that.

"How much is that?" she asked Erika Stadt-Ellis, the team's logistics chief.

"That gets us to 64%. As long as the incubators don't run into problems, we can have full coverage by morning. Of course, that assumes everyone is getting inoculated right away."

And why wouldn't they? Schleizen is a nasty way to die, Esther thought with a shudder.

"Then what? I mean, what do we do?"

"We've got to hang around for another few weeks. We've got people still coming in . . ."

Which was true. Just ten minutes prior, a young woman was carried to the gates, her tearful husband softly begging them to cure her. It was too late, however, Esther knew. She was admitted, but her prognosis was poor.

". . . and UAM-Health needs to certify the treatment. There may be—scratch that, will be—tweaks to the vaccine, at least, but this is the easy part. We've tackled the demon yet once again."

"How many times have you done this?"

"For a new disease? This will be number 14," Erika said with pride.

As she should have. Esther was no different than many in the military in that she hadn't given much weight to civil servants such as those in FAID. She knew of their various missions, if vaguely, but somehow, being a Marine, sailor, or even FCDC trooper seemed to her a more valuable way to serve the Federation. But right here on Lorton-Delos AD, this team of which she was part, had saved some 30,000,000 people, maybe more if the virus had managed to escape the planetary quarantine.

Esther hadn't had any direct impact on the development of the vaccine and treatment, but still, she'd participated, and that was something of which she could be proud. It was different from assaulting an enemy position, but what was a virus but an enemy of humanity? It was all a war, and the doctors and techs of FAID were the front-line soldiers in that war.

Esther was not about to resign her commission and join the agency. Her expertise was as a Marine. But she was proud of having worked with them, and offered an opportunity, she'd be proud to work with them again.

Chapter 35

Esther sat on a crate watching the local crew start to assemble the load out. Erika ran around like a mother hen, haranguing them to be careful.

"I feel a little guilty just sitting here," Jim said from where he sat on the adjoining crate, then added, "Well, not too much," when Esther gave him a sidelong glance. "Erika's got everything under control."

The last two weeks had been rather relaxing, all things told. For three days after first the anti-viral, then the vaccine had been distributed, patients had still arrived, begging relief. Twelve of them had not survived, but the rest were saved and had since been discharged.

Things could have been worse. Only—and Esther didn't like to use that word—only 300,000 people had died during the epidemic. That was a huge number, but in the history of pandemics, it was barely a drop in the bucket. Even with the lightly settled world, that number comprised slightly less than 1% of the population. That number could have been halved if the planet-wide quarantined had been put into place earlier. Panicked people fled the three main centers of the disease. Many of them were infected and spread the virus to smaller population centers. An earlier implementation of quarantine procedures would have saved lives, but with the infection rate growing in geometric numbers, Bing told her that had the officials waited one more day, he guessed the death rate would have approached a million souls.

UAM-Health declared the planet safe, and after taking samples of the virus to their pathogen library out in the deep reaches of the Black, had returned the medical administration to the local government. FAID was in the process of sending teams to assist in the aftermath, but as for Bing's team, they were done.

Tomorrow, they'd be lifting off planet for the return to the home system.

"So, are you coming with us tonight?" Esther asked Jim.

"Is this a date, Captain?" Jim asked. "While we are on duty? I'm shocked, I am. Shocked."

"Oh, yeah, that's right. Penelope and I've got the hots for you. Can't keep our hands away."

With normal life returning to the capital, Penelope Smith had invited Esther and Jim to a local restaurant. Esther had become close to the woman during her time on the planet. The woman was a rock. Esther couldn't imagine losing a child as she had and still function as well as she'd done. It was a little humbling that Penelope wanted to thank the two for coming to the planet when they hadn't managed to save Krysandra.

"I can't blame you. Is it my sparkling wit or my devilish good looks that draws you?"

"I'll give you 'devilish good looks,'" she said, trying to kick up a rock at him.

Her legs weren't long enough to reach anything, and she was too lazy to get off the crate at the moment. She gave up and looked over at him.

He is a good-looking guy, she thought, studying his profile. *But such a baby! Even Penelope's got him by three years.*

She wasn't sure why that thought had come unbidden into her mind. Penelope had gone through some emotional trauma and would not be looking for a hook-up. At least she thought she wouldn't. She didn't need to be playing matchmaker, even if she had to admit Jim would be a pretty fine catch for most women. Penelope would be a great catch for any guy, she thought. Logic would dictate that they would be a good match.

The Universe rarely unfolded in a logical manner, however. Neither one of them had expressed the slightest degree of interest in the other, and that wasn't going to change in one last evening.

"Captain, can you come to the gate?" Michelle asked.

"What's up," Esther asked, idly watching the next crate appear from the lab. "Erika won't be getting to your gear for another couple of hours, I'm guessing."

"We've got someone at the gate. He's sick."

Esther didn't need to be told how the man was sick.

She jumped off the crate, telling Jim, "Come on. We've got another patient."

"Veta, are you free?" she passed to the doctor.

"No. I'm up to my ass in alligators with the load out. Why?"

"Michelle just called me. She says we've got some guy at the gate. He's sick."

"Now? He just showed up now? Shit, that means we've got another pocket somewhere. I'll meet you there."

UAM-Health had declared the planet free from the virus. If this really were another case of Schleizen, the planet would be slapped with another quarantine.

"Maybe it's something else?" Jim asked as they hurried to the gate. "Another disease."

"Yeah, maybe," she said despite not believing it.

The gate had been dismantled, but none of the equipment had been crated yet. Michelle's team had gathered around three people. Two were supporting a third who seemed to be having a hard time standing. As soon as Esther came up, she knew. The man had Schleizen. She'd seen enough people die from it that she didn't need any scanner to confirm it.

Chapter 38

"What's the zeta?" Bing asked.

"I'm getting 24.7," Lori said, her head bent over the readout.

"Damn!" Bing shouted, throwing his stylus across the room.

"What's that mean?" Esther quietly asked Veta.

"Anything over a 15 means this is not just a variant, but a new virus."

"You mean this planet's being hit with something entirely new?" Esther asked, aghast at the horribly bad luck.

"No, not entirely new. Schleizen's mutated. The anti-viral we've created is programmed to adjust to normal mutation, up to a zeta of 10, but it can't make a 24.7. We've got to come up with a new one targeting the virus."

Esther didn't have a clue as to what a "zeta" was, nor how bad a "24.7" was when compared to a "10," but from the expressions on each of the team members' faces, this would not be an easy fix.

"Veta, I need you to get on the hook with UAM-Health. Get Dr. Glory to Him, not that Confed asswipe leading their delegation. Tell him we've got three newly-infected patients."

"And the zeta? Give her that?"

Bing barely hesitated, but said, "Yes. We might need their help. See who she can spare."

From conversations with the team over the last two weeks, she knew that their rapid development of the vaccine and anti-viral would have been a huge career boost for Bing, in particular, but for all of them. So, to have to face failure could not be a good thing, she knew. And to ask for UAM assistance would be even worse, yet he'd just opened that possibility.

Not many bureaucrats would do that so readily.

"OK, people, start setting up again. We've got a lot of work to do."

Esther gave Jim the high sign as the medical team burst into a flurry of action. She left the lab and waited for Jim to join her.

"OK, tell Michelle that we're going to need the gate fully functional again. Erik's here for the tear-down, so I'm going to ask him for help."

"Roger that. We'll get it up and running."

She split from Jim and headed back to Ward 2 where she'd seen Erik and his crew gathering. To her surprise, half of the ward had already been dismantled, and one of his crew was spraying the back half of the pad with the catalyst. The foamcrete was disintegrating right before her eyes.

"Stop!" she shouted, breaking into a run. "Erik! We need the ward back up. We're not done yet!"

Someone should have stopped the break-down when the first patient arrived. She didn't know whose task that would have been, but she'd seen the Open Arms crew arrive, and she could've taken the initiative.

Erik turned to her looking confused.

"We've only got today to break all of this down," he said.

"We're not breaking down. We've got more cases."

"Miles, stop!" Erik shouted to the man on the catalyst, then to Esther, "You're sure about this? Did Dr. Bao say that?"

Esther didn't have time to get into a snit because Erik questioned her. The mission was too important for that, and she had a feeling they'd be needing the ward again soon. Already, another ambulance was approaching the compound, and more would be coming.

"Yes, Dr. Bao ordered the camp set up again."

He hadn't exactly ordered Ward 2 to be set up, but she was pretty confident that had been part of what Marines called the "commander's intent."

"OK, you've got it. We'll foam up the pad again, then put up the building."

"Thanks, Erik." She started to leave to go to the gate when she realized there was one more thing yet to do. She turned to Erik and said, "And get everybody PPE'd up. This is a hot zone again."

Chapter 39

"I don't like the memory wire on top of the fence," Jim said to her as the two walked the perimeter.

"Neither do I. I asked Erik before they took off if we had any more somewhere, but nada."

"A simple set of wire clippers and they're in under the wire. We've got zero security."

"Not zero. Any break in the fence sets of the alarm."

"Come on, Esther. You know what I mean."

And she did. They simply didn't have the means to secure the compound. Sure, they'd know the instant someone cut the fence, but what could they do about it? Not much.

"Yeah, I do. But if anything goes down, it's going to be up to us to do something about it."

And two days into the new outbreak, it looked more and more that there could be an incident. Crowds had gathered, and most seem to be accusing the FAID team of not only failing to cure the disease, but of actually spreading it on purpose. As one blowhard haranguing the crowd had said, what better way to shift the planet to a full member of the Federation than to kill off the present population? Esther, who'd been listening from inside the compound had almost snorted in disbelief, knowing no one could believe that, but many of the people out there had shouted in agreement.

Only an hour ago, an ambulance had been waylaid outside the gate. The crowd had rushed it, rocking it until its skirts hit the ground. A very sick person had emerged, and after what looked to be an intense conversation, the person was led away.

From all reports, the current outbreak of Schleizen 2 was exploding, and this time, the local government was taking action. Infected people were required to enter quarantine at any of the 179 camps planet-wide. But the people were not coming in any significant numbers, despite the fact that the existing anti-viral could slow down the progress of the disease, even if it couldn't cure it. Of the 118 patients who'd arrived at the compound, either by choice or escorted by the police, only nine had died so far. The rest were hanging in there, thanks to Veta and her three-man team.

Despite this relative success, the protestors called the compound the "Death Camp," where horrible experiments were being conducted on people before they were "eliminated" once the experiments were completed. Whether people believed it or simply because they feared to go through the gauntlet of protesters, the numbers of new patients had dwindled when every computer model showed the numbers of infections were skyrocketing.

Esther and Jim stood together, looking at the back fence. So far, no one had gathered on the other side, but she knew both Marines were thinking the same thing. If the crowd was determined to break in anywhere along the back fence, there wasn't much they could do about it.

"We could pre-position a couple of the M99's back here, say, in back of the incinerator."

Esther thought about it for a moment before saying, "I don't think we're at that point yet. I wouldn't want to leave them unattended so that if anyone did break through, they could pick them up."

"Trigger locks?"

"Which we didn't bring. No, let's leave them in the shed, right where we put them. Easier access to any point in the compound."

The two Marines had brought six M99's in the case now in the shed. She was sure Bing didn't know about them. They'd only told Michelle an hour ago, who hadn't been too happy about it, but had grudgingly identified herself and three others who could use the weapons in a pinch.

The two Marines turned to head back to the gate. Esther had spent most of the last 40 hours there, just observing. It hadn't been difficult to convince Bing that the entire team, along with Dr. Glory to Him and her two techs, needed to stay on the compound. No one was leaving. For all of them, it was pretty much around the clock anyway as they worked to break the virus.

"Go on ahead," she told Jim. "I want to check the status."

She broke off to enter the lab. It was surprisingly quiet, but she knew that was just the outward appearances. Each of the doctors and techs was pouring over readings, making adjustments, and running tests.

"Anything?" she asked Gene, who looked up from a scanning microscope.

"We think we've identified the marker that's accelerating the mutation rate. If we can turn that off, then we can adjust the anti-viral to handle this strain."

Most of that went over Esther's head, but she understood the gist of it. If they could keep the virus from mutating so quickly and so severely, then the anti-viral could keep up with it.

"When will you know?"

"If we're right? Twelve hours, I'd guess," he said, then asked, "How're things out there?"

"Still the same. Lots of shouting. They kept a patient from coming in an hour ago."

"Idiots," he said. "Veta can at least slow down the progression, and if we're right, in twelve hours, we can start on a cure."

"How's the UAM doc?" she asked, nodding towards the woman who was in an intense-looking conversation with Bing.

"Dr. Glory to Him? She knows her shit, that's for sure. I'm glad we have her on board. She was the one who steered us to where we needed to search from the marker."

"OK, that's good. Anything to help, I guess. Well, I'd better get back out there and leave you guys to crack this nut—and the sooner, the better."

"That's what we're trying to do. You just keep them on the outside of the fence. I've been on projects where things can get ugly really quick."

Esther took one last look around the lab. There was more brainpower in there, the best and the brightest from the Federation, and with Dr. Glory to Him, from the Brotherhood as well, all working to defeat the virus, all working to save lives. Esther may not be a doctor, she may not even be a lab tech, but she was a Marine and she'd do whatever it takes to make sure they would not be interrupted in their search for the cure.

Chapter 40

"Another one just died," Esther told Jim as he walked up, still rubbing the sleep from his eyes.

"How many is that now?" he asked, turning to check the space between Ward 2 and the incinerator.

"Thirteen, and we're not bringing the bodies out right now. It gets the crowd going."

"Looks like twice as many as when I left," he noted.

After almost two full days of being awake, Esther had sent Jim to the lounge to catch some sleep. The Marines could brainwash, something that Esther had done in her recon training, which could keep a body going for up to a week, but it was something no one ever wanted to do. She was almost happy the team didn't have that available to them, but that meant they had to get natural sleep in order to function. Stimsticks could help in the short term, but not for any significant length of time.

"They keep coming. And that makes them all potential vectors to spread the virus even quicker. Veta's been on the hook with the locals trying to explain that, and they sent some deputy mayor to try and tell them to disburse, but he got shouted down pretty quick, and he left. Now, we've got those three sterling examples of Lorton-Delos police to control the crowd."

The three police were huddled together, as if for mutual support, and off to the side. Esther had no false feeling of confidence that they would react if the crowd erupted.

"Well, I think I've got it now. Why don't you get some shut-eye."

Esther took one more quick look around, then nodded and said, "OK, you've got it. Wake me if anything happens."

She left the gate, but made a detour back into the lab. Gene was still at his station—he might not have even moved from his seat since Esther was last inside.

"Any progress?"

Gene looked up, rubbed his eyes, and said, "Don't know. We've started programming the anti-viral, but that all depends on the sequencing. If that doesn't give us what we need, it's back to the drawing board."

"How long is that going to take?"

"Another three hours or so. Maybe a bit more."

Gene looked horrible, and Esther was going to suggest he get some sleep as well. If the sequencing or whatever was going to take more time before they could start on the anti-viral, then he'd be better off getting some rest so he could function. Looking around the lab, she expected most of them could use some sleep as well, but that was Bing's call, not hers.

"Is it still bad out there?" he asked her.

"More come every hour."

"You can't let anything interrupt the sequencing. A power surge or drop, and we'll have lost ten hours and need to start from scratch again."

The power for the compound was internal. The small fusion generator was pretty much foolproof, and with the switch locked, it would take a significant effort to turn it off. The power lines that transported the electricity to the lab, however, would be a vulnerability. If someone was intent on shutting down the lab, all they would have to do would be to sever the lines.

Ah, shit.

The cot in the lounge was a siren call, trying to suck her into Morpheus' embrace, but Esther hadn't considered the power. She knew she had to bring that up with Jim. She thanked Gene, then headed back to the gate.

"That was a short four hours," Jim noted as she walked up.

"Yeah, I know. But we need to make sure the power to the lab isn't cut."

"They're not going to be able to take down the generator, not unless they're hiding some pretty big pieces of equipment out there."

"They don't have to. All they have to do is find the cable and cut it."

She could see realization dawn over his face as he said "Ah, shit!"

"That was my exact reaction when Gene brought it to my attention."

"So, what do we do? We can't very well dig it up to put bigger conduits around it."

"No, but we've got to keep it in mind if there's a breach. That's our Maginot Line."

"And the German's bypassed that."

"OK, bad analogy. How about Horatius at the Bridge?"

"Better, and I get it. Let me talk it over with Paul and see what we can come up with."

"OK, and now I really need to get some sleep."

"Sweet dreams."

"Yeah, right. I'm just sure," she said.

Halfway to the lounge, Michelle met her coming from her own nap. Esther stopped her and briefed her on the power issue. Just as Michelle said she understood, a roar sounded from the crowd.

"What now?" Esther said.

The mass of people, who had been standing a good 20 or 30 meters away from the compound, had suddenly rushed forward and were right at the fence, peering inside and yelling.

Esther turned around, wondering what had set them off, and behind Ward 2, someone was trundling not one, not two, but three bodies, all stacked on top of each other, on the gurney, heading to the incinerator.

"Holy Mother of God!" Esther shouted. "I told Bing to hold off on any burning!"

She and Michelle bolted for the gate, her weariness washed away in the surge of adrenaline.

Jim, Paul, and three more of the security team, were lined up, almost shoulder to shoulder, at the gate. The crowd was pushing on the fence, though. If they broke through, and they could if they had it in their mind, it would be somewhere along the fence line, not at the gate.

"See what they're doing?" an amplified voice echoed over the heads of the mob. "They're murdering us, right there."

"Bing, we've got a situation. Lock the wards and the labs," she passed.

"How bad?"

"We might get overrun."

"Keep them away from the lab. We need three more hours at a minimum if we're going to start on the anti-virals."

Easy for you to say.

"We'll try. No one goes out of the buildings until I give the all-clear."

The amplified voice kept up the litany of sins the Federation was imposing on the people of the planet, and the mob was eating it up. They started pushing in unison on the fence making the entire thing sway.

"I'm getting the M99's," she told Michelle. "Get ready."

Michelle grabbed Esther by the upper arm, stopping her.

"You can't."

"What do you mean, I can't? This is a life and death situation."

"I know, but it's in our charter. No deadly force."

"Better to kill a few if we can save thousands, hell, millions. Bing needs to finish the sequencing."

Esther was not inured to death, and she hoped she never would be, but she also understood that sometimes lives were sacrificed for the greater good. This had to be one of those times.

"I know, but we can't."

"But you gave me four names, including you, who can handle a weapon."

"And that was a mistake. I let you push me, and I can't any more. We cannot use deadly force."

Esther was shocked, and she was about to tell her to blow sand, that she and Jim would use the 99's, but the look on Michelle's face, both hopeful and determined, gave her pause. She shifted her gaze to the people pushing on the fence, and she realized that Michelle was right. Not just because of FAID regulations, but because the Federation was there to help the people, not kill them. They were part of her responsibility, just as much as the team itself.

OK, maybe not as much as the team, but I'm still responsible for their safety.

"So, what are we going to do?"

"Our best. And nothing says we can't crack a few heads," Michelle said.

Esther started pulling ideas out of the air. Marines were trained to kill, not to merely restrain, so she didn't have some pat procedure she could pull up. The obvious thing was the memory wire, which would slow anyone down. But it was still attached to the fence, and the moment she tried to free it, the crowd would understand exactly what would happen.

What about a barricade? she thought, looking back into the compound for what she could cobble together.

There wouldn't be enough to cover the perimeter, but she could give up real estate to possibly set up a defensive perimeter around the lab and the generator. Maybe the mob would be happy with trashing the out-buildings and leaving a more heavily fortified lab alone.

"Veta, get your personnel into the lab," she passed.

The doctor didn't argue, but only asked, "What about the patients?"

"Your call. But I think they'd be safe if left in the wards. The mob is angry at us, not them."

"How many super-skunks do we have?" she asked Michelle as she scanned for things she could use as a line of defense—when she saw it.

"Twenty-three—" Michelle started when Esther waved her silent.

"Paul had construction experience, right?"

"Well, yes, before he joined the agency."

"Send him to me. You do whatever you can to slow them down, because they're coming, one way or the other."

She spun around and sprinted to where Erik had left his equipment beside Ward 2. She was poring over the foamcrete dispenser when Paul came running up, breathing heavily.

Jonathan P. Brazee

"Is this the catalyst to break up the foamcrete or the foamcrete itself?"

Paul took a look, then said, "The cat."

"I need foamcrete! Can you switch it?"

"Uh, yeah, if they have some. Let me look."

Esther waited impatiently and Paul rummaged through the supplies. Behind her, the mob was in action. There was a concerted effort to push down the fence, and it was swaying a good two or three meters on either side of center now. She was surprised that no one had used a truck to simply blast through, although the simple mass of bodies in the way probably explained that.

"I've got it!" Paul shouted, pushing some compressed tanks forward.

"Get it hooked up, and now."

"They don't hook up. We just refill."

"I don't care what you call it, just get the foamcrete in the dispenser thing. And hurry."

While Paul was refilling the dispenser, she examined the wands. They looked pretty straight-forward. There was a lever to open the flow, then a trigger to shoot it out. From what she'd seen during the setup, the foamcrete shot out about five meters.

"OK, done!" Paul shouted. "Now what?"

"Now, we move this thing by the lab."

The dispenser probably massed 300 kilos, and the two got behind it and started pushing. It was on a set of four wheels, but the dirt ground was not the best surface. It took some effort from the both of them. There was a crash from up by the gate, but Esther didn't raise her head. She had to trust Jim and Michelle to take care of whatever happened.

The PPE, while better and more comfortable than and EVAS suit of a PICS, was still hindering her, and the sweat was building up.

"Wait," she said, then quickly shed it.

She didn't think success would come down to being protected from the virus or not, and she was much more mobile without the PPE.

208

In just her Marine Corps gym shorts and a Globe and Laurel Tavern t-shirt, she said, "OK, let's go."

Up ahead, she could see people starting to clamber over a portion of the fence that had been knocked almost to the ground. There were puffs of mist as the first of the super-skunk detonated, and people scattered, but not all to the rear. Some pushed forward, only to be met by Jim and two others. Esther could see blows being landed, but it was hard to tell who was coming out on top.

"Keep them off my ass for a few more minutes," she said as she grunted pushing the dispenser. Finally, she stopped it about over where she thought the power cable ran, then had Paul help her strap the wand harness on her back.

"Now what?" Paul asked.

"Now, we stop anyone coming at us."

"With the foamcrete?"

"Yeah, with the foamcrete."

"Awesome! I've always wanted to do that," he said, shedding his PPE as well and harnessing up.

"You take the rear, I'll take the front."

The two of them, with a single dispenser, could not cover the entire lab and generator station. But there were no entrances into the lab except for the front door. Expeditionary building or not, it was quite secure, and it would take some powerful tools to break through. All Esther and Paul had to do would be to keep the mob from the power cable and the door. Nothing else mattered.

She gave the trigger a little squeeze and was rewarded with a small stream of foamcrete which hit the ground and immediately started to expand.

"Keep the stream low. Too high and the wind can scatter some of it before it solidifies," Paul told her.

Up ahead, a second section of the fence came crashing down, and more people started pouring in. Two of Michelle's team rushed to meet them, but were immediately bowled over. She had a clear view of Jim, and the man was a berserker. Esther would never have guessed he was a brawler, given his runner's frame, but he looked to be giving much more than he was receiving.

Esther saw Michelle go down, but then the mass of people from the second breach streamed into the compound and rushed towards the lab.

"That's where they're doing the experiments," one man shouted, pointing.

He was ignoring Esther, though as he led a group of half-a-dozen to the lab. She was surprised that they didn't even give her a second glance, but that was to her advantage. With a steady stream of foamcrete, she hit the ground at their feet. There were shouts of confusion, and the men and women started to struggle for a step or two before it expanded and hardened. Their cries of anger turned to confusion, then anger again as they realized what had happened.

It works! she thought as she felt a tiny burst of achievement.

"Get her!" the first man shouted, waving his arm and pointing. "Hector, over here, get that bitch!"

Five men and two women—probably including Hector—rushed Esther. But she triggered the wand and sprayed them, going a little higher than the first time. It didn't matter. The foamcrete hit them, and seconds later, they were trapped, cursing and screaming at her.

"What's the situation out there?" Bing asked over the comms. "We can hear shouting."

"We've been breached. You stay locked inside and keep working," she answered as she let out another stream at a woman who'd tried to sneak in from the side, a piece of lumber in her hand.

Once she realized she was stuck, she hurled the wood at Esther, but with her feet in an odd position, she couldn't get anything on it, and the chunk of wood fell short.

Behind her, Esther could hear the splat of Paul's wand, but she didn't waste a glance. There were 20-25 people in front of her, trying to figure out what do.

"Come on, just rush her," the first man she hit egged the others on. "What can she do? Look, I'm fine. I'm not hurt."

"Who's next," Esther shouted out with heartfelt bravado. "Step on up."

The group looked from Esther to the man, who continued to harangue them. Finally, the damn broke, and they spread out to rush her en masse.

"Get her, get her!" the first man yelled as Esther started sweeping her wand.

The first pass made people duck, but she didn't get enough on most of them to stop them. She had to slow down and concentrate the stream. She depressed the trigger all the way, making a slow, low sweep that trapped a good fifteen of them. One young man, barely more than a boy, stumbled as his feet hit the foamcrete and fell face-down, to be covered by the expanding foam. Erik had told her the safety valves in the foamcrete would keep it from adhering to a person, but she wasn't sure what would happen if someone was encased.

One of the men trapped to her right managed to pull his leg free, leaving his shoe behind. He lunged at her, too closed to be foamed, but Esther was not helpless. Without thinking, she swung the wand's handle up in a wicked uppercut, connecting solidly with the man's jaw and dropping him.

"Come on, what are you waiting for?" she shouted. "It just two of us here and how many of you?"

A group of at least 30 people was in front of Ward 1, chanting while four men were smashing the door with what looked to be part of the scanner that had been at the gate. The door gave way, and the people disappeared inside. Other people were wandering around, almost as if they were playing tourist, while several were taking selfies with the ruined gate as a backdrop. But surrounding her and Paul were at least fifty people, all talking over each other as they tried to figure out what to do. With one firm leader, they could have rushed the two, but mobs rarely had that, and too many people, including the first guy who was encased up to his right knee, wanted to be in charge.

Esther risked a glance back. She had another ten meters of slack hose connecting her wand to the dispenser. Marines always preferred to be on the offense rather the defense, so with her best battle cry, she charged forward, jumping up on chunks of hardened foamcrete and past the grasping arms of a trapped man. The mob surged back, but not fast enough. Three people fell to their backs as Esther foamed them, trapping six people like flies in amber before the rest were able to dart out of range.

"Sergei's in there," a woman screamed, rushing forward to kneel where a knee was sticking out of the foamcrete. She started pulling at it with her bare hands. Esther let her be.

She retreated to her position when a thought struck her.

"How much more of this stuff do we have." she whispered into her mic.

"We're at 92%. You know, maybe we should just cover up the ground over the cable. That would stop them," Paul said.

Esther considered it for a moment, then said, "No, they've broken into Ward 1, so they could get into the lab, too."

She shot a stream at a man who'd been sidling around her, missing him, but making him retreat. Someone else threw a rock at her, but she was able to twist so it missed her. If they started with smaller rocks that they could fling at her with some oomph on them, she knew they'd start connecting. Once again, she was glad this was a mob instead of an organized group—at least for the moment.

For several minutes, they were at a standoff. Several of the group gathered to discuss the situation while the rest kept up a litany of threats, cat calls, and pleadings. Esther ignored them, focusing on the ones in the discussion. When they broke up, she knew something was coming. The core group of about a dozen spread out covering the gap between the lab and the generator.

"They're getting smarter," she whispered into her mic.

"Turn your aperture to the right. That'll give you a wider spray," Paul told her.

She started to comply, then held off. When they started their move, she'd try for a couple of longer sprays before switching to wide. She didn't have long to wait. As soon as the middle-aged man in the blue shirt opened his mouth, Esther darted forward and nailed him with a shot to the hips. He fell with the extra weight dragging him, but he managed to shout out to charge her.

Esther nailed two more at the feet before she dropped back and twisted her nozzle as a veritable shower of debris was thrown at her. Something hit her high in the back, but she shrugged it off as she started sweeping her front in broad waves, laying a quagmire on the ground. Most of those charging danced back, but two more were caught. Someone got around her, though, a large man with a bar from the gate in his hands. Esther didn't even see him until something flashed by her to flatten the man. She immediately sprayed the two prone figures, only realizing that one of them was Jim as the foam encased both men.

Shit! Jim!

But she didn't have time. More people were rushing her, and she was busy for the next two minutes, laying out sheet after sheet of foamcrete. She wasn't trapping many, but she was keeping them at bay. Finally, the assault petered out, with 20 people pulling back and staring at the two.

"Where are we at," she asked Paul.

With a very labored voice, he said, "Down to 31%."

"You OK, Paul?" she asked.

"Took something to the head. But I'm still standing."

Esther took a quick look back. Blood was streaming down the side of his face, but he smiled and gave her a thumbs up.

The initial frenzy of the mob had abated. A few people ran out of Ward 1, carrying a piece of equipment as a trophy of some sort while shouting aloud, but for the most part, the people around Esther and Paul were a little more wary. The 30 or so people who were trapped in the foamcrete either looked resigned or where issuing dire threats of what was going to happen when they got free.

A wave of weariness swept over her and the adrenaline that had kept her going petered out. But she had to put up a good front.

A 30-something woman, her red hair almost unnaturally bright in the sun, came running from the back of the lab. She spoke with a few of the mob, and after a moment, most of the group followed the woman. A few moments later, Esther could hear pounding from the other side of the building.

"What's going on out there?" Bing asked.

"You've got some people wanting to get in. I don't think they can, but if it looks like they will, let me know."

"Can't you do anything about it?"

Esther looked at the ground between her and the building. It was covered with differing levels of foamcrete—as well as trapped bodies. Whatever feature had kept the pads level during construction could not deal with the haphazard spraying she and Paul had done. Esther didn't think there was a way for Paul and her to haul the dispenser to the other side.

"That's a negative for now," she told him.

"We still need time."

"Understood."

"Ma'am, can you please help me? I promise, I'll just leave," a heavyset man called out.

His leg was bent backwards, his body leaning forward. He must have been trying to yank his leg free when the foamcrete set, and the position had to be uncomfortable, even painful.

"I'm sorry, I can't," she said.

"I promise, I'll leave. I won't come back."

"It's not that. I don't have the capability."

The man started softly crying, his left leg, which was free and holding the bulk of his weight, trembling.

"I've got a chisel," someone called out. "Will you let me free Deke?"

Another man was standing out of her range. He'd stayed when most of the rest had left for the other side of the lab. In his hand was a power-chisel he'd scrounged from somewhere. Esther immediately knew he'd searched for it as soon as this Deke had been trapped. The chisel could be used as a weapon against her, but she felt the man was sincere.

"Go ahead."

She kept her wand trained on him as he hesitantly made his way forward to his friend. He gave her one last wary look, then knelt and started the chisel. Bits of foamcrete flew with each blow, and within a couple of minutes, enough had been knocked away that Deke could pull out his leg. He collapsed on the ground, crying.

His friend helped the heavy man up, and his leg held. Esther had been curious about it, but evidently, Erik had been right in that the man had only been trapped, not injured by the foamcrete.

Other trapped people started crying out, but with a tenderness that indicated something more than casual friendship, the smaller man helped Deke off the field of foamcrete. He dropped the chisel on the ground and headed for the ruined gate.

"Can I get freed?" and "What about me?" hammered Esther from all sides, many of those pleading for help being those who were wishing her graphic violence only five minutes prior. She was not about to let any of them free.

But matters were taken out of her hand. As Deke and his partner exited the compound, two trucks came up and settled onto the ground. Moments later, the pink helmeted figures of a UAM peacekeeping team debarked. Each of them had sidearms on their thighs and carried riot batons. Immediately, loose groups started scattering, rushing to get out of the way.

Two platoons of disciplined troops marched into the compound. One of the officers scanned the area and locked eyes with her. He marched up, and Esther saw the Brotherhood patch on his right arm in counterpart to the pink UAM patch on his left.

"Where is Dr. Glory to Him?" he asked without introduction.

Esther's pride prickled, but only for a moment, and she pointed to the door.

As he marched over to it, she called out, "Don't interfere. They've almost got a cure."

He ignored her, so she called up Bing to let him know that UAM was on the scene.

"Paul, can you hook up the catalyst?" she asked.

"Give me a moment," he said to her, then to someone else, "Hey, you, if you want your friends freed, I need your help."

Esther didn't look to see to whom he was talking. She went right to where she knew Jim was buried. She'd been able to keep his image, trapped in the foamcrete, out of her head when she was still fighting, but now, with the UAM peacekeepers taking over, her heart was heavy. Once again, he'd saved her ass, and once again, it had cost him.

"Hurry up, Paul!" she shouted.

"I'm going as fast as I can!"

After an eternity, Paul told her she was hooked up. She immediately started spraying the catalyst over where she thought Jim was located. It had only been about 30 minutes, so there was time to get him into stasis and back for a resurrection.

Some of the Brotherhood troopers looked on with interest but didn't volunteer to help. Most of the other trapped people watched in silence as the foamcrete turned to dust where the catalyst hit it.

She swept the spray back and forth, and when she saw what looked like a thigh, she adjusted to face.

Within moments, the foamcrete had fallen away—and a dusty Jim said, "Took you long enough!"

"Jim! You're alive!"

"Hell, yeah, I'm alive, but pretty freaking uncomfortable. Can you get me out of here?"

She looked to Paul in amazement. He was already working on the feet of one of the people he'd trapped, and he said, "It's porous. You can survive for maybe a couple of days inside, if it comes to that."

She turned back to Jim and asked, "You could breathe?"

"No, I held my breath. Yeah, I could breathe. It was an effort, but doable. And if you're done with your amazement, I'd really like to get out of here."

She hit him again with the spray, and within a few moments, he was able to straighten up and stand. Two legs had been underneath him, and both were kicking. Esther freed the man who Jim had tackled. With a roar, the man jumped up, ready to fight—until he saw the peacekeepers. That put a damper on his anger. He positively glowered, but when one of the peacekeepers said he could leave or wait around to go through processing, he took off, but not without a few choice phrases as he exited what was left of the compound.

"Hey, can we go, too?" one of the trapped women asked.

Esther looked at the peacekeepers. It was pretty obvious that they were in charge now.

She offered one of them her wand, and he demurred, saying, "You put them in there. It'll be better for you if you released them in case any civil charges come up."

Civil charges? They attacked us! I did what I could to stop them without deadly force.

Once again, she had to control her anger. Blowing up at some Brotherhood UAM goon wouldn't do anyone any good.

"Can you go check on Michelle and the rest? I saw her go down," she told Jim. Then turning to the 20 or so remaining trapped people, asked, "OK, who's next?"

Chapter 41

Four hours later, the entire FAID team was on a UAM truck getting taken to the shuttleport. Their mission canceled, they were being recalled. The UAM had taken over with Dr. Glory to Him as the new joint project coordinator. The time Esther and the others had bought Bing and his team, however, had been enough. The genetic code had been found and analyzed, and the prospective anti-viral Gene and the others had mapped out had been pretty close to what was needed. The UAM-Health team simply took over the process, and the first batch of the drugs should be coming out of the medical fabricators within a few hours. After validation, which might take another two hours if things went well, the drug could be replicated at local medical centers and distributed.

"Not quite what I expected," Jim said from beside her as the hover made its way through still mostly empty streets. "But pretty rewarding, all said and done."

"I'm surprised to say I agree with you," she said, turning to look at him.

He still had the dust from the foamcrete on his face. Reaching into her pack, she pulled out a semi-clean T-shirt and reached over to wipe the bulk of the dust off.

"Thanks, mom!" Jim said, turning his face away.

"Appearances, young captain, appearances."

He took the T-shirt out of her hand and took over, rubbing his face, but smearing more than removing.

"Better?" he asked, a smile on his face.

She shook her head, then said, "Yeah, perfect," resisting a surprising urge to wet the edge of the T and do a better job on him.

Hell, am I turning into my mom?

"What's next for you?" she asked, changing the subject to something safer.

"Who knows? I'll find out when it happens, I guess."

"Same here. I've still got another nine months or so before I find out."

"TAC 1?"

"Doing it correspondence."

"Really?" he asked, and Esther could hear the question in his voice.

"What with my APOC orders delaying me, I'd be a major when I graduated."

"Oh. So, no company," he said, immediately catching her drift.

"It's probably too late, anyway. Between recon and this, I kind of took that off the table for myself."

"But recon, I mean, we all know what you did on Elysium," he said.

"Out of sight, out of mind. Now with the gap in reports, well . . ."

"That kind of sucks," he said. He paused, looked at the others sitting alongside and across from them, then barely whispered, "I don't mean to pry, but can I ask you something personal?"

Esther stiffened, and she was going to say no, but there was something in his voice that she couldn't place. She just nodded, still wary, but willing to listen.

"I don't mean to be, well, critical or anything. I mean, everyone knows you've got the chops, but well, the . . . uh . . . the general rumor about you is that you're something of a glory hound, you know, someone looking to climb the ladder without caring about who you have to step on to get up there."

He paused as if trying to see how she was accepting it. She kept her face stoic. She'd have expected that some people might think of her that way—she wasn't blind as to how some people reacted to her—but it still didn't feel good to hear it.

"But, and this is a big but, if that was true, why did you accept the APOC orders? You could have played it safe, and you'd be getting your ticket punched right now with a company. So, why'd you do it? Why are you in this, well, dead-end job?"

"Why'd you do it? You're in the same boat."

"I'm asking you. You're the Commandant's daughter, not me."

Esther leaned back onto the hard slats that served to make a bench seat in the bed of the truck. With their personal gear piled in the middle, it was crowded with nine medical staff, six security, and the two Marines. Somehow, it seemed a little empty with Josiah and Michelle gone, Josiah incinerated and Michelle taken away by ambulance. There were some haggard faces there, faces of people running on empty. But there was something else coming through as well. Everyone was smiling, everyone had that last rush of adrenaline, and the reason was simple. They'd won. They'd defeated the enemy just as much as a Marine battalion defeating an armed enemy. The fact that the UAM was coming in to take the bows and credit seemed immaterial to them. There'd be no medal ceremony, no gathering to welcome the troops home, no declaration of peace for them. Another virus, another medical emergency would pop up, and they'd be sent off again to save lives, even lives that might resent their presence.

"This is why I accepted the orders," she said, nodding at the rest of the team. "We actually did something here. We were a part of saving lives, lots of lives.

"I mean, I'm proud of being a Marine, and I'm pretty good at it, if I can risk sounding vain. And when the time comes again, I'll march to the sound of the guns. This, though, this gave me an opportunity to serve in another way, and it's opened my eyes, even the crap missions."

"And your career?"

"I'm a better Marine for this tour, and if the selection boards can't see that, then they're not doing their job. And if I stall out at major or lieutenant colonel, so be it. Success is what you accomplish, not how high up the ladder you climb.

"Grubbing hell, as my dad might have said. Here I'm pontificating like a preacher on Sunday morning. So, tell me, why'd you accept your orders? To the Third Ministry, of all places."

"Pretty much the same as you, Esther."

"My friends call me Ess."

"OK, Ess. My reasons are pretty much the same as yours."

There was nothing more to say. She'd said her piece, and that was good enough. She closed her eyes as sleep overtook her, only vaguely aware that she'd slumped over to lean up against Jim.

MARS

Chapter 49

Esther whistled as she sauntered down the corridor to her office. The debrief on Earth had gone surprisingly well. The chairman himself had attended the overview given by Bing, and he'd taken the time to shake each person's hand and offer his appreciation of their service. The individual debriefs took a little longer, but they were conducted with a decidedly light air.

An FCDC brigadier had attended as a guest, and her actions with the foamcrete seemed to take most of his attention. By now, Esther had found out that the FCDC had an actual riot foam, not unlike what Esther had used on Lorton-Delos and able to deploy in huge quantities, but he seemed impressed with her field expedient solution.

When Esther saw the recordings, particularly the sat view, she was fairly impressed herself. On the ground, she hadn't quite grasped how touch-and-go the entire fight had been. A few more people making it a few meters closer, and she and Paul would have gone down. With a clear route into the lab, there was no telling what would have happened. At the very least, the sequencing process would have had to start over again. At the worst, the equipment would have been destroyed and the team . . . well, she hadn't wanted to contemplate that. Whatever happened, tens of thousands if not more people would have died until a new anti-viral could have been developed and deployed.

She slowed down at the D4 office, stuck her head in the door, and yelled at Major Lent, who looked to be neck-deep in work, "Hey Major, ready to get your ass kicked?"

He looked up, saw her, and smiled.

"Welcome home, the prodigal daughter, and no, I'm not ready to get my ass kicked. I'm ready to do some ass kicking of my own, if you can take the humiliation."

Esther snorted, then said, "In your dreams, Major, with all due respect, of course. Seventeen hundred?"

"See you there."

Top Forrester had caught her when she entered the building, telling her that the major had actually been taking lessons. He'd beaten the top two days earlier, taking two out of three games. The top was good; he had been the best player among the Marines when she arrived, but after more than two years, Esther was better than him now. The fact that the major had beaten him didn't mean much to her, and she was going to enjoy keeping the major from getting too uppity.

She entered her office, which was empty, and sat down at her desk. Her AI had already informed her of her 156 Cat 2 messages. She could have read them on her PA, but she didn't like using the small screen when she had a 30cm display on her desk. Cat 1 messages were answered immediately, but Cat 2's could be put off.

"List messages," she said as she leaned back in her chair.

The list of senders scrolled down the display. She paused on a personal message from Miriam, asking her to call. It was 0430 for her, so she flagged that for action in five hours. One of the last messages that arrived was from Helen-Lee, telling her to report to Mr. Byzantine at her earliest convenience.

Orders? Those are usually Cat 1's, she thought.

She'd just returned from Earth, and if there'd been another mission for her, she wasn't sure why they hadn't just told her instead of having her go back to Mars.

Can't be that important, then.

She scrolled through more of her messages, dictating out a few answers, marking others for action. There was a personal from Jim, facetiously asking if she got back OK. She laughed and wrote that she'd somehow made it all the way back to Mars without adult supervision and without causing an intergalactic incident.

The return trip to Earth and the three-day debrief had been a pleasant interlude. Without the mission hanging over their heads,

Jim had proven to be a man with a great sense of humor and a wide range of knowledge—much of it useless, but interesting none-the-less. She'd known from his past history that he had to be some sort of genius, but his little anecdotes and facts were never presented in an overbearing manner or with a sense of superiority. And when presented with something he didn't know, he eagerly drank in every word Esther said.

He'd even invited her on a date, sort of. He'd told her about some sort of water festival, Songkran, he'd called it, that was celebrated in SE Asia. In ancient times, it was a ceremony to bring back the rains; in more modern times, it was a vast party where people threw water on each other. Esther didn't quite understand why they did that, but the way Jim had explained it made it sound like fun. In three weeks, he was going to Bangkok on leave for five days to join in the celebration, and he'd invited her to go. She was tempted. Jim was good company, and she could use the down time, but duty called, and she thought she had to be available for the next BTG contingency.

As she slowly cleared—or put off—her list, her eyes kept darting to the message to see Byzantine. Finally, she couldn't put it off any longer. She didn't think it was another mission, and she wasn't due another fitrep, so curiosity was overcoming her. She shut the display and left the office, walking down the corridor to Byzantine's office.

"Captain Lysander," Helen-Lee said in her perfunctory voice. "If you'll take a seat, I'll tell Mr. Byzantine that you're here."

"Do you know what this is about?" Esther asked as soon as she was finished.

"That's not for me to discuss, Captain," she said, almost frowning as she buried her head in some read-outs.

Well, excuse me!

Helen-Lee could be somewhat robotic in her manner at times, but Esther would bet dollar to donuts that she knew exactly why she was being summoned. There shouldn't be any reason why the woman couldn't give her a heads up.

So Esther cooled her heels for twenty minutes, wishing she'd just stayed in her office clearing her list, when Captain Wrangle Ploeffer came out.

"Hey, Ess. I didn't know you're back," he said, stopping to shake her hand as she stood.

"And you're off, I'm guessing, Wran?"

"You got it. We're like two ships passing in the night. But let's get together and do dinner when I get back."

"If I'm not gone by then. I've got a meeting with him now."

"Yeah, I know. He asked me to send you in."

"Well, then, I'd better get on in. Keep your head down wherever you're going."

"You know me," he said, crouching, arms outspread as he mimed dodging back and forth. "I don't let anyone get a bead on me."

Esther rolled her eyes, holding back a laugh.

"Yeah, that's the only way to keep the law off your ass."

"Captain, Mr. Byzantine is waiting," Helen-Lee interrupted.

Esther rolled her eyes again, then said, "See you on the rebound," before entering the office.

"Captain Lysander, thank you for coming. I've got your orders," Byzantine said, handing her a set of plastisheet orders.

All of her previous missions had been tapped onto her PA—the secure PA, granted, but still a PA. She'd never received physical orders. Curious, she picked them up and immediately saw that they were from the commandant, not the Office of the Chairman. Wondering why the change, she read on.

From: the Commandant of the Federation Marine Corps, To: Captain Esther Lysander . . . blah, blah, blah . . . NLT than 27 May . . . you are ordered to report to the commanding general, Fourth Marine Division . . . for duty with Second Battalion, Eleventh Marines, as a company commander . . .

Esther almost dropped the orders.

Company commander? What? How?

"But I've got nine more months here," she said, looking blankly up at Mr. Byzantine.

"You *had* nine more months, captain."

Suddenly, she wondered if she'd done something wrong.

Am I being fired?

"What . . . I mean, why the change?"

Byzantine could obviously see the concern etched across her face, and he gave a small smile.

"The commandant won, Captain. He pretty much demanded that you be released to serve as a company commander before you made major."

"Major?" she asked confused. "I'm not up for major for another year."

"I believe you have something you in the Marine Corps call 'deep-selected?'"

"I'm deep-selected?"

"I would have to assume so. That was your commandant's line of reasoning, that you needed company commander time to continue in your career. The third minister, on the other hand, asked for you to be extended here with us."

Esther's mind was awhirl. Deep-selected to major? The third minister and the commandant were fighting over her? And most of all she was getting her company? The last one of those made her giddy.

"I . . . I don't know what to think. I can't believe that the commandant and the third minister were arguing about me."

"Not just them," he said. "Someone had to make a decision, after all."

It dawned on her what Byzantine was saying.

"The chairman."

Byzantine nodded and said, "None other. You've made some waves here, if I might say so. Of course, I'm not privy to the details of your missions, but you've made friends with the Third Ministry, and evidently, your commandant thinks highly of you."

Esther didn't know what to think. She'd have to digest what she'd just learned. She had thought—truly thought—that accepting the APOC orders had been a career mistake, orders she'd accepted as the right thing to do. General Simone had warned her of the possibility that accepting the orders could stall her rise through the ranks, but evidently, the commandant himself had watched out for her.

For her, Captain Lysander, not for her, daughter of Ryck Lysander.

As far as she knew, the commandant had never served with her father, and he wasn't one of her father's posse. He was simply watching out for her as one of his junior Marines.

She felt the slightest wetness forming in her eyes, and she hurriedly wiped them with her sleeve.

"So, what now?" she asked.

"Well, you accept or decline the orders. I'm sure the third minister would be more than happy to keep you around here."

For a moment, she was tempted. Initially, she hadn't wanted to take the orders. Duty compelled her to, though. This was a tour to be endured, not enjoyed. But over the last two-plus years, she had enjoyed them. More specifically, she'd enjoyed what she'd done, and she'd developed a tremendous sense of respect for those who served out of uniform. And from the tone of Byzantine's voice, she knew that if she jumped ship now, she could have a pretty good career in the civil side of the government.

As good as the tour had turned out, though, she was still a Marine, and she couldn't think of anything else she wanted to do.

She turned the orders over to the retinal scan (which was why they'd been printed on plastisheet). She looked into the tiny lens, then waited for the dim red LED to turn to green.

The orders were official.

"So . . . uh . . . now what? I mean, what's up for me here?"

"The chairman has requested—please note the word 'requested'—that you accompany him to the G-12 Summit next week. There won't be any side mission," he said with a knowing smile, "but simply to show the flag. If you accept, you are free to institute your orders back to the Marine Corps at your convenience. If you do not want to accompany the chairman, then you may institute the orders at your pleasure."

Esther was tempted to leave immediately. If she had been deep-selected to major, she'd be at the end of the promotion list, which meant pinning on her oak leaves in a year or a few months longer. That meant she'd be limited to a year or slightly longer with her new company. Every moment would be precious, and she didn't want to squander any of those. But she was astute enough to realize that a 'request' from the chairman was rarely, if ever, a mere request.

"I'd be honored to accompany the chairman," she said with a smile.

"I thought you might," Byzantine said. "I'll have those for you tomorrow."

"Well, I guess that's that," Esther said, standing up.

To her surprise, Byzantine stood as well, his hand out.

"It's been a pleasure working with you," he said.

She shook his hand, then almost waltzed out of the office, giving Helen-Lee a hearty, "Have a great day!"

She almost floated down the passageway, her mind singing.

I'm a grunt again!

She'd honestly thought she'd blown her opportunity to command a company, hoping against hope that her career could recover. She'd never thought that by doing her duty, by doing the right thing, her career could be enhanced. She knew without a shadow of a doubt that her experiences during this tour made her a better Marine, especially if she should rise beyond major. She just hadn't thought that she'd get the opportunity.

Maybe, trying to pull all the strings simply to further her career, as she had to admit she'd been doing ever since boot camp, was not the way to advance. Maybe it was even counterproductive.

Maybe simply doing the best job she could, whatever her orders were, was the best way to succeed.

She threw open her office door with a slam, full of energy.

Major Lent better stand the eff by, she thought. *No one can beat me today!*

She sat at her desk and called up her list of messages. Staring at them, none of them registered with her. She didn't even felt guilty when she closed the list, pushing them to tomorrow.

She should make a call, though.

It wasn't technically official, but she didn't think anyone would care as she placed it.

Within moments, Noah's voice answered, "Hey, big sis, this is a surprise."

"Did I wake you?"

"Wake me? It's 0515. No, you didn't wake me. We're on a maintenance stand-down, so all hands are at full tilt. So, what's up? You didn't call me to be my alarm clock."

"I . . . I just had to tell you. I've got my orders. I'm going to 2/11, as a company commander."

"Really? That's great, Ess. Congrats. But I thought you, well, didn't you have another year there? And Miriam said you told her you weren't going to get a company command."

"Yes, I know. I thought so, too, but I'm being released early so I can get my command time in before I . . . well, there's another thing. I've been deep-selected for major."

There was silence for a moment, then "No grubbing way, Ess. Deep-selected?"

"Yeah. It caught me by surprise. I'm still gob smacked."

"A grubbing major. Dad would have been so proud. And I guess that trumps me. I've been selected for staff sergeant, but just the regular route."

"Didn't the board come out two months ago?" she asked, suddenly ashamed she hadn't even checked to see if her brother was on the list.

"Well, yeah. I guess I thought Miriam would have told you. You two talk all the time, after all."

Something in his voice gave her pause, and she asked, "Are you two all right?"

"Ah, I don't exactly know. She was pretty pissed when I reenlisted, and now with three kids and her job, and with me deploying half of the time, I guess it's rough on her."

Esther didn't quite know what to say. She still knew her twin, even if they weren't in contact much. There was a lot more involved than what he was saying, she knew.

"But hey, I don't want to be a buzzkill. This is a good day for you, and you should be happy. Two-Eleven? Good battalion, that. Their patron unit is the German Marineschutzkräfte."

Esther had to smile. This was the Noah she remembered, the guy who knew the history and traditions of the Corps inside and out. In that way, he was much more like their father than she was.

"When do you report in?"

"It's somewhat up to me. Soon, though."

"If you get a chance, come stop by before you report in. You've never met your niece Shiloh yet. And with that, I've got to cut this off. I've got to get a move on if I'm going to make formation.

"But thanks for calling, and I'm proud of you. Major Ess. It's got a nice ring to it."

"OK, take care. And I'll see if I can swing by before reporting in."

Esther stared at her PA for a moment after the connection was broken. She'd been ignoring Noah and Miriam, knowing that they were having problems. That was the easy way out. But Noah was family, and she had a duty to him. To Miriam and the kids, too. She made a promise to herself to make time to stop by for a couple of days.

With that decision made, whatever clouds caused by her knowing she'd been ignoring family dissipated, and her excitement level started rising again. She was back to the grunts, and in command of a rifle company. Each and every senior officer who'd expressed an opinion to her had told her that their company commander tour had been the highlight of their career. She'd wondered how flag officers could say that, and now she'd find out.

She was brimming with energy, too much to contain. A trip to the gym might calm her down before she met Major Lent at the squash court. There was one more thing, however, she realized, that she had to do. There was one more person with whom she wanted to share her news.

From Mars, Earth was a normal call, one she could make on her personal PA.

She asked for the connection, and in a few moments, a familiar face appeared, and with an insolent voice, Jim asked, "Miss me already? It's only been what, less than a day?"

"Are you still going to Bangkok on the 14th? For that Songkran thing?"

"Yeah. I've gotta get it checked off my bucket list. Why?"

"Well, Captain Aylsworth, Marine extraordinaire, if your invitation still stands, I'd like to go with you."

Esther almost laughed at the shocked expression that came over his face. For once, Jim seemed at a loss for words. She knew it had taken a lot of courage for him to suggest she go with him the first time, and she also knew that despite his outward appearance, he'd been more than a little disappointed when she'd declined. She'd told him she couldn't because of her duties, which was the truth, but she knew he thought there was something a little more to it. And maybe there had been.

"Of course, the invitation stands," he said hurriedly as his brain finally slipped into gear. "But why the change of heart?"

"Well, as it turns, out, my situation here's changed. All for the good," she said quickly when she saw the concern cross his face. "But as I've got the time, well, I'd love to spend it with you in Bangkok. Or anywhere," she added, surprising herself.

Jim started to say something, then stopped as he realized what she'd just said. His mouth gaped open, undoubtedly trying to say something clever.

But for once, he didn't have a snappy comeback, as he simply said, "Ess, I'd truly welcome your company."

As a Marine, Esther was comfortable with the friend zone. Was she ready for something else? Something more?

Well, I guess you'll find out, Lysander.

Thank you for reading *Special Duty*. I hope you enjoyed it, and I welcome a review on Amazon, Goodreads, or any other outlet. The series continues will conclude with the final book, due for a late July release.

If you would like updates on new books releases, news, or special offers, please consider signing up for my mailing list. Your email will not be sold, rented, or in any other way disseminated. If you are interested, please sign up at the link below:

http://eepurl.com/bnFSHH

Other Books by Jonathan Brazee

The United Federation Marine Corps' Lysander Twins
Legacy Marines
Esther's Story: Recon Marine
Noah's Story: Marine Tanker
Esther's Story: Special Duty
Final Volume (Coming soon)

The United Federation Marine Corps
Recruit
Sergeant
Lieutenant
Captain
Major
Lieutenant Colonel
Colonel
Commandant

Rebel
(Set in the UFMC universe.)

Behind Enemy Lines
(A UFMC Prequel)

Women of the United Federation Marine Corps
Gladiator
Sniper
Corpsman

High Value Target (A Gracie Medicine Crow Short Story)
BOLO Mission (A Gracie Medicine Crow Short Story)

The Return of the Marines Trilogy
The Few
The Proud
The Marines

The Al Anbar Chronicles: First Marine Expeditionary Force--Iraq
Prisoner of Fallujah
Combat Corpsman
Sniper

Werewolf of Marines
Werewolf of Marines: Semper Lycanus
Werewolf of Marines: Patria Lycanus
Werewold of Marines: Pax Lycanus

To The Shores of Tripoli

Wererat

Darwin's Quest: The Search for the Ultimate Survivor

Venus: A Paleolithic Short Story

Secession

Duty

Non-Fiction

Exercise for a Longer Life

Author Website
http://www.jonathanbrazee.com